THE PYTHAGOREAN SOLUTION

THE PYTHAGOREAN SOLUTION

Joseph Badal

ibooks
new york

DISTRIBUTED BY PUBLISHERS GROUP WEST

A previous edition published in a different form is copyright © 2003 Joseph Badal.

Copyright © 2005 Joseph Badal

An ibooks, inc. Book

Distributed by Publishers Group West
1700 Fourth Street Berkeley, California 94710
www.pgw.com

ibooks, inc.
24 West 25th Street
New York, NY 10010

The ibooks world wide web site address is:
www.ibooks.net

ISBN: 1-59687-113-X
First ibook printing 2005
10 9 8 7 6 5 4 3 2 1

Printed in the USA

THE PYTHAGOREAN SOLUTION

ACKNOWLEDGEMENTS

The critical feedback I received from Karla Ponder, John Badal, Rosalie Sherman, Shirley Londer, Liz Wertheim, Nick Franklin, Nick Pica, Marie Badgley, Julie DuBois, and David Livingston made *The Pythagorean Solution* a better read.

My thanks go to:

Frank Zoretich, Editor Extraordinaire. The red ink helped.

Steve Brewer and Parris Afton Bonds. You told me it would happen.

Jim Riordan, Betty Frovarp, and Heather Buchman. You did exactly what you promised to do, and then some.

Byron Preiss, Roger Cooper, Dwight Zimmerman, and Maria R. Reyes, for your vision and hard work in making this edition a reality.

Danny Simon and Barry Rosen for your support and confidence.

Maureen Walters and Curtis brown, Ltd. for your counsel and assistance.

Finally, my thanks to the citizens of Samos, Greece. Your glorious history and your wondrous ability to make a stranger feel welcome inspired this book.

PROLOGUE

1945

PROLOGUE

March 13, 1945

"Thank you, Allah, for the Great War," Mehmet Arkoun intoned once again in the privacy of his cluttered cabin, while he prepared to return to the deck above. Clothes lay draped haphazardly over a chair, on the bunk, even on the floor. He frowned at the day-old dregs of Turkish coffee in the small cup in front of him. This place needs a woman's touch, Mehmet thought. He twisted one end of his mustache while he stared at his image in the small, ornately framed mirror fixed to the bulkhead. He smiled at himself, feeling a warming wave of satisfaction.

Every day he praised Allah for the World War, and especially for Nazi generals and Swiss bankers. Before the war, his life had never been as good. He knew he would still be earning pennies ferrying peasants and produce around the Black Sea, the Aegean islands and Turkish ports—picking up a little extra cash smuggling opium and black market goods. In the four years since 1941, he had become a wealthy man—thanks to his German and Swiss clients. He kicked at one of the sealed metal boxes the German general had loaded aboard the *Sabiya* and wondered what each box contained.

He fastened the buckles on his slicker, then turned and looked at the Swiss francs piled high in his open safe and daydreamed about the future Allah prepared for him. This one last shipment would suffice. He would build the grandest house in Finike, on the Turkish coast, and finalize arrangements for marrying Sabiya, the daughter of that ignorant goat herder, Mustafa Barak.

Mehmet could never understand the tricks Allah played. How could a girl as beautiful as Sabiya have a father as ugly as Mustafa? He gazed at Sabiya's framed photograph tacked to the bulkhead next to the mirror and imagined the feel of her lush figure. Her long, black hair and hazel eyes.

While his boat rocked in heavy seas, Mehmet scooped up his gloves and counted the things he had already done for Sabiya's ungrateful, camel dung-of-a-father: *I fixed their shack-of-a-home; I gave him twenty young goats and two fine Akbash guardian dogs; I even named my boat after his daughter. And now he wants 1,000 Turkish pounds for me to marry Sabiya. I'll give him his money, but that's the end of it. If he asks for one thing more, I'll kidnap his daughter and not pay him a lira.*

He envisioned Sabiya lying next to him while they watched the sun set from the balcony of the home he would build on the shore of the Mediterranean--when someone pounded on his cabin door.

"*Kaptan, Kaptan*, please come. The storm is getting worse."

Mehmet calmly crossed the room. He replaced the ship's log in the waterproof safe, laying it on top of the high stacks of Swiss francs and the letter from the German general. He closed the safe, then fastened the buckles on his rubber boots and slipped on his gloves. Staggering across the rolling floor of his cabin, he opened the door. In the narrow passageway, his ashen-faced first mate stared at him with fear-rounded eyes.

"Calm yourself, Ali! What could the sea throw at us that we haven't seen before?" Mehmet said. "Besides, my friend, Allah will watch over us."

He patted Ali's shoulder reassuringly and slowly stumbled down the passageway, struggling to keep his balance against the boat's violent pitch and roll. Mehmet and Ali climbed the stairs to the *Sabiya's* main deck just when a mighty gust of wind tore a hatch cover loose and sent it spiraling into the pitch-black night like a kite torn from its string. Mehmet shuddered when a wave washed across the deck, dumping thousands of gallons of seawater into the aft cargo hold. In that instant, he knew the *Sabiya* would be doomed if they didn't cover the hatch and start pumping out the water.

Screaming at Ali, Mehmet ordered him to rouse every crewmember. "Close off that hatch and get them working on the bilge pumps." Then he ran up to the wheelhouse and yelled, "Metin, what's our position?"

The navigator shot Mehmet a forlorn look. "*Kaptan*, I didn't realize until a few minutes ago, but the compass is broken," he said, his voice breaking. "I've been using incorrect readings for hours. With this storm, I can't see the stars or the coastline to navigate. I don't know where we are." He shrugged. "My best guess would be east of Samos."

Mehmet cursed both Metin and the storm under his breath. "You'd better pray we are well east of that island. The reef off Pythagorio would crush this boat."

While he watched Ali and a crewman jerryrig a cover for the open hatch, Mehmet jerked a flare gun from its holder on the wheelhouse wall and stepped out into the howling wind and driving rain. The *Sabiya* continued to sway violently in the heavy seas. Mehmet's breath caught in his throat at the sight of the boat's booms touching the sea at the same time that the boat tipped starboard. Then the *Sabiya* rolled in the opposite direction. It took all of Mehmet's strength to hold onto the wood rail attached to the outside of the wheelhouse. He raised the flare gun and pointed it skyward.

A giant swell suddenly approached on a collision course with the *Sabiya's* bow. It rushed at them with incredible speed, like a dark marauding monster. Mehmet yelled at Ali to hold onto something, but the wind scattered his warning over the deafness of the sea. The massive wave crashed against the *Sabiya* and lifted her twenty feet, twisted her around a full ninety degrees, and rolled a deluge of water over her main deck. Still holding the rail on the upper deck, Mehmet watched the water carry Ali and a crewman over the side. The motion of the boat lifted Mehmet in the air. He lost his grip on the rail, and slammed onto the deck. "Unnh," he moaned.

With the passing of the swell, the sea and the storm seemed to calm a bit, although the sky all around them appeared ominously black. Mehmet gasped painfully. He started to stand, when a fearsome sight filled his eyes and heart with horror. A wave twice the size of the one that had nearly capsized his boat only moments ago was charging directly at them. But this time the *Sabiya's* starboard side sat directly in the wave's path. Mehmet saw with painful, desperate clarity that the *Sabiya,* his remaining crewmen, and he and his future, were doomed.

In that split second, before the watery dreadnought overwhelmed the *Sabiya,* Mehmet Arkoun thought about the money in his safe and Sabiya Barak's beauty. The swell rolled the boat over, carried her two hundred yards, and threw her against the reef protecting Pythagorio Harbor. Her hull broken, the *Sabiya* sank into the roiling sea.

Mehmet did not have the chance to ask Allah why.

LAST YEAR

CHAPTER ONE

April 21

Butros Pengali looked like a Turkish Ichabod Crane—with style. Slicked black hair, bushy eyebrows, sharp Roman nose, thick mustache, and a long neck with a prominent Adam's apple. He wore rimless wire glasses perched on the end of his nose, had an ascetic look, and rarely showed any emotion. Butros lived an austere existence on a civil servant's pay. His only extravagances were the clothes he wore. Butros believed that clothes made the man.

Butros' heart pounded with excitement. He realized that good fortune had just come his way. He adjusted his reading glasses and pulled a file from his desk drawer. He began constructing the file twelve years ago—immediately after the call from Switzerland reached him at the Turkish Maritime Bureau. He looked at the label and ran his finger over the name typed there: SABIYA.

Butros knew his co-workers considered him a drudge; but little did they know he was about to become a very well-to-do drudge. He chuckled under his breath and went through the facts: The *Sabiya* was a Turkish-registered and crewed tramp steamer; captained by a Turk—Mehmet Arkoun; it disappeared in 1945 somewhere in the Aegean after leaving Turkey en route for the Tyrrhenian Sea. Butros wondered about the Swiss gentleman's interest in the boat, but he wasn't about to ask him why he wanted information about some ancient piece-of-crap Turkish steamer. Butros was being paid for information, not to ask questions.

The man from Switzerland had paid him a nice bonus each year for many years now just to keep his eyes and ears open for any word about the *Sabiya*. All Butros had to do was wait for someone to write or telephone the Turkish Maritime Bureau and mention the name of the long-lost boat. Candidly, Butros thought the possibility of anyone finding the *Sabiya* was slim. But, what the hell! He'd been more than pleased to take the Swiss gentleman's money.

He closed the file in front of him and thought, *My ship has finally come in.* He snickered at the play on words, but immediately stifled the laugh when he saw one of his co-workers staring at him. He cleared his throat and looked at his wristwatch. Exactly 1:00 in the afternoon. He removed his glasses, carefully placed them in a leather case, and inserted the case into the breast pocket of his navy, pinstriped suit jacket. He smoothed the sides of his hair with his hands, and adjusted his tie. Putting the file in his briefcase, along with the letter that had been put on his desk that day from a Petros Vangelos on the Greek Island of Samos, Butros stood, snatched his umbrella from the corner by his desk, and walked out of his Istanbul office.

The thought of the letter in the briefcase made Butros sweat. The humidity of the warmish spring day was made worse by a light, steady drizzle. What if someone tried to steal the briefcase? What if the man in Switzerland is no longer interested in the boat? No! Hadn't Leidner recently sent him his annual check? Butros balled his fist and clenched his jaw. "Calm down," he told himself. "This is your lucky day."

Butros entered the front door of the Pasha Hotel and wound his way through the lobby to the bank of pay telephones at the far corner. He tried to stop his hand from shaking while he dropped the coins into the phone. He dialed the number in Zurich from memory and waited.

"Leave your number at the tone," a recorded voice said.

Butros did as instructed, inputting the pay telephone number. While he waited for the return call, he opened his briefcase on his lap and extracted the Vangelos letter. He read the man's awkward Turkish: He claimed salvage rights. Wanted to know who the owner was. What cargo was the boat carrying? Was there anything dangerous on board—explosives, chemicals? Vangelos advised he had a map of the boat's location and would provide a copy to both the Turkish and Hellenic Maritime Bureaus with formal applications for salvage rights.

When the phone rang, Butros nearly jumped out of his skin. He dropped the letter on top of the file in his open briefcase, snatched the handkerchief from his suitcoat pocket, wiped his forehead, and grabbed the receiver from its cradle.

"He… hello."

"Your name!" the man on the other end of the line demanded.

"Butros Pengali."

The voice moderated in tone. "Yes, Mister Pengali, what can I do for you?"

Butros rubbed the perspiration from his upper lip with his handkerchief, mopped his brow again, swallowed. "It's about the boat you are interested in."

"Of course!" the man said, in a suddenly harder, impatient tone.

"The *Sabiya*, sir. Someone has found her."

Butros heard the man gasp.

CHAPTER TWO

April 21

Fritz Leidner passed the large brown envelope to the blond Amazon in front of his desk. Theodora Burger was six feet tall, trim and sinewy. Her perfect face—high forehead, sculpted cheekbones, brilliant-blue eyes, small straight nose—and full-breasted, long-legged body would have been at home on a Versace runway. She was impressive looking and seemingly non-threatening in her ivory silk pants and sleeveless blouse, until one looked into her eyes. They were truly the windows to the blackness inside her. Leidner had used Burger's people on numerous occasions, as bodyguards when he traveled outside Switzerland, as investigators when he needed confidential information, and once for "muscle" when the husband of a woman he was seeing on the side threatened to kill him. He felt his heart speed up as he thought of his first experience with Theo, when she accompanied him on a business trip to New York fifteen years ago. She worked for another security company at the time, and he had been skeptical when she reported for duty. After all, she didn't look like the typical bodyguard. The trip had been the most tense of his life. All he could think about was finding a way to get her in bed, but was afraid to come on to her out of fear she might kick his ass. It wasn't until they had returned to Zurich that he generated the nerve to ask her to join him for dinner. Three dinners and his offer to fund her own security operation got him what he wanted: Theodora in bed. Their relationship had grown until his father had discovered the affair.

Leidner felt a tingling run up his back. Fifteen years ago. That's when his life had changed. His father, Friederich, had threatened to disinherit him, to fire him from the bank if he had any more indiscretions. The old man was a prude who demanded pristine behavior from all of his employees, including his son. When his father learned about Theodora, he no longer threatened. He informed Fritz that he was going to call his lawyer to start the process of terminating Fritz's position with the bank, and as his father's principal heir.

Fritz had explained the problem to Theodora and she had calmly draped an arm around his shoulder and told him she would fix things. On her instructions, he drove her to the street where his father lived, dropped her off, and drove to a spot one hundred feet up the street. Fritz wiped a hand down the car window to remove the condensation that had formed there and watched.

Friederich always walked the one mile from his office to his home, good weather or bad. He was just a few steps from the gate that accessed the gardens that separated his home from the street, when Fritz saw Theodora step from behind a hedge and lunge at his father, her arm extended, a long-bladed knife in her hand. She reversed direction and briskly walked toward him, while Friederich Leidner convulsed on the icy pavement.

Fritz stared open-mouthed at Theodora as she returned to his car, while his father's body spasmed behind her.

Theodora opened the passenger door of his car and, in a throaty voice ordered, "Drive." She was breathing hard, which he had thought was unusual because she had not seemed to have exerted herself.

"Where to?" he'd asked.

She'd smiled, placed her hand on his thigh, and said, "To your father's office."

The heat of her hand made its way to his crotch, he felt her other hand on the back of his neck, her fingers combing his hair.

It took them five minutes to reach the office, and another two minutes to undress. Theodora guided him to his father's desk chair and pushed him down into it. She moved him into position and mounted him. He had never been more excited, and the more he thought about his father's twitching body on the sidewalk in front of the old man's home, the better the sex became.

Theo had taken care of everything, and he had made her rich in the years since then.

He involuntarily shook his head as though a chill had hit him. He refocused on the woman and stared as though mesmerized by the prominent tendons and veins and rock-hard muscles showing in the woman's hands and arms while she broke the seal on the envelope and pulled out the sheaf of papers. Glancing at the cover sheet, she read aloud from the typewritten information. "The man's name is Petros Vangelos? A fisherman on the Island of Samos in the eastern Aegean?"

"Everything you need to know is in that envelope, Theo," Leidner said, calling her by the shortened version of her name that she preferred. He felt a sudden twinge in his groin while staring at her classic Nordic features. *It has been a long time since I've enjoyed the warmth of her hard body,* he thought.

"What do you want of this man?" the woman asked.

"He has information about a boat that sank years ago. I want to know where that wreck is. My information tells me he has a map showing the boat's location. And then I want him eliminated. If you handle this matter in your usual competent fashion—quickly and confidentially—there will be a five hundred thousand franc bonus," Leidner said.

"Forgive the presumption," Theo said, "but why not pay the man for the information. Everyone has his price."

Leidner had considered this option, but decided that if the Greek fisherman opened his mouth about the boat, the results could be catastrophic. He couldn't afford to let the man live. "I want this matter handled within twenty-four hours, Theo. I assume you can do that."

Theo Burger shrugged, then stood. "Of course, *Herr* Leidner."

Leidner followed Theo Burger's tight ass with his eyes when she exited his office. After she closed the door, he swiveled in his chair and stared out at the Zurich skyline, as his long dead father used to do, and his grandfather before that. The power and wealth that three generations of Leidners had accumulated was in terrible jeopardy.

He picked up the telephone receiver and called a number in Athens from memory. The man at the Greek Ministry of Public Affairs was an additional insurance policy.

CHAPTER THREE

April 21

Theo Burger had an uneasy feeling about this assignment. It wasn't the killing that bothered her; it was the fact that she felt it was unnecessary. She again went over the file that Fritz had given her and wondered what Leidner's interest was in this Greek fisherman and a sunken boat. She had known the banker in intimate terms and knew that with Leidner what you see is not always what you get.

He had enabled her to live a life that was well beyond anything she had ever imagined. She knew things would be different today if she had saved some of the money he had paid her. But she liked spending more than she liked saving; so her relationship with Leidner was one of co-dependency. She needed his money like a junkie needed narcotics.

But they weren't equals. He demanded that she address him formally: *Herr* Leidner. He was the boss and she the employee—a very well paid employee.

Theo typed a list of instructions on her computer and then hit the print icon. She walked to the printer and retrieved the single sheet of paper. After returning to her chair behind her desk, she buzzed her secretary on the intercom and ordered her to send in the two men waiting in the reception area.

The men knocked and walked to Theo's desk. They came to parade rest, their legs apart and their hands braced behind their backs.

She passed the paper and Leidner's file to one of the men and said, "That explains your assignment. Have Lisle draw funds for your trip." She paused for a moment and then added, "The weather should be nice in Greece at this time of year."

CHAPTER FOUR

April 22

"Flight attendants, please prepare for landing." The announcement over the airplane's intercom startled John Hammond out of a fitful, dream-filled sleep. He checked his watch: 9:00 a.m., Athens time. He looked out the window. Except for the smog-distorted view of the Parthenon, he could be over Los Angeles. Automobiles inched along like merging ant armies on inexorable food gathering marches.

It was the middle of April—John's favorite time in Greece, when the weather was warm, but not hot. And the tourists were sparse.

John found his way to the baggage claim area and noticed once again how every city had its own peculiar sounds and smells. The rat-a-tat of Greek spoken at a furious pace, backed up by the sounds of car engines and horns in the street outside the terminal seemed almost mellifluous. The odors of a city without vehicle smog devices and unleaded gas, mixed with the fragrance of meat cooking somewhere in the airport, seemed, in some way, pleasantly aromatic.

There was something about Athens, despite the smog and noise, which put him at ease. As though he'd only been gone a day, rather than nearly three decades. It always amazed him that it had only taken eighteen months in Greece so many years ago for him to fall in love with the country and its people. He'd studied the language, and the country's customs. When the Army transferred him to Vietnam after only eighteen months in Greece, memories of the country helped to balance his perspective of the world.

And, now that his divorce from Sonya was final and the pain still occupied parts of his heart and mind, he had come back to Greece to find peace. Sonya had told him he was "unexciting." That he had changed, shut down when he returned from Vietnam. He guessed that was the reason for her infidelity. She wanted someone who wasn't boring. His marriage over, his business sold, and plenty of cash in the bank, he was now ready for the next phase of his life. He had no way of knowing what role Greece might play in that next phase, but he did know that putting ten time zones between him and Sonya felt good.

John turned and caught the eye of an attractive woman in her late thirties. She'd been on the same flight. Probably American, he thought, noticing her clothes, the way she carried herself—with brash confidence. He returned her smile, but then looked away. She reminded him too much of Sonya—tall, long-legged, reddish-brown hair, a Dentyne smile. He happened to see his reflection in a kiosk window and thought about the difference between the John Hammond today and the John Hammond who landed in this same terminal so many years ago. It pleased him to know he was as trim now as then. There were lines in his face now; but he'd been told they lent character to his features. His hair was peppered with gray, except at the temples, where it had gone totally gray.

At six foot one, with a complexion that made him appear to have a perpetual mild tan, John knew he was attractive, if not outright handsome. Between his looks and his money, he received plenty of female attention back home. But, since Sonya had dumped him, he'd really not shown much interest in the opposite sex. He looked back at the woman and read the invitation on her face, but nothing sparked inside him.

He collected his bags, cleared Customs, and taxied to the Olympic Airlines Terminal, a couple miles down the coast.

The plane to Samos seated twenty, had minimal air conditioning, no legroom, and smelled like bad coffee. John calculated he'd been in the air from California, or waiting for connections, more than eighteen hours. He could not have cared less about the plane's ambiance. All he wanted was sleep.

▯

John's tongue clung to the roof of his mouth, which seemed to have an aftertaste that, for some reason, made him think of cold chipped beef on toast. He shook his head; his mind felt befuddled by sleep and fatigue. He couldn't remember the plane taking off. Was he still at the gate in Athens? He was puzzled until he looked out the plane's window and saw crystal-clear blue skies had replaced the polluted Athens air. He saw dark blue water etched by white caps in the distance.

The walk down the center of the plane and down the stairs to the tarmac seemed like an Olympic event. He was beat. Still, he marveled at the azure sky, the brilliant sunshine, and the clean air. A strong breeze caressed his face and he detected a slight trace of salt from the sea. While he walked toward the Samos terminal and deeply breathed in the slightly cool air swirling around him, an errant thought picked at a recessed corner of his brain. Premonition or omen, he suddenly felt as though he'd stepped through a time warp, as though he'd left his old life behind.

John took a cab to the Soula Hotel in Vathi, Samos' principal town. Most of the large hotels wouldn't open until May, so he'd settled for this out-of-the-way twelve-room *pensionne,* on a narrow paved road leading down to the sea, one kilometer from the center of town. The room had a low-slung double bed, an end table on either side of the headboard, a wide and shallow two-drawer chest, a small desk and chair, and a tiny balcony. The bathroom was just inside the entry door and held a cramped shower, a small sink, and a "john."

Stripping down to his shorts, he stretched out on the bed. The Aegean breezes wafting through the balcony's open French doors made the sheer, floor-length muslin curtains seem to dance while they reached out for him.

John slept comatose for seven hours and would have slept longer except for a braying burro tethered below his second floor balcony. After a shower and shave, he put on a fresh change of clothes and hiked down the road to the center of town. It was just a few minutes past ten p.m. Cool air floating off the sea made him glad he'd draped a sweater over his shoulders. An enormous white cruise ship lay anchored in the harbor—a reminder that this was a place people visited to relax. So relax, he told himself.

The shops and restaurants along the quay appeared relatively quiet—only a few couples taking late night walks, or sitting in some of the restaurants.

John selected a taverna with a dozen white-tableclothed tables on a covered patio. He took a seat at the rear. The cooking odors drifting from the kitchen behind him had penetrated his brain and were causing his stomach to growl. He didn't need a menu; he knew exactly what he would order: *Horiatiki* salad of lettuce, tomatoes, olives, cucumbers, and *feta* cheese; grilled octopus; *dolmades*—stuffed grape leaves; and *baklava* for dessert. He'd waited three decades for this meal.

CHAPTER FIVE

April 22

"You think the old Greek is ever going to leave?" Josef asked Hans. "It's almost eleven o'clock."

"You're too impatient, my friend," Hans replied. He glanced over at the old man seated two tables over and saw him take a few bills from his wallet and drop them on the table. "See," Hans whispered, "Vangelos is leaving now."

The two men hung back, following the old man, waiting for the right opportunity. They tracked him through the funereal darkness of Vathi's silent streets and alleys. With the locals and the scattering of tourists already tucked into their beds, Hans and Josef had the streets to themselves. Hans watched Vangelos walk into a narrow, cobblestoned lane. There were no streetlights here, no light coming from any of the houses.

Rushing like two lions after prey, they pounced on the old man and dragged him into an alley between two buildings.

While Josef pinned the old man's arms behind his back, Hans held a knife to the man's throat and spoke slowly in German. According to the briefing Hans had received from Theo Burger the night before in Zurich, Vangelos spoke some German. "You have been very troublesome, *Herr* Vangelos."

Due to the intermittent cloud cover, there was only a little light coming from the moon. But there was enough for Hans to detect confusion in the old Greek's eyes.

"You found something of interest to our client. I suggest you tell us about it. Things will go much easier for you if you do."

"What the hell are you talking about?" Vangelos said.

Hans drove his fist into the old man's mid-section, just below his ribs. Air burst from the man's lungs. Vangelos sagged toward the ground, but Josef jerked up on his arms, forcing the old man to remain erect.

"The *Sabiya*," Hans rasped. "Do you know what I am talking about now?" He pricked at the man's neck with his knife, knowing without seeing that he'd drawn a bead of blood.

The old man groaned, straightened, then surprised Hans by kicking him in the shin, at the same time trying to free his arms from Josef's grip.

Hans absorbed Vangelos' kick; Josef released his arms and punched the old Greek in the side of the head, dropping him to the alley floor as though he'd been poleaxed. They placed Vangelos on a wooden bench, propped against a wall, and stuffed a handkerchief in his mouth. Hans slapped the man's face to try to rouse him, but Vangelos just moaned and sat there, his head hanging limply to one side.

"You must have really hit him," Hans said.

"Not that hard," Josef responded. "He's probably faking." Josef pulled his pistol from his shoulder holster under his jacket and pressed its muzzle hard against the old man's forehead. "Hey, asshole," he hissed, "wake up."

"Oh good, Josef, put a bullet in his brain," Hans said. "That ought to get us the information we need."

"I don't see you doing anything," Josef said, turning to look at his partner's face, stepping close to Hans so that their chests were mere inches apart. "I'm sick and—"

The old fisherman suddenly leaped off the bench, driving his compact, powerful body into the two younger men. Although more than a foot shorter than his assailants, he was stocky and solidly built. The old man hit them like a bowling ball striking bowling pins. Hans flew backward toward the opposite wall, thudding heavily into two large wooden barrels and crashing to the alley floor. Josef was knocked to the ground, too. When his right arm collided with the alley's uneven stone surface, his trigger finger jerked, discharging the weapon. Vangelos turned and ran from the alley, disappearing into the night.

CHAPTER SIX

April 22

B y the time John had finished his meal, he was the last customer in the taverna and he relished the quiet. Most of the establishments visible along the quay had shut down by then. The night was quiet except for the creaking sounds of the fishing boats tugging at their lines, and the lapping of water against the seawall.

After paying his bill, he began the walk to his hotel. The air had cooled even further, so he put on his sweater. Turning off the main street and away from the seawall, he took the road paralleling the coast. It rose up and turned sharply to the left on a semi-circular spit of land protruding toward the bay. At the point where the road turned to the right, he saw a five-tiered, marble staircase that climbed to the top of the hill. The full moon showing between clouds illuminated the steps as though they were floodlit. Although steeper than the road grade, the steps appeared to offer a more direct path to his hotel. When he started the climb up the first tier of steps, a scudding cloud hid the moon again and threw the steps into murky darkness.

The white-walled, flat-roofed houses on either side of the steps, with their barely discernible colorfully painted doors and shutters, were silent and unlit.

Narrow cross streets, wide enough only for pedestrians or small vehicles, separated the tiers of steps.

John began whistling, then laughed at himself. Sure it was night and he was in a foreign land, but he knew that Greece was one of the safest countries in the world. John passed the second cross street and was about to begin climbing the third set of steps—the scent of flowers coming to him as he thought about finding a secluded beach the next morning—when a rattling, choking sound startled him. His heart seemed to stop, and then beat so fast he thought it would burst. He jumped sideways, away from the noise.

His eyes, by this time, were more accustomed to the dark, but he didn't notice any movement. He felt foolish, thinking he'd overreacted to some cat on its nocturnal rounds. Taking a deep breath, he put one foot on a step, intent on resuming his ascent, when his heart did a somersault in his chest. A man lurched out of the shadows and wrapped his arms around him. John smelled the odors of fish and sweat on the man while he struggled to break free from his grasp.

The stranger hung on; the rattling sound again burst from his throat. Then his grasp loosened and he slid to the ground, falling backward onto the marble-paved cross street. A gurgling sound escaped his lips. The moon suddenly appeared from behind a cloud, highlighting an older man's face. Light-colored red foam bubbled from his mouth and his gray-stubbled face looked waxen and stiff.

When John bent closer to see if the man was still breathing, the man grasped the front of John's sweater and pulled him down toward him. Their faces were only inches apart and John detected the coppery smell of blood. Pain showed in the man's eyes. When John put his hands on the man's stomach to push him away, the man cried out, making a sound like a creaking door. John felt wetness on his hands. Blood. The man held on, then cried out again and pulled harder on John's sweater. He coughed, spraying John's face with a fine mist. Finally he managed to say, *"Eepotheema... hartees."* The effort to say the two words seemed to be almost too much for him. But after a moment he spoke again: *"Pythagorio... evpalin ..."* He coughed violently again and blood spurted from his mouth. John lifted the man's shoulders off the ground to ease his breathing. The man sucked in air and spoke again. *"Ee eekoyenya mou. Ee zoë mou."* A venting of air burst from his lungs and blood flowed from his mouth. He was dead.

John understood some of the words. The first meant "boot" and the second "map." *"Ee eekoyenya mou"* meant "My family," and *"Ee zoë mou"* meant "My life." He was trying to figure out the other two words—*"Pythagorio"* and *"evpalin"*—when the sound of approaching footsteps startled him.

Two very large men approached along the narrow cross street, speaking in low, guttural tones sounding like German. They were about thirty yards away. John guessed they were tourists off the cruise ship in the harbor and was about to call to them for help. But then he noticed moonlight glinting off something in one man's hand. A pistol. His heart pounded even faster.

John checked the dead man's pants pockets. He found a wallet. He removed it and slid it into his own pants pocket. Then he moved on hands and knees to the man's feet. His socks and boots were bloodstained. White paper protruded a quarter of an inch above the top of the right ankle-high boot. He gripped the edge of the paper and slipped it from the man's boot.

John rose to a crouch and moved away from the corpse, toward the steps. Once shielded by the corner of a building, he sprinted—two steps at a time—hardly breathing while he raced upward. He slipped when a piece of marble stone broke loose from a step. John caught his balance and heard the solitary stone tumble down the steps. In the dead night-quiet of that small seaside town, the stone sounded like an avalanche. Still a dozen steps from the top, he realized, with a sinking feeling, he must be perfectly silhouetted against the now moonlit sky.

"Halte!" someone screamed. A pistol shot roared as John reached the top step. He ran like a madman, dodging around parked cars, racing up dark alleys and narrow, ancient streets. Propelled by a surge of adrenaline, he ran all the way to the Soula Hotel.

Dashing through the hotel's front door, he hurried past the empty lobby, then climbed to his second-floor room. After tossing the wallet and paper he'd taken from the dead man into the bathroom sink, he turned on the light and bent over to look in the mirror. Dried blood spotted his face and streaked his hands. Dark red blotches and spots covered his sweater, shirt collar, and pants. His fingers felt sticky. He stepped out of his shoes and into the shower. The spray of cold water washed blood off his clothes, hands, and face, swirling it around the bottom of the shower and down the drain. John, his body trembling, undressed and left his clothes in the shower pan.

⬛

Hans had sprinted up the marble steps, pistol in hand. He'd caught a glimpse of the man he'd fired at just before the bastard raced around the corner of a building. He slapped his thigh with his free hand, then slipped his pistol back into his shoulder holster. The guy had too much of a headstart. Mumbling curses, he reversed direction and descended the steps to the alley where his partner knelt, searching the fisherman's body.

"Eh, Josef," he said. "Find anything?"

"Nothing. Whoever that guy was, he even took Vangelos' wallet. And if the old man was carrying the map, well…." He let the thought hover. "Did you see where the man ran to?"

"In the direction of the strip of hotels that border the water on the far side of the hill. But there are houses down there, too. Hell, we don't know if the guy's a tourist or a local resident."

Josef nodded and expelled his frustrations on a loud stream of air. "What do you want to do with the body?" he asked.

"We'll take it back to the boat and dump it out at sea. No point in leaving evidence for the police."

While Josef ran off to retrieve their rental car, Hans dragged the fisherman's body further into the shadows. He tried to put himself in the place of the man he'd shot at. What would he do, whether he was a tourist or local, if he came across a dead man and then got shot at? A smile came to his face. Any law-abiding citizen in a democracy, once his heart rate had returned to normal and he'd changed his underwear, would call the police, of course.

CHAPTER SEVEN

April 22

While he put on clean clothes, John dialed the local operator and asked to be connected to the police. After a minute and no one answering, he was tempted to hang up, to forget the whole thing. Why get involved? A voice finally came on the other end of the line.

"Embros!"

"Hello!" John said. "Do you speak English?"

"Of course." The man sounded sleepy. "How can I help you?"

"My name is John Hammond. I am a tourist and was returning to my hotel and found a man who was badly hurt. He died before I could call for help."

Pause. "Where are you located at this moment, Mister Hammond?" the voice asked, suddenly alert and agitated.

"The Soula Hotel. Room eight."

"And where is the body?" the man asked.

"Halfway up the steep marble steps going down into Vathi. You know where—?"

"I know where you mean, Mister Hammond. Stay where you are. The Inspector will come to your hotel. Understand?"

John understood all right. The policeman's suspicious tone made it clear he'd identified at least one suspect. A stupid American tourist named John Hammond.

He retrieved the wallet and the bloodstained document from the bathroom sink, put the document on a towel he'd spread out on the bed, and turned the wallet over in his hands. Although dried blood spotted the outside of the wallet, none had seeped inside. He found a photograph of an older man surrounded by people he assumed to be the man's family. The man in the picture looked like the one who had died in his arms. In the photo, the man stood next to a woman of about sixty—perhaps his wife. Two other men and a woman, all appearing to be in their thirties, stood behind the couple. Everyone was smiling. A Greek driver's license in the wallet told John the dead man's name was Petros Vangelos.

He replaced the photo and drivers license in the wallet and put it on the towel. Then he picked up the document, a folded piece of plain white paper, spotted and smeared with blood from John's hand. When fully opened, it appeared to be a carefully drawn map of what looked like a portion of coastline—the word *"thalassa"* indicated the sea. No place names, reference points, or roads were marked. Three small circles were drawn on the land and one on the sea. Straight lines connected the three circles on the land into what looked like a right triangle about the size of a common protractor. A dotted line connected the circle on the sea with the apex of the triangle. Without a scale present on the map, John couldn't tell how far apart the circles were. Nothing on the map explained the meaning of the lines, the small circles, or the triangle they formed. He carefully turned the map over and found words handwritten in Greek on the back: *An kovo sta dio ena orthogonio, tha eho theeo trigona. Kai otan pandrevoun theeo trigona, eho ena orthogonio. Themase pos O Pythagoros eenay o filos sou.*

John's hands began to shake. He recognized the symptoms. He'd experienced them before. There was nothing like finding a dying man in a darkened alley and getting shot at to bring on a surge of adrenaline.

"What the hell is going on?" he asked himself. "First, I find a dying man, then I get shot at, now I've got nursery rhymes." He glanced back down at the words on the map. They made no sense. The ramblings of an old man? *When I cut a rectangle in two, I will have two triangles. When two triangles marry I have a rectangle. Remember that Pythagoras is your friend.*

A knock startled him. He moved toward the door, but remembered the map in his hand and dropped it on the shelf in the open closet by the door.

A short, thin, stern-faced man dressed in a poorly tailored black suit, a soiled tie, and badly scuffed brown shoes stared up at John with coal-black eyes. His carefully trimmed hair and waxed mustache contrasted with his unkempt appearance.

Without waiting to be asked in, the man pushed past John and announced, "I am Inspector Christoforos Alexandros Panagoulakos." He said this in perfect, only slightly accented American English.

It crossed John's mind it was a lot of name for a man not much more than five feet five inches tall.

Panagoulakos walked over to the bed, picked up the wallet from the towel, and checked the ID inside. Then he replaced the wallet on the towel.

He surveyed the room, then moved to the bathroom, where John had left the pile of bloodstained clothes in the shower. John trailed the man and watched him pick up his clothes, inspect them, then drop them back on the shower floor. John had to quickly backtrack when the man turned and walked out of the bathroom.

"Sit down in that chair," Panagoulakos said gruffly, sounding like someone used to giving orders and having them obeyed. Panagoulakos glared at John with an implacable stare. "Your passport!" he demanded.

John reached for his passport on the dresser and handed it to the Inspector before taking a seat. Panagoulakos looked at each page. He slipped the passport into a jacket pocket, and pulled out a small notebook and pen.

"Mister Hammond, I warn you it is imperative to hold nothing back. Is that clear?"

"Yes, Inspector, it's clear," John responded. "I assure you I have no reason to hold anything back. What I experienced tonight was shocking and I want to help you in every way I can."

"Humph!" he said. "What's your full name?"

"John Andrew Hammond." John almost added, "Just like it says in my passport," but decided this was not the time to be a smartass.

More questions followed, rapid-fire.

Where are you from? Why are you in Samos? Where did you say you saw the murdered man? What were you doing at that location at such a late hour? Did you see any weapons at the scene? Was Mister Vangelos dead when you arrived on the scene? Did he say anything to you before he died? Did you see anyone else in the area? Do you know who killed this man you say died in your arms?

John answered all of them as completely as he could. Then he asked, "Inspector, does any of this make sense to you?"

He skewered John with his stare and ignored the question.

John shrugged. The little guy was really starting to piss him off.

"Why did you take the man's wallet and then leave the scene of the crime?" Panagoulakos asked.

"I took his wallet because I assumed from his words he wanted me to get something out of his pocket. I might have returned the wallet to his pocket if those two other men hadn't shown up and shot at me."

"Tell me about those two men," Panagoulakos said, his eyes widening just a bit.

"I've no idea who they were. I heard them talking to one another—in German, I think—before they saw me. However, I can't be sure because they were about thirty yards away and they spoke softly. They must have heard me run away. I just didn't have time to do anything but run like hell." Then John had an afterthought. "I can tell you they looked enormous." He hesitated a moment, then said, "Not that they were so tall. They looked like bodybuilders."

"Why did you run away when you first saw these two men? What did they do to frighten you?"

"Inspector, I ran because, as I said before, I saw that at least one of them had a pistol." John tried to control his anger, but he did so with only limited success. "Tell me what you'd do," he said, his voice rising, "if you were kneeling next to a dead man who had bled all over you, you were unarmed, and armed men were approaching you?"

"After you ran off, what happened? After you were supposedly shot at."

"Let's get one thing straight," John said, feeling his face go hot. "I wasn't *supposedly* shot at. They shot at me."

Panagoulakos narrowed his black eyes, put a balled-up hand to his mouth and bit down on one of his fingers while he appeared to think. He fixed his shark-like eyes on the wall above and behind John and did not respond for about ten seconds. Finally, he laughed. It wasn't much of a laugh, but John welcomed it.

"All right, Mister Hammond, I thank you for your time and cooperation." He looked at his wristwatch. "I want you to come into the station at 10 o'clock tomorrow morning. I'll have a written statement typed out for your signature. Here's my card."

Panagoulakos did an about face. He walked over to the bed, folded the wallet in the hotel towel, stripped the pillowcase from one of the pillows on the bed, and walked into the bathroom. He picked up John's sopping-wet clothes and placed them in the pillowcase.

Following Panagoulakos to the door, John said, "Inspector, may I ask you something?"

Panagoulakos turned, looked at John, and smiled. "Of course, Mister Hammond."

"May I have my passport back?"

"No, Mister Hammond, you may not," he said, still smiling. "Any other questions?"

John paused for a second, then said, "Did you find anything on Mister Vangelos' body or in the area that might lead you to the murderers?"

The smile left the cop's face. "No, Mister Hammond. No clues, no murder weapon—and no body either."

CHAPTER EIGHT

April 22

Hans and Josef stood in the shadows of the Soula Hotel, screened from the street by a row of oleander bushes. They watched the little man walk down the steps, get into the police cruiser, and drive away.

Josef patted Hans on his massive shoulder. "That was a good idea, waiting in the plaza to see if a police car would go by. Someone did call the police."

"*Ja*, Josef, and I'll bet you a thousand francs it was the man we saw run away from Vangelos. We need to find out if that man is staying in this place and what room he's in." Hans scratched his nose and said, "I was hoping there would only be one lighted room showing through the windows."

"I counted three lights," Joseph said. "We can't just knock on every door. Someone might remember our faces."

Hans slapped Josef on the back. "We'll return in the morning. Perhaps we can question one of the hotel employees then."

"But what if he had the map and gave it to the policeman?" Josef asked.

"One way or the other we'll find out where the map is, won't we? Whether he has it or if he gave it to the policeman, the guy's dead. If the cop has it, no problem. There are ways to make even the toughest cop cooperate."

Josef chuckled. "*Ja,* Hans. You're correct."

Hans slapped his partner on the back. "Let's go dump the body, then get some sleep. I think tomorrow will be a good day."

CHAPTER NINE

April 23

John didn't sleep much that night. He didn't remember until three in the morning that he'd never mentioned the map to the cop. Panagoulakos had irritated him enough that he'd forgotten the map on the closet shelf. He made a mental note to take the map to the police station at 10:00.

John replayed Petros Vangelos' last words: *Ee eekoyenya mou.* My family. And he guessed the old man was mourning his own death when he said, *Ee zoë mou.* My life.

He staggered out of bed at a few minutes before 9:00 a.m., feeling like a zombie. His tongue felt swollen and his eyes burned. After showering and dressing, he departed for the police station.

The Soula Hotel sat on the north side of a steep, narrow street that dropped down to the left, past olive groves, to the sea, and rose uphill to the right to a cluster of shops and other small hotels. John lingered for a moment and stared down at the sparkling blue Aegean and then, reluctantly, began climbing the hill. So much for relaxing, he thought. After two blocks, he noticed a sign in the window of a storefront: *"Feela/Copies-50 DR."* He patted his pocket, felt the map, and then stopped in the store. He'd make a copy for Vangelos' family.

John then followed the meandering road downhill toward the harbor. He spotted three police cars parked outside a building sandwiched between a restaurant and a souvenir shop. The sign over the entrance read "POLICE" in Greek, German, and English. After entering the station, he saw Inspector Panagoulakos wave at him through the open door of his office.

John stopped in the office doorway. The Inspector had a telephone to his ear and apparently the party on the other end of the line was doing all the talking. When Panagoulakos finally spoke, he said soothingly in Greek, "Calm down, madam." He repeated this twice more and then asked for her telephone number and told her he would call back. He hung up and waved John into his office.

The ten-foot by ten-foot room was furnished with a desk, three chairs, and a tall file cabinet. Papers were stacked on nearly every flat surface. The Inspector removed one of the stacks from a chair and told John to sit.

Panagoulakos slowly shook his head and ran a hand through his hair. He looked sad. He wrote something on a piece of paper, then looked across his desk at John. He forced a smile. "I hope you didn't eat anything at your hotel this morning. Soula Demetridakis is famous for serving inedible food. She's probably the only Greek in the world who can't cook."

John laughed and said, "No."

"Good," Panagoulakos said. "But we can't have travelers to our island starve." He got up from behind his desk and told John to follow him.

John wondered about the policeman's sudden change in demeanor. Panagoulakos was no longer treating him like a suspect.

The Inspector led the way across the street to a small, outdoor kafeneio. There were a half dozen men in their fifties and sixties crowded around a table in a back corner, fingering worry beads, sipping coffee, and arguing about something. John was able to pick up the Greek words for "politician" and "stupid." John smiled. He knew from reading about Greece's history that the Greeks had been arguing about their politicians for thousands of years.

The men all looked toward the Inspector and greeted him respectfully. A waiter came over, half-bowed, and showed them to a corner table. The deference all the men showed the Inspector spoke volumes about his authority and reputation.

"Our American visitor is the unwitting guest of Soula Demetridakis," Panagoulakos announced in Greek, after taking a seat.

John smiled. He'd picked up enough of what the Inspector said.

The waiter and the other men laughed. Then the waiter said in a serious tone, "Inspector, the government should revoke that woman's business permit. She's going to kill someone one of these days." He then disappeared into the back of the café.

"Have you come up with anything new?" John asked.

"Mister Hammond, this business is becoming more and more curious by the hour," he said. "I believe your story about a dead man; but, without a body, it's difficult to know where to go first.

"We found blood on the stones of one of the narrow crosswalks where you said you left Mister Vangelos. That was Mrs. Vangelos on the telephone when you came into the station. She's terribly upset. She says her husband took a small boat out yesterday morning and was due back home late last night. Apparently, her husband has never failed to come home without calling. It's pretty clear Mister Vangelos returned to shore yesterday and got into some sort of trouble."

"What did you tell the man's wife?"

"Nothing," the Inspector said. "I need to find the body, then I'll talk to her in person."

"Isn't what I told you enough?" John asked. "Do you need the body to start your investigation?"

"There are a few things we can do, all of them a waste of time. If you mean that you want us to interrogate every man on Samos who speaks German, you don't understand the importance of tourism to our little island. About seven hundred Germans got off a ship yesterday. Three hundred of them were men. If I start questioning that many German tourists, I'll have an international incident on my hands. And, if the culprits aren't from that ship, then they have more than likely left the island by now."

John gritted his teeth. "Have you found Vangelos' boat? He had to have docked somewhere in Vathi."

"He did." The Inspector's face flushed. "We found it tied to the seawall, right across from the police station. The Coast Guard is searching along the coast on the chance his body was dumped in the sea. But, with the Aegean currents, a body could be halfway to Turkey by now. If it was weighted down before being tossed in the sea, the odds are we'll never find any trace of it."

"Where did Mister Vangelos live?" John asked. "Was his home close by?"

Panagoulakos rubbed his cheek. "The Vangelos family lives quite a distance from here. He would have had a very long boat trip from Vathi to his home on the other side of the island. And it wasn't like him to have his dinner alone, away from his wife. But one of my men saw him standing outside the telegram office yesterday, just a few blocks from where we are now. The owner of the office told me that Petros Vangelos had waited all day for a telegram he claimed would come from Turkey. He seemed highly anxious. Apparently, nothing ever arrived for him." Panagoulakos' eyes shifted away from John's and he looked as though he was thinking about something. Finally, he met John's gaze. "One of Vangelos' friends here in Vathi called this morning and told us he had been expecting Vangelos to spend the night with his family. When he didn't show last night, he assumed Vangelos had gone home. But, when he called the Vangelos home this morning and learned that Vangelos never arrived there, he called us to report him missing. Vangelos obviously never had the chance to call his wife about his change of plans."

The waiter brought a tray of pastries to the table, along with glasses of fresh-squeezed orange juice and two cups of coffee. Panagoulakos sipped his coffee and watched John dive into the food. He had barely finished one of the croissants when the waiter returned with a plate laden with ham, eggs, and potatoes.

"Do the police treat all visitors to breakfast?"

Panagoulakos smiled. "Why Mister Hammond, I'm sure you're well acquainted with Greek hospitality, having lived here for a year and a half."

John took a bite of egg and finished chewing it, all the while looking the cop in the eye. "I see you've been checking on me, Inspector. What else have you discovered?"

"The computer is a wondrous thing, Mister Hammond. With the cooperation of our NATO ally, the United States, I learned all about your military assignment here in Greece—and about your tour in Vietnam. I also learned you're an only child and that your parents live in New Mexico. You built a very successful business in California, which you recently sold, and are now financially well off."

"Very impressive," John said. "Anything else?"

The cop's eyes turned sad and he wagged his head. "Well, I'm sorry to say that I also learned about your recent divorce." He turned slightly in his chair and crossed his legs.

"Sounds as though you got the whole story," John said. Then he decided to change the subject. "I've been trying to place your accent. You must have spent some time in the States."

Panagoulakos gave John a wry smile. "My father emigrated from Thessaloniki to Chicago in the early fifties. Met my mother—a good Greek American girl, married, and started a printing business. I was born two years later and went through the eighth grade there. Then I came back here to Samos to live with my grandparents."

"Must have been tough leaving your folks in Chicago?" John said.

"Yes, it was," Panagoulakos said. "They were both killed by a drunk driver one night returning home from work."

"Jesus!" John said. "I'm sorry."

Panagoulakos waved a hand. "It was a long time ago."

John looked out at the harbor for a moment, then turned back to the Inspector. "So where do we go from here?" he said.

The Inspector pulled John's passport from his jacket pocket and dropped it on the table. "I trust you won't leave the island without checking with me first," Panagoulakos said.

"You have my word on it," John responded. Thinking that this would be the perfect opportunity to hand over the map, John began to reach into his jacket pocket—just when an uniformed policeman rushed up to the table.

The policeman made his apologies for interrupting, then told Panagoulakos that a fisherman had found a body floating in the sea.

The Inspector must have been able to tell from John's raised eyebrows and open mouth that John had understood the policeman. "Since you now know we have a body, perhaps you should come along with me. You can identify it if it's the same man you saw last night. Besides," he said with a smile, "I think it will be a good idea if I keep an eye on you."

CHAPTER TEN

April 23

Back at the police station, John followed Panagoulakos into his office. The same police officer who had come to the café brought one sheet of paper to the Inspector. Panagoulakos seemed to go over it several times before he spoke.

"We found no identification on the body," he said, pacing around the office, stepping over piles of paper. "A fishing net had been wrapped around it. Apparently, whoever dumped the corpse in the water didn't weight it down properly. It takes body weight plus seventy-five kilos to weigh a body down under water. Instead, it washed ashore near Karlovassy, about forty kilometers from here. If someone dumped the body near here it could have floated all the way to Karlovassy between last night and this morning. The tides can be quite strong around here."

"If it *is* Vangelos, why would they have taken the body? Why not just leave it on the steps?" John asked.

Panagoulakos shrugged. "Maybe they wanted time to thoroughly search it. They must have assumed you would call the police. They couldn't wait around the crime scene. Anyway, the body's being transported by truck to the pathologist at the Pythagorio Army base."

Then John remembered the map. "Inspector, there was an item on Vangelos' body that I took to my room last night. I should have turned it over to you, but forgot to do so." He pulled the original map from his pocket and handed it over.

Concentrating on the map, the Inspector seemed to be intentionally avoiding looking at John. His mouth was closed in a grim line. Eyes squinted, brow furrowed. He appeared to be angry, but trying to control it. Finally he looked up.

"I'm going to write this off as an innocent mistake, Mister Hammond. Consider yourself lucky. But, if I discover you're withholding any other information, I'll see to it you're prosecuted for obstructing my investigation. And, I promise, you will not like the inside of a Greek prison."

John apologized profusely and swore he had no other information.

Panagoulakos returned his attention to the map. "Without any place names," he said, "I have no clue where this is supposed to be," pointing at a spot on the map. Then he turned the paper over and scanned the words on the opposite side. "The words on the back look like some sort of nursery rhyme."

"I had the same impression," John said.

Panagoulakos ignored John. His lips moved while he again read the handwritten script to himself. Then, as though thinking out loud, he said, "This business about triangles getting married and rectangles being cut in two sounds like gibberish. And the only Pythagoras I've ever heard of died thousands of years ago." He scratched his head and dropped the map on his desk. He looked up at John as though he'd just remembered he was there. "Does any of this make sense to you?"

"I know the words, but I don't understand their significance," John replied.

"They may not *have* any significance. Their literal meaning is 'If I cut a rectangle in two, I will have two triangles. And when two triangles marry, I have a rectangle.' The next sentence seems to be a separate thought. 'Remember that Pythagoras is your friend.'"

He pulled a plastic evidence bag from a desk drawer and inserted the map. Then he walked over to the file cabinet and used a key to unlock the top drawer. He placed the map in the drawer and noisily slammed it shut and relocked it. The telephone on his desk rang just when the Inspector returned to his chair.

The Inspector picked up the receiver, listened for a few seconds, then hung up. "The body just arrived at the military base. We can be there in less than thirty minutes. It won't be pleasant to look at after having been in the sea for so many hours. I would rather not put the Vangelos family through the ordeal of identification until we're sure it's Petros. I would like you to come with me to see if it's the man from whom you took the wallet and," he added with extra emphasis, "the map."

John didn't bother to remind the good Inspector that identifying a bloated body that had probably been fed upon by all sorts of sea creatures would not be pleasant for him either. Perhaps it was his way of making John pay for not turning the map over to him last night. Then John thought it might not please Panagoulakos to know he'd made a copy of the map.

CHAPTER ELEVEN

April 23

Theo Burger raised her free hand to her forehead and gazed down at the polished wood floor of her Zurich apartment. She felt acid build in her stomach.

"How could you have allowed this to happen?" she demanded. Then she screamed into the telephone receiver, "If you two screw this up I will cut off your balls."

"Calm down, Theo," Hans said in a remarkably quiet voice for a man of his size. "We will take care of everything. You're right, we messed up. But we think we know where the map is. We'll call you the moment we get it."

"What do you mean, you *think* you know where the map is?"

Hans expelled a loud stream of air that whistled through the receiver. Then his tone changed and he growled, "Look, if you don't think we can do the job, then why did you send us down here? How about getting off my ass and let me go to work?"

"You sonofa—" Theo heard the connection broken. She slammed the receiver down onto the cradle and leaped from her chair. She clenched her fists, then methodically cracked the knuckles of both hands, one finger at a time. She forced herself to bring her anger under control. Then, while pacing the room, she made up her mind that she would cut off Hans' nuts, whether he succeeded in this mission or not. No one talked to Theo Burger like he had.

CHAPTER TWELVE

April 23

Inspector Panagoulakos drove John in his Fiat from Vathi over the steep spine of the island. The road serpentined away from them all the way to the coast near Pythagorio. The views were spectacular—a scattering of blue-roofed shrines and churches, white-walled houses in small villages, patchwork vineyards, and olive groves with rock wall borders, all set against the distant Aegean. The water was a deep, sparkling blue; shading in the shallows along the shoreline turned the water's color to jade.

The Turkish coast was visible just a few miles away across the sea. But there was just enough haze over the Turkish coast that John couldn't make out anything but the outline of hills.

Panagoulakos pointed out to sea, in the direction John had been looking a moment earlier. His mouth scrunched into a sour look and he grunted as though he'd tasted something foul. "You ever visit Turkey?" he asked.

"No," John said. "I'd like to some day."

"Don't bother," he said. "There's nothing over there but barbarians."

Letting the comment pass, John chose not to remind the Inspector that the Turks held the Greeks in equal esteem. They were like the Hatfields and the McCoys—except a thousand times worse. And the feud had been going on for centuries.

Pythagorio, on the eastern side of Samos, is just a few miles from the Turkish coast. Considering the animosity between the two countries, it was no wonder, John thought, the Greeks maintained a military base near Pythagorio.

Then another thought intruded. What had Petros Vangelos said? One word in particular: Pythagorio. Why would Pythagorio have been one of the last words gasped by Petros Vangelos?

CHAPTER THIRTEEN

April 23

H ans left Josef sitting in the car on the street outside
the Soula Hotel. He entered the small lobby and
noticed a woman standing behind the reception desk.
She was plump and dark-skinned, with black hair falling
to her shoulders. A pair of glasses tied to a chain around
her neck perched on her nose. She appeared to be doing
paperwork. The sound of the door opening distracted her
and she stared straight at Hans as he walked toward the
counter.

"*Sprechen sie Deutsche?*" Hans said.

"*Ja, einwenige,*" the woman answered.

"I represent a tour group," Hans continued in
German, "and we are interested in taking ten rooms this
weekend."

She waved her hand in a circular motion, as though
to say, Do I have rooms! "There are only five rooms taken
now," she said. "Four English couples and an American

man. The English all leave tomorrow, so I'll have eleven open rooms."

"I hope the American isn't noisy," Hans said. "You know how some of them can be."

Soula nodded her head in an understanding way, but then held up her hands. "Oh, not Mister Hammond. He is quite the gentleman."

Hans made a sour face and said, "I heard there was some trouble here last night. Something about the police."

Soula made a clucking sound. "It was nothing. A policeman friend of mine told me that Mister Hammond found a body near here. It has nothing to do with my hotel."

Hans now knew the name of the man who had found Vangelos. Perhaps the one who now had Vangelos' map.

"Can you tell me which room the American is in?" he asked. "I'd like to be able to pre-assign the other rooms to my group."

"Of course," she said. "He's on the second floor. Room eight. How many nights will your people be staying?"

"Six nights. If the rate is reasonable."

The woman smiled. She placed her right hand over her heart. "You won't find a better price on the island."

"Perhaps you could give me a tour of the premises."

The woman closed the ledger on the counter, removed her glasses, dropping them against her ample bosom, and quickly came around to the other side. "Please," she said. "Follow me."

The tour took less than ten minutes. Once Hans had located the American's room, he told the woman he'd seen enough. After they returned to the lobby, he handed over five hundred euros as a deposit, gave the woman a fictitious company name, and left the hotel.

Josef put the car in gear after Hans closed the car door. "Well?" he said.

Hans snapped his fingers. "Nothing to it," he said.

CHAPTER FOURTEEN

April 23

The *Banque Securité de Swisse's* boardroom spoke volumes about the financial institution and its chairman, Fritz Leidner. The Persian carpet that covered almost the entire area of the thirty by forty-foot room, the original oils—by Goya, Vermeer, and Renoir, the view of Zurich from atop the thirty-story *Banque Securité* Tower, and the industrial titans who occupied the seats around the enormous mahogany table were all symbols of Fritz Leidner's wealth and power. And of the bank's influence.

Leidner gazed at the men around him and felt a surge of satisfaction run through him. These men controlled the most successful businesses in Switzerland—but they deferred to him. After all, he'd made them even richer than they already were. And he held major ownership positions in all of their companies.

"All right, gentlemen," he said, bringing an immediate hush to the room. "We have an extensive agenda before us and I don't want to be the cause of any of you missing lunch appointments." He smiled and the others in the room reciprocated.

Leidner guided the board through the agenda with little comment from the others, and never any opposition. He'd just completed a review of the financial statements when the door behind him opened. He looked back over his shoulder. His assistant stood just inside the door, a look of sheer panic on his face.

His assistant stepped forward and visibly swallowed. "My apologies, *Herr* Leidner." The man handed Leidner a slip of paper. Leidner looked down at the piece of paper: *Hans is calling from Greece. Says it is an emergency.*

After crumpling the note in his hand, Leidner stood. "Please forgive me, gentlemen. I have an urgent matter to attend to. I should be back in just a few minutes." He walked out of the boardroom and went to his private office. Once seated, he pulled a set of keys from his suitcoat pocket and unlocked the center desk drawer. He withdrew the Vangelos letter he'd received from Butros Pengali at the Turkish Maritime Bureau and scanned it. Vangelos' questions about the *Sabiya*—its cargo, ownership—his claim for salvage rights. Then Leidner reached for the telephone and lifted the receiver.

"What has happened?" he demanded.

"We found the old man, but he got away."

"What about the map?"

"He didn't have it."

"So go find him. That's what you should be doing instead of wasting my time. That's what I'm paying you to do."

Hans paused. "If Theo finds out I've been talking to—"

Leidner laughed. "You don't find that fisherman and his map, and I'll call Theo myself."

"The old fisherman is dead," Hans said. "We found him in an alley. We saw another man run away from where we found the body."

"Did you check to see if the map was on the body?" Leidner demanded. Something told him that Hans' story wasn't the entire truth.

"Yes, sir. It wasn't there."

"Then find this other man."

Leidner slammed the receiver into the cradle and worked on getting his breathing back to normal. He swiveled in his chair and looked at the paintings of the bank's former Chairmen—his grandfather, and, of course, his father. His gaze fixed on his father's eyes in the painting. He could only meet the old man's eyes for a second. He would have removed the damned portrait if it wouldn't have raised too many unwanted questions from board members and bank staff. His father had been about to disinherit him; instead, at the age of forty-six, he inherited a world-class fortune, the chairmanship of the bank, and a potential problem that had ticked like a timebomb for years.

Fritz had grown up in the bank; he was ready to take over when Theo killed his father. But what he wasn't ready for was the sealed envelope he found in his father's safety deposit box. The letter inside warned him about the danger aboard a boat named *Sabiya*. It explained how his father had laundered wealth the Nazis had stolen, how his father had hired a Turk who owned the *Sabiya* to transport Nazi loot, and how the boat had sunk in a storm in the Aegean in 1945. On board that boat was a fortune in gold and jewels—and a letter in a waterproof safe that could bring down the Leidncr empire.

CHAPTER FIFTEEN

April 23

Razor wire topped the ten-foot high chain link fence surrounding the Greek Army base on the eastern side of Samos. Built on a promontory above the sea, the base looked out across the Aegean toward Turkey. Armed sentries patrolled rocky paths cut into the side of almost sheer cliffs. The blue and white Greek flag fluttered in the light breeze from a flagpole planted outside the entrance gate.

After the guard checked their IDs at the gate and called someone to announce their arrival, Panagoulakos drove into the military complex. They passed a half-dozen Greek Army platoons marching quick-time along the side of the road.

Panagoulakos parked in front of a small block building sitting directly behind the main hospital and led John inside. A bright-eyed Greek Army lieutenant named Porras greeted them. He led them along a tiled corridor with pale yellow walls lined with portrait photographs of anonymous men in uniform. At a set of double doors, they turned right—a sign said *Nekrotomeeo/Morgue*—and entered a large room equipped with six stainless steel, wheeled tables.

Three of the tables held bodies laid out with feet protruding from under sheets. Each body had a tag attached to one of its big toes. The smells of antiseptic and other chemicals in the room were not strong enough to disguise the rot of flesh.

That odor brought back terrible memories for John. He flashed back to the time his unit in Vietnam discovered a dozen dead Vietnamese villagers roped together and floating in the Mekong River. They'd been sent down the river by the Viet Cong—a message to other villages not to cooperate with the Saigon government, its troops, or its American allies.

Inspector Panagoulakos must have noticed something was wrong. He stepped over and put a hand on John's shoulder. "Are you all right?" he asked.

Returning to the present, John rubbed his hands over his face, as though to wash away the unwanted memory. "Yeah! Thanks!" But he was thinking that if he looked the way he felt at that moment, Panagoulakos could not be particularly well assured.

Porras walked to the far corner of the morgue and tapped on an office door. The side walls of the office were windowed, but the Venetian blinds on the insides of the glass were closed. Porras' light knock brought no response, so he knocked much harder.

From behind the office door came a thunderous shout of something unintelligible, followed by a string of curses.

The young officer might have been able to face enemy fire without pause; but, whoever was behind that door had him cowed. "Doctor," Porras said hesitantly, his voice squeaking, "there are some gentlemen here to see you."

More curses emanated from the office, followed by the sound of something heavy, as though a chair had been thrown against a wall. The young officer quickly backed away and retreated to the far side of the room, where he took up a position behind Panagoulakos.

Based on the booming voice that came from the office, John expected at least a giant to walk through the door. Instead, a tiny, elderly man only a couple inches taller than the diminutive Panagoulakos flung the office door open and strode into the morgue. He had a wild shock of thick, white hair. His white lab coat sported multi-colored stains. He wore light-blue booties over his shoes and his eyeglasses hung on a chain around his neck. He bellowed in a deep, resonating basso voice, "You better have a good reason for interrupting me."

Panagoulakos, without saying a word, walked toward the doctor. It appeared a confrontation might occur. The older man put on his glasses and then smiled and clapped his hands once. Panagoulakos stopped directly in front of the man and put his arms around him. They hugged each other for about fifteen seconds while asking after the health of one another's families.

Panagoulakos released the old man and turned to John. "John Hammond, meet Doctor Socrates Theodorakis," he said, "Chief Pathologist of the Army Medical Corps… and my uncle."

John stepped forward and took the doctor's hand. When he stepped back, he noticed that Porras seemed more at ease.

"So, Christo," the doctor said, "I assume you are here about the fisherman pulled from the sea. Tragic case. Would you like to inspect the body?"

They followed the doctor over to one of the tables. John looked up at shelves built into the walls while he trailed behind Panagoulakos. Anything to avoid staring at the bodies. Dozens of bottles and jars lined the shelves. They contained what appeared to be human body parts—some recognizable, others not. John shuddered.

The pathologist picked up a jar and removed the lid. It smelled of strongly scented salve—menthol and something else—maybe eucalyptus. After applying a small amount to his upper lip, he passed the jar around to the others. After they all imitated the doctor, smearing some of the goop under their noses, he explained, with a smile, that the reason he did not have a mustache like so many Greeks was because of the mess the salve made. Both Porras and Panagoulakos looked sheepishly at the doctor, having coated their own mustaches with the goop.

After donning rubber gloves, the doctor drew the sheet off one of the cadavers with a flourish. Porras immediately began to change color. First pale, then gray.

Theodorakis jabbed a finger at the soldier and ordered him out of the room. Then he looked at John. "If you cannot handle this, leave now. I do not want you throwing up in here."

John merely shook his head.

The naked corpse was hideously bloated and a surreal milky-white/blue in color. Sea creatures had obviously chewed on it. As distorted as it was, however, there was no question in John's mind. The high cheekbones and the large, straight nose. The mustache. "That's Vangelos," he said.

"You're sure?" Panagoulakos said.

"Absolutely!"

Panagoulakos nodded and then turned back to study the body.

Doctor Theodorakis began his inspection. A microphone hung from the ceiling over the middle of the lab table, near the doctor's head. He spoke into it. "Greek male identified as Petros Vangelos. Approximately sixty-five to seventy years old. Decomposition has already begun. Adipocere evident. No lividity apparent. Past the point of rigor mortis. From the condition of... well, well, what do we have here?" Theodorakis said, poking the dead man's abdomen with a stainless steel probe. He inserted the tool into a small mark that appeared to be a hole that had been sealed by coagulated blood and the swelling of the corpse. "Looks like a wound of some sort. Maybe a bullet. Help me roll him over," he ordered Panagoulakos. They rolled the body up on its side and inspected Vangelos' back. There was a larger, puckered wound there. "Exit wound," the doctor said in a matter-of-fact tone. "See the lividity on this side," he added, pointing at the dark color of the man's back where his blood had settled after death.

He rolled the body onto its back again and began probing the abdominal area. The metal probe suddenly broke the seal on the wound and gas erupted from the abdomen. The salve on his upper lip did nothing to cut the odor. John turned on his heels and left the room when the smell hit him and his already roiling stomach threatened to revolt. Panagoulakos was not far behind.

Panagoulakos lit a cigarette as soon as they stepped outside the building.

"Hell of a way to make a living," he said, inhaling deeply of the pungent Greek tobacco. "I've been trying to quit this disgusting habit," he said, waving the cigarette in the air. "But at times like this, I'm glad I smoke. There's nothing like a Greek cigarette to kill the odor of the morgue."

John stared at Panagoulakos and tried to smile. "That cigarette smells like shit," he said.

"That's the point," Panagoulakos said.

They walked down the road past the hospital until they reached the one-story, cinder block Army headquarters building. They passed through the front entrance and immediately saw Lieutenant Porras. He'd still not recovered his natural color. John tried to remember the Greek word for "nauseous" but could only come up with the word for "sick"—*arrostos*.

"I've asked Doctor Theodorakis to deliver his autopsy report to you," Panagoulakos said to the lieutenant. "Do you think you could arrange to have it brought over to my office in Vathi?"

"Of course, Inspector," Porras answered, his voice weak.

Panagoulakos gave the lieutenant his card.

They walked back out the front entrance, retrieved the Inspector's car, and left the base. After driving a short distance, John said, "Inspector, if you'll pick the restaurant, it would be my pleasure to buy lunch." He wasn't sure if he'd actually be able to eat anything after seeing Vangelos' body and after the morgue smells, but he badly needed a stiff drink.

CHAPTER SIXTEEN

April 23

Hans and Josef took turns napping in the back seat of their rented car. They had no idea where Hammond had gone. But they had learned from the hotel owner that the American's things were still in his room. They knew he'd return sooner or later. They'd parked on a side street, twenty meters up from the Soula Hotel, where they had a clear view of the hotel entrance.

The hours dragged by and the afternoon sun raised the temperature in the car.

"What are we going to do, wait here all day and night?" Josef complained. "Maybe the sonofabitch isn't coming back. I mean, after all, he's probably scared shitless after you shot at him last night."

Hans slowly turned his head and glared at his partner, who was shifting in the back seat of the compact car in an attempt to find a comfortable position. "What do you suggest?" Hans growled. "Going down to the beach and getting a nice tan?" He poked a sausage-sized index finger against his temple. "Think for a change. We have one good chance of finding this guy Hammond. If he was so frightened after last night, and took off, then he's probably not only left Samos, but also the whole damned country. If that's the case, then we're wasting our time. So what! We waste a day sitting on our asses. But if the sonofabitch didn't run, he's bound to show up sooner or later."

"Yeah, and what if he never returns?" Josef said in a petulant tone.

Hans reached between the front seats and pointed his finger at Josef's forehead. Josef knocked his hand away. Hans laughed. "Then we will find out where the Greek policeman lives and convince him he should give us the map."

"If there is a map," Josef said.

"Well, we'll find out one way or the other, won't we?"

CHAPTER SEVENTEEN

April 23

A half mile from the Greek Army base, Panagoulakos turned right at a sign that read, *CHORA/MYTILINI*. This put them on a road leading inland, and within a few minutes they came to the village of Mytilini.

The village appeared to be deserted, not unexpected considering the time of year, the time of day, and the Greek custom of taking a siesta. The main street through town was paved, but was no wider than would allow two small cars to pass at the same time. The cross streets they passed all seemed to be unpaved. A few gnarled, ancient olive trees occupied places of honor in yards fronting the main street. A mixture of wrought iron fences separated some of the residences from the pavement. There were no sidewalks.

Panagoulakos stopped at a small establishment called *Taverna Bacchus*, a white-washed affair with blue window trim and a blue door facing the street. Panagoulakos left the car in a small dirt lot on the right side of the property. He walked down a driveway toward the back of the building. John followed him into a small, flower-bedecked courtyard, half-shaded from the sun by a trellis burdened with the arms of a twelve-foot tall grapevine. In that shade, a gray-haired, ruddy-faced man of about fifty-five, with an enormous belly slept in a hammock.

The Inspector put his finger to his lips, gesturing to John to be quiet. He pointed at a small table set in the middle of the courtyard and they both took seats.

He nodded toward the sleeping figure. "The old man who owns this place has a very beautiful, very young wife," Panagoulakos said conspiratorially, in a tone slightly louder than necessary. "He keeps her on a short leash. Never lets her out of his sight. But, if we're careful, we should be able to sneak into the house without him knowing. Maybe grab a quick kiss. Are you game?"

John certainly knew that messing around with another man's wife in Greece could get you killed. But, before he could respond, a voice came from the hammock.

"If either of you motherless dogs takes one step toward my house, I'll be forced to protect the good name of my goddess-of-a-wife and turn you both into eunuchs." The man spoke without opening his eyes. When he did open them, and looked at Panagoulakos, he said, "Oh, never mind. It's only that runt police Inspector. What harm can he do? He's so short, he couldn't screw a Chihuahua."

He rolled out of his hammock laughing and walked over to Panagoulakos, grabbed him around the chest, and lifted him out of his chair. He hoisted him in the air so that the Inspector's feet were dangling two feet above the ground. They both laughed uproariously.

Panagoulakos introduced his friend. "This *arkoutha's* name is Pericles Vlacopoulos." Pericles took John's hand in both of his, making John's hand disappear, and shook it enthusiastically.

John thought the Inspector's description of Pericles as a bear was plenty appropriate. The man stood about six feet four inches tall, had shoulders so broad he looked as though he wore football pads under his shirt. His head seemed too large even for his already oversized frame. Only his enormous paunch seemed to go with his skull. Despite the man's stomach, he exuded power.

Pericles laid a hand on Panagoulakos' shoulder and led them inside to a large table in the middle of the taverna's main room, served them wine, and then left them alone for a minute. When he returned, he had in tow a gorgeous woman who appeared to be about twenty years his junior. She had olive skin and green eyes, and her lush, wavy brownish-red hair hung just past her shoulders. Her figure was full.

"This is Marika, my wife," he said to John. "Marika, our guest is John Hammond. I hope you won't hold it against him that he is accompanied by our midget Kojak."

Marika Vlacopoulos looked confused and, after saying hello to John and hugging Panagoulakos, asked her husband in a whisper, "Who is this Kojak?"

Vlacopoulos laughed at his wife's question and dismissed it with a wave, as though to say, "It's not important." He took her hand and led her back into the kitchen.

After only a few minutes, the Vlacopouloses began carrying in dishes loaded with Greek delicacies:

taramosalata—fish roe puree, *spanakopita*—spinach pies,
tiropitakia—cheese pies, *melitzanosalata*—eggplant dip,
tzazeekee—yogurt and cucumber dip, *eliesse*—olives,
pita bread, and *kaseri* cheese, and bottles of Monte Nero
red and Robola white wines. The simple lunch John
had offered to buy Panagoulakos threatened to become
an orgy of food and drink when the first serving dishes
were removed and Marika replaced them with plates and
bowls of chicken, green beans, potatoes, and *pastitsio*—
macaroni and meat pie. John's past experience with
Greek hospitality told him there would be no way he'd be
allowed to pay for the meal, as he'd offered to do. When
Vlacopoulos introduced John to his wife as his "guest," he
meant it literally. Panagoulakos had set John up.

At some point during the meal—probably after
the second bottle of wine and two glasses of Ouzo
each—John realized he'd stopped calling Panagoulakos
"Inspector," and the cop had stopped referring to him as
"Mr. Hammond." It was now Christo and John. Pericles
sat down with them about halfway through the meal.
There they were, Pericles, Christo, and John—life-long
friends.

"How do you know about Kojak?" John asked
Pericles. "Were the episodes of that old cop show shown
here in Greece?"

"No, no," he said. "I spent twenty-eight years running
my own restaurant and bar in the States. God knows I
couldn't make a living here in Greece. Between the taxes
and the bribes for the bureaucrats, I don't know how any
business survives over here. This restaurant is nothing but
a hobby. I used to watch Kojak on the television I put

on the wall behind the bar at my place in Boston. Never missed a show. I still love Telly Savalas."

"So, what brings Samos' top cop to our pissant village?" Pericles asked.

"We've had a murder in Vathi. Our friend John found the victim just before he died."

Pericles gave John a sympathetic look. "That must have been a terrible experience."

John nodded.

"The victim apparently escaped from his murderer or murderers after they'd shot him," Panagoulakos continued. "Some time after he got away, John found him on the marble steps by the sea. You know where I mean?"

"Yes."

"Two men who we assume were the killers found John with the victim, and one of those men took a shot at him. It was a miracle he got away unharmed."

"What were these men after?" Pericles asked.

"We don't know for sure," Panagoulakos said. "The dead man had a map on him. Stuffed in a boot. Perhaps that's what the men wanted. But it has no information on it of any use, at least as far as I can tell."

"Who was the victim?" Pericles asked.

"A local fisherman by the name of Vangelos."

"Petros Vangelos?" Pericles said. He looked stricken—jaw dropping, eyes squinting, forehead furrowed. "I know... knew Petros. I bought fish and sponges from him over in Kokkari. His family has lived in that village for generations. He was one of the hardest working people I've ever known. His family must have taken the news pretty hard."

"They don't know about the murder yet," Pana-goulakos said. "That's one more task I have to perform today."

"Does his whole family live in Kokkari?" John asked, remembering the photograph he'd pulled from Vangelos' wallet.

"No, one of his sons is an air force officer stationed at a base near Kerataya. His daughter is some kind of professor at the University of Athens. Antiquities, or something like that. Only the oldest son, Nicolaos—Nick—lives in Kokkari with his wife and two children. He's worked with his father on their boats his entire life. Petros has been sort of semi-retired for the last year or two. Petros' wife, Layla, is going to be devastated."

The mood in *Taverna Bacchus* had suddenly turned dark and oppressive. John was relieved when they finally said their farewells and started back toward Vathi. They'd traveled for about fifteen minutes in silence and had come to the turnoff for Kokkari. Christo stopped the car.

"How do you feel about going to the Vangelos house with me?" he asked.

"In for a penny...."

"Does that mean yes?" he asked.

"Sorry. Yes!"

CHAPTER EIGHTEEN

April 23

John and Christo arrived in Kokkari just before sunset. The road took them into the past. Christo explained that the buildings were as they'd been for centuries—flat-roofed, whitewashed, the ubiquitous bright blue shutters. Other than the narrow main drag through the fishing village, all of the side streets were cobblestoned or unpaved. They stopped at a small house three doors from the beach. A man sitting on a screened-in porch got up and came out to the car. Christo introduced him to John as Constable Raisis.

"Raisis," Christo said, "we need to find the Vangelos home. I have the unpleasant task of notifying Mrs. Vangelos that her husband is dead. It would be a good idea if you summoned the local priest."

Raisis grimaced at the news of Vangelos' death. He provided directions to the Vangelos home and then said he'd find the priest.

The drive to the Vangelos property took less than

two minutes. The family lived on high ground across the road from a narrow, rocky point of land jutting about one hundred yards into the sea. A dock had been built at a right angle to this natural seawall and tied to it were an eighteen-foot motor-powered boat and a small rowboat. Then John saw another boat—a large motor-powered fishing craft—approaching the seawall from around a bend in the shoreline. It looked to be about fifty feet long. The name printed on the bow read *Penelope.*

He might not have noticed the arriving boat had he not already been staring at a figure at the end of the seawall. John strained to make out the person in the distance. A woman wearing a white dress that made her appear wraith-like. Her slim body was visible in silhouette through the fabric of her dress, made almost sheer by the setting sun behind her. The woman's thick, jet-black hair trailed behind her in the evening breeze coming off the Aegean. Her left hand shielded her eyes from the sun's glare, while she waved her right arm in slow, exaggerated arcs as though to welcome the arriving boat, to welcome her man coming home from the sea. John felt a twinge of embarrassment at the sudden envy he felt toward the man on the boat. In all the years he'd been married, he couldn't remember one time when Sonya had greeted him at the front door. As likely as not, she would come home well after he'd already arrived, down a drink or two, and head for bed. He shook his head as though to clear it of the unwanted thought and turned to look up at the house across from the sea.

Christo drove up a steep, crushed-seashell driveway to a one-story house, built on a flat spot two hundred feet up the hillside. An elderly woman stepped out of the front door and waited for them to stop. Short, heavy set, and closer to seventy than she was to sixty, she had her salt-and-pepper hair pulled back in a neat bun. She looked like the grandmother everyone would want to have. While the Inspector drove the car closer, John saw the woman's features were etched with worry. He recognized her from the photograph in Petros Vangelos' wallet, and thought, while he watched her standing there in her brightly colored dress, drying her hands on her apron, that this might be the last time she would wear anything but black. One more member of the Greek widows' brigade.

The woman, now wringing her apron with her hands, stared at Christo. As soon as the Inspector showed his policeman's badge and introduced himself, she turned to John, but apparently found no safe harbor in his face. She moaned, seemingly knowing the news was bad. Christo and John reached out to grab her when she began to collapse. They supported her while they walked to the house.

They helped Layla Vangelos to a sofa in an immaculate and orderly sitting room. Christo sat next to her. John walked into the kitchen and fetched a glass of water. When he placed the glass in front of the old lady, she began crying over and over, *"Petro mou, Petro mou,"* all the while beating her left breast with her right hand. Her voice became hoarse and then her words devolved into wails.

Then the woman from the seawall rushed in through the front door. She glared at them and shouted in Greek,

"What have you done to my mother? Get away from her right now. Who are you? What are you doing here?"

She was the most beautiful woman John had ever seen. She looked to be in her late thirties, had green eyes, a straight nose, a generous mouth, and a light olive complexion. John's view of her on the seawall had been tantalizing. The sight of her face and swimsuit model-perfect figure from a distance of only a few feet was breathtaking. John averted his eyes, forcing himself to remember the circumstances that had brought him to the Vangelos home. But, as though possessed, his gaze reverted back to the woman.

Without trying to answer any of her questions, and feeling self-conscious about his reaction to her, John walked outside, leaving her to Christo. He made his way across the road and down to the beach. Climbing onto a boulder about half the size of a Volkswagen, he watched the bottom edge of the sun melt into the sea. He could just barely hear wailing coming from the house.

From his vantage point, he watched a procession of people make its way to the Vangelos home. The priest, in Greek Orthodox black robes and headpiece, and Constable Raisis arrived together. Elderly women dressed in black also began to arrive—the official mourning troop. Widows who knew what Mrs. Vangelos was going through.

Meanwhile, the fishing boat he'd seen approaching earlier had dropped its anchor by the dock. A powerfully built, fortyish man climbed down a ladder to the dock. A second man stood in the boat's wheelhouse. After tying up the boat, the man on the dock moved in John's direction, walking along the seawall. They acknowledged one another with nods. He seemed to be about to say something, but then the sight of visitors approaching the house seemed to catch his attention. He sprinted across the road, up the driveway to the house. After a moment, Christo came out, spotlighted by the last of the sunset. John whistled to get his attention. Christo looked from side to side, then seemed to spot John, waved, and yelled for him to wait. He drove the car down the hill and picked him up by the side of the road.

They spoke only a few words during the return trip to Vathi.

"I appreciate you coming along," Christo said. John could tell from the tone of his voice that he really meant it.

"*Teepota,*" John responded. "It was nothing." But they both knew it was not *nothing*.

When they crested the hill overlooking Vathi, the lights of the town sparkled below and provided a small lift to John's spirits.

Christo dropped him at his hotel, making him promise to meet in the morning for an uninterrupted breakfast. John made it halfway to the front door before remembering he'd left his jacket, with the copy of Vangelos' map in its pocket, on the back seat of the police car. He turned, but the taillights of Christo's car were already disappearing around the corner at the end of the block.

John climbed the stairs to his second-floor room and pulled his room key from his pants pocket. He was about to insert it into the lock when he noticed a light showing under the door. He thought for a moment he'd forgotten to turn off a lamp in his haste to get to the police station that morning, or perhaps the maid had left a light on. But, after all that had already happened, he hesitated, wondering if he should call the police. He remembered the old saying, "You may be paranoid, but that doesn't mean there isn't someone hiding behind every bush." He began to think he was being ridiculous, when the door suddenly flew open.

"Ah, is it Mr. Hammond? Please come in and join us."

John noticed the pistol in the man's hand, then the size of the man wielding it. The guy was enormous, like Arnold Schwarzenegger on steroids.

"You can't know how much we've looked forward to meeting you," the man said, stepping into the hall and pointing the weapon back at the room.

John walked into his room. A second man sat in the chair by the balcony doors, calmly smoking a cigarette, lightly tapping what appeared to be a matte-black sap against his thigh.

"Yes, please join us, Mr. Hammond," the second man said.

John had a sudden realization that these were the men who had murdered Petros Vangelos.

"Mr. Hammond," the seated one said, "we think you have something that our employer wants very badly. We're going to give you one opportunity to tell us where it is. If you are smart, you will do so quickly, with no bullshit."

John looked from the one doing the talking to the

man with the pistol, and back again to the seated one. Something told him that all the cooperation in the world wasn't going to make one iota of difference. These men had the look of hired guns, and they were not about to leave a witness who could identify them, especially after killing Vangelos. "I would be happy to give you whatever it is you think I have," John said, "but I can hardly think with a gun pointed at me."

"Ach, mann," the seated one said, "please put away the pistol. I can see that Mr. Hammond is more than willing to help us. Isn't that so, Mr. Hammond?"

John nodded his head and made a show of swallowing. Just a thoroughly frightened, middle-aged man who was not used to being threatened by gun-toting assassins.

"Good, good," the man said.

John saw out of his peripheral vision the man behind him shoulder holster his weapon. He wheeled and charged the man, lowering his shoulder, hitting him square in the chest, and driving him backward past the foot of the bed and into the closed entry door. The sound of cracking wood exploded in the small room. John slammed a fist into the side of the man's face, grabbed the front of the man's shirt as he was starting to sag to the floor, and spun him around to block the path of the second man. John lurched for the door, knowing he only had a second or two to make his escape. He grabbed the door handle and jerked the door open, throwing it back. Then something vise-like clamped around his ankle. The one with the gun was stretched out on the floor, arm extended, fingers wrapped around John's ankle. John tried to wrench himself loose, but the man was too strong.

John looked toward the second man. He was amazed to see that he was still sitting in the chair, legs crossed, smoking his cigarette.

The man looked back at John, shook his head, stubbed out his cigarette on the chair arm, and then stood. "You surprise me, Mr. Hammond," the man said while walking over to where John stood, his leg still in the iron clasp of the other man. "I hoped you had more sense." He reached around John and calmly pushed the door shut. "Get up, Josef," he said, "you're embarrassing me."

John looked down at Josef, then started to turn his head back toward the other man, when fireworks went off in his head and he felt himself falling.

CHAPTER NINETEEN

April 23

After dropping John Hammond off at his hotel, Christo drove to the other side of the island, back in the direction of the airport. It had been a long, tiring day. Although he'd gotten used to handling homicide cases and to the long hours associated with them when he worked with the Athens police, he was now out of practice—both from the standpoints of time required and emotional impact. And he didn't have the support staff here he'd had in Athens. He thought over every step he'd taken and couldn't think of anything more he could have done. He smiled while he thought about how Hammond had gone from suspect number one to an unofficial assistant. He was beginning to like the American.

The road dropped quickly toward the sea, then led away from the coast. Here Christo made a sharp turn onto a dirt driveway that climbed precipitously. Olive trees bordered both sides of the drive and grape vines showed through the moonlit trees. He felt pride and a sense of belonging every time he followed this drive. This was home. Where his father and his father before him had made a living from the land. The Panagoulakoses had owned this land for generations before the Turkish occupation of Samos that ended at the beginning of the twentieth century, and ever since.

A light shone in the distance. Sophia would be working off her anxieties about his work schedule. Christo guessed she was baking as usual. He smiled at the wonder of it all. Sophia baked enough for an army, he ate everything she put before him, and he was still just as rail-thin as he'd been as a teenager. He checked his watch and sighed when he realized it was hours past the children's bedtime. Another night of lost opportunities to be with his son and daughter.

Sophia Panagoulakos met her husband at the front door of their one-story house, set in the middle of forty acres. "Christo, you are late again," she said, sympathy, rather than complaint evident in her voice.

"I'm sorry, Sophia. *Tee na kaname?*"

"You can let someone else handle some of the cases. You can't do everything yourself."

Christo kissed his wife's cheek. "I'll try," he said, knowing he wouldn't. There was no one else on Samos to assign his cases to.

Sophia knew it, too. She gave him a look that said she'd heard that before and didn't believe a word of it. "Go get changed, I've got a nice *kalamaria* casserole in the oven."

Christo blew her a kiss and walked into his bedroom. The telephone rang while he unbuttoned his shirt.

"Christo," he heard, turning to see Sophia standing in the doorway, "it's for you."

He walked back into the living room and picked up the phone. "Panagoulakos," he growled. He listened for several seconds, feeling the blood rise to his face. "Is he alive?" he asked. Then he replaced the receiver and turned to Sophia. "I've got to go out," he said.

CHAPTER TWENTY

April 24

*T*he rocket exploded, raining wet earth, metal, and yellow and white sparks. The shrapnel cut through Jim Eastly, his driver, and Ernie Baca, his machine gunner. Like marionettes dumped by a thoughtless puppet master, they lay unnaturally bent, half-in, half-out of the jeep. Something— the explosion itself or some debris—had knocked John from the vehicle, up against a giant, twisted tree. The tree had leaves as big as elephant ears; he knew its name, wanted to remember it for some stupid reason, but couldn't think of it. Confused, bleeding—red drops cascaded onto his hands lying like useless bowls in his lap—he watched everything around him move in slow motion. Even the little man dressed in black pajamas approached him with dream-like speed— slowly, deliberately, floating.

There was nothing that missed his attention—not the butterflies stirring the air six feet above the little man's head, not Jim and Ernie's bodies already going pale from loss of blood. Come on guys, it's only a dream. You can get up now. He squinted at the bright early morning sun and felt amazement at the sight of sparkling crystals the sunlight fabricated out of the dew. He wondered what was wrong with his arms and legs, and questioned why the little man in black pajamas pointed a 1903 Springfield rifle at him. The man shoved the muzzle of the Springfield toward the middle of his forehead, making his eyes cross. He felt a stab of pain and his head bounced back against the tree.

His stunned mind processed information in slow, asymmetrical pulses. Leaving gaps. This is…VC. Oh-oh,… not good. The black-clad man smiled triumphantly, evilly, showing John his blackened, betel juice-stained teeth, and pressed his finger on the trigger. He screamed something. It didn't process.

Amazing, John thought, matter-of-factly, calmly, I'm going to die.

The clack of the striking hammer sounded like an explosion. Misfire. That clack wiped away the VC soldier's smile and brought John out of his hypnotic stupor. Suddenly, all the electric circuits in his body sparked and adrenaline washed through him like a flash flood quenching a dry riverbed. He pulled the .45 from his shoulder holster and aimed it at his enemy's startled face.

Then everything around him turned pale yellow.

▯

John awoke drenched in sweat. His head throbbed with pain and there appeared to be a yellow aura surrounding him. This is a new twist to my dream, he thought.

"John, can you hear me, are you all right?" a man's voice asked. He sounded worried.

What's wrong? John thought. *What happened?*

He tried to respond, but his throat was too dry. His tongue felt glued to the roof of his mouth. He rasped out, "Water." Someone placed a straw in his mouth and he sucked on it reflexively. Water had never tasted better.

His eyes began to focus enough to recognize Christo. A second man, standing behind Christo, pushed forward and announced, "I am Doctor Stavros Pappas. Mr. Hammond, you are in the hospital at the Pythagorio Army Base. You have had a nasty knock on the head and have a concussion, along with a gash on the side of your head that took thirty-four stitches to close. I assure you that you are going to have a vicious headache for at least several days and I would not be surprised if you experience some nausea."

John seemed to get the gist of the doctor's speech, but his brain felt fuzzy. For some reason he imagined his skull stuffed with cotton candy. He scrunched his eyes shut, willing himself to focus on the doctor's words. He looked back at Christo. The Inspector looked worried. With some effort, John smiled at him and gave him the thumbs-up sign.

"How long will he have to stay here?" John heard Christo ask.

The doctor skewered Christo with an impatient, incredulous look, which John found humorous. He giggled, but then wondered what he had just found so funny.

"Mr. Hammond is lucky to be alive!" the doctor said. "The blow to his head was just indirect enough to avoid crushing his skull. Either the person who clubbed him had poor aim or Mr. Hammond turned his head at just the right moment. A direct hit would probably have killed him. He will be our guest for several days… at least." He made the speech sound like a scolding. Then he made a noise that sounded like "humph" and walked out.

"Wh… what hap…pened, Chris…to?" John asked, knowing that his words slurred, but unable to do anything about it.

"All I can tell you," Christo said, "is that Soula Demetridakis heard a noise and got out of bed. She found you lying in a pool of blood just inside your open doorway. All of your things were thrown around the room and someone even slashed open the bedding. Whoever hit you on the head thought you had something he wanted and, from the looks of the knot on your head, he meant to kill you to get it. Do you remember anything?"

Christo's voice sounded to John as though someone was playing a 45 RPM record on 33 RPM speed. His eyelids felt heavy, then everything went black.

⧠

John awoke feeling less stuporous. He noticed Christo slouched in a chair at the foot of the bed. "Christo."

The Inspector started, but quickly came wide awake. "Thank God!" he exclaimed, leaping to his feet. "You look almost human again."

John smiled. "I only feel half-human." He gingerly touched the side of his head and moaned. "Damn! I've got quite a lump."

Christo laughed, but his face turned suddenly serious. "You know how lucky you were?"

John hunched his shoulders. "I guess."

"You feel up to telling me what you can remember?"

John blinked several times, as though he were trying to make his memory zoom in on something. Then he said, "I found two guys in my room when you dropped me off last night. There was a scuffle. That's the last thing I remember."

"In another month, the hotel would have been full and someone might have seen something. The bastards got away," Christo said.

Not until Christo finished speaking did John remember the copy of the map he'd made. He'd put it in his jacket pocket. Where was the jacket? The men who'd assaulted him must have found it.

As if able to read John's mind, the Inspector said, "Oh, by the way, John, I found your jacket on the back seat of my car. I brought it with me." He pointed toward a corner of the room. "It's in the closet."

John recalled only then he'd left the jacket in the police car. The map was safe. He felt reprieved until Christo looked at him with his cop eyes and said, "Guess what fell out of your jacket when I lifted it off the back seat?"

It took all of the backbone John could muster just to look Christo in the eyes. The Inspector gazed back sternly for several seconds, then laughed.

"You should see your face," he exclaimed. "Priceless, that's what it is. Absolutely priceless."

"You son of a bitch," John moaned. "What's so damn funny?"

"You are. I haven't seen anyone look so guilty in a long time."

"Well, I'm glad you find it so amusing."

"I forgive you for your little white lie. I think you've been punished enough already."

John settled back into the pillows and sighed in relief. Then a new thought struck him. "Where am I?"

"The Greek Army Hospital," Christo answered.

John now recalled the doctor saying something about the Army Hospital. "Why the Army hospital?"

"Two reasons," Christo answered. "First, this is the best hospital on the island. Second, this base has a chain link perimeter fence and is guarded twenty-four hours a day. Someone tried to kill you and I can't think of a safer place than right here. I think it's fair to assume whoever broke into your room wanted the map and assumed you had it. He didn't find it, obviously. For all he knows, he did kill you. With you dead, he has no hope of getting it from you. Besides, from the way they trashed your room, they've probably figured out that you didn't have it after all."

John was wondering how the men had tracked him down. Then another thought struck him. "If those men saw you arrive at my hotel after I called about finding Petros Vangelos, then they must know I met with the police."

Christo finished his thought. "And they also must know that, if you found a map on Mr. Vangelos, you would have turned it over to the police."

"You'd better watch your back, Christo," John said. "These men don't seem to be the type to care who they kill."

Christo's eyes went diamond-hard. "I'm counting on that, my friend," he said.

Suddenly, the doctor's prediction came true and a wave of nausea swept over John, accompanied by a jackhammer of a headache. Without having to be asked, Christo went into the hall and came back with a nurse. Whatever she gave John knocked him out until the early hours of the following morning.

☐

Between the drugs and his injuries, John felt like hell. Although it was still dark outside, he could see a faint hint of dawn through his window. He had one overriding need—to get to the bathroom. Cautiously, he slid off the bed until his bare feet touched the cool tile floor. He steadied himself by holding onto a wheeled intravenous rack next to his bed. Overcome by dizziness, he would have fallen to the floor but for that rack. When the room stopped spinning, he slowly made his way to the bathroom.

While washing his hands, he hazarded a glance in the mirror and was shocked by his appearance. A bandage was wrapped around his head--stained where blood had seeped through. Both of his eyes were blackened.

He slowly made his way back to the bed. His hospital gown rode up his legs, barely covering his butt. Negotiating the climb into bed, his rear end exposed to the world, he heard giggling behind him. He rolled onto his side, buttocks turned away from the door. The beauty from the Vangelos house stood in the doorway. John groaned. Nice impression I'm making here, he thought.

The woman stood in the doorway and, in excellent British English, asked, "Would it be all right if I come in?"

"Yes, please," he said, arranging his bedclothes as best he could, and pulling the sheet up to his chin.

She stepped forward into a ray of sunshine slicing through the window, spotlighting her as though she'd entered a stage. John felt his breath catch.

"Mr. Hammond, I came here this morning to thank you for what you did for my father... and my mother. Inspector Panagoulakos told me you were the last person to talk with my father, and that your injuries are probably a result of your trying to help him. I cannot put into words the gratitude my family and I have for you."

John blushed like a kid at his first dance. "You don't need to thank me," he said, "but I appreciate you coming here."

"Mr. Hammond. I will always be in your debt."

Wonderful, he thought. Just what I need. A gorgeous married woman in my debt. In a land where husbands castrate you for merely staring at their wives. She took a seat in the chair at the foot of the bed.

"How are you feeling?"

"Great!" he lied.

"Forgive me for saying so, but you look as though you lost a wrestling match with a tiger."

"Actually, madam, I feel like I look."

She laughed in a way that reminded John of wind chimes--full of life and good humor.

"Mr. Hammond, you need not call me 'madam' since I am not married. Please call me Zoë."

John felt suddenly light-headed, yet exhilarated. She had not been waving to a husband when he'd seen her on the dock. Maybe a fiancé? He tried to come up with a way to ask about the man she'd been waving to on the boat, without sounding like an idiot, but a nurse came into the room just then, ruining the chance for further conversation.

The nurse glared at Zoë. "You are not supposed to be in this room without permission. Wait out in the hall until I can find the guard." Turning on her heels, the nurse ran square into Inspector Panagoulakos.

"Thank you for your concern," Panagoulakos said, "but Ms. Vangelos is here with me. I will escort her off the base."

The nurse recognized the voice of authority and backed off immediately.

Zoë smiled and assured John she would return for a visit the next day. She walked out of the room ahead of Christo, who turned his head and winked at John, then followed her out.

CHAPTER TWENTY–ONE

April 25

John found showering and shaving an ordeal, but one he would have performed if he'd actually been on his deathbed, rather than just feeling as though he were dead. No way in hell he'd let Zoë Vangelos see him again looking like a skid row bum. He did the best he could to clean off yellow antiseptic stains from his face and neck, avoiding getting the bandage around his head wet. After repeated efforts, he gave up trying to make his hair presentable. Unruly tufts stood up like miniature sheaves of wheat, framed by the white bandage.

He awaited Zoë's promised return with the anticipation of a lovesick adolescent, increasingly anxious and impatient while the minutes turned into hours. He'd expected her to arrive in the morning as she had the day before, but by noon she hadn't shown up and John had fallen into a full-blown funk.

Christo and Zoë arrived at four in the afternoon. She had the same electric effect on John as the first time he had seen her. Her smile seemed to light up his room and obliterated the frustration and depression he felt all day.

"How's the patient?" Christo asked.

"Great," John said. "I'm ready to get out of here."

Christo opened his mouth, about to say something, but Zoë beat him to it. "Oh no! You cannot leave the hospital yet. You must stay here until the doctors are sure you are well."

"I thought you might be here earlier," John said to both of them, changing the subject.

Zoë gave John a sympathetic look. "I met with Inspector Panagoulakos this morning and gave him a statement about what we knew about my fath . . . my father's state of mind and activities. I am afraid I was not much help. Then, for most of the day, I helped my mother arrange for the funeral and burial. It has been a very long and tiring day."

John felt stupid then for having shown his impatience, when he should have been thinking about what she must be going through. The dark circles under her eyes and the fatigue showing in her less-than-erect posture provided ample evidence of the stress she was under.

Zoë said she had to call her mother and left the room to find a phone. When she was gone, Christo began to half-dance, half-walk around the room, singing a little tune. "Oh Zoë, I love you very much. You make my heart melt like ice in the hot sun. You put the lead in my pencil. La, la, la."

"Asshole!" John muttered.

"What's the matter, John? You're not going to thank your good friend Christo for bringing the love of your life to visit you?"

"What the hell are you talking about? So I like the lady's company. What's the big deal?"

Christo snorted. "What do you think, I'm some kind of *kolokeethas?* I look like an eggplant to you? You got that look about you all men get when they've lost their minds. You got it good. And you know what else? I don't blame you. Zoë is one hell of a woman. So don't play stupid with me. You got the bug, buddy, and you got it bad."

John stared at the little Greek cop standing there in that ugly yellow room, laughing his butt off. Finally he said, "No, I don't think you're an eggplant. You're a royal pain in the ass."

"Now that's something I will admit to, my friend. But that doesn't make me wrong."

CHAPTER TWENTY–TWO

April 30

John developed a fever on his third night in the hospital, his temperature climbing to 103 degrees. Doctor Pappas started pumping antibiotics into John's system. The drugs worked, but the ordeal delayed his release from the hospital. Zoë showed up every one of the seven days of his confinement, even on the afternoon of the day that Petros Vangelos was buried.

On the day of John's release, Christo picked Zoë up at her mother's house before coming to the hospital. John was still terribly weak and had to be helped to the car. Just a week in the hospital and he felt ninety years old.

Instead of taking the road to John's hotel in Vathi, Christo drove over the top of the island toward Mytilini. He pulled around behind the *Taverna Bacchus* and honked his horn. Pericles instantly appeared at the back door and swiftly stepped to the car.

"Welcome to our home, my friend," he said to John after opening the car door.

John glanced quizzically at Christo.

"Let's go inside and I'll explain everything to you," Christo said.

When they were all settled around a table in the taverna's dining room, Christo said, "I'm concerned that whoever attacked you may still be a danger. You can't return to your hotel. Also, your doctor wants you watched over for another couple of days. Pericles and Marika have agreed to put you up. Marika will make sure you get plenty of good food and rest. If anyone is after you, this is probably the last place they'll look."

"I thought you said the bad guys probably think they killed me," John said.

"Probably, but not absolutely," Christo answered.

About to protest, John judiciously shut up when Zoë added, "Besides, Mytilini is close to Kokkari, so it will be quite easy for me to visit every day."

It was about five o'clock in the afternoon and the taverna had not yet opened for the evening. John detected cooking odors coming from the kitchen. He sighed with something close to ecstasy when Pericles and Marika brought platters of hors d'ocuvres, *horiatiki* salads, and a stew—*youvetsakia*—into the dining room. He was again confirmed in his opinion that the food in Greece is reason enough to travel there.

"Christo told me what happened to you in your hotel," Pericles said. "I'd love to get my hands on the bastards."

John smiled in appreciation of the sentiment, but he was so worn out he couldn't muster the energy to say anything. The place in his scalp where the stitches had been now itched like crazy. But he couldn't stand the pain every time he started to scratch the itch. And he seemed to have a perpetual headache. He'd barely begun to sample the meal when fatigue overcame him.

Every time he looked at Zoë, he found her staring back at him, worry lines etching her forehead and the corners of her eyes. She now appeared even more worried, the lines in her forehead had become furrows. She whispered something to Marika, who immediately left the room. Zoë came around to his place at the table. "I think it's time we put you to bed."

John offered no resistance and, with Zoë holding his arm, walked to the spare bedroom in the quarters behind the taverna. Zoë gently nudged him toward the bed. He stretched out on the cool, clean sheets. The last thing he remembered was someone tugging off his shoes.

CHAPTER TWENTY–THREE

May 1

The next day John awoke to the strong smell of Turkish coffee. After washing up and putting on clean clothes, he looked around the house for Pericles and Marika. He found them seated in the courtyard behind the taverna with Zoë.

"Sleeping Beauty has awakened," Pericles said. "How are you feeling this morning?"

"Not bad," John replied.

"For a while there we thought you had died," Pericles said with a laugh. "It's not often a guest sleeps for fifteen hours."

"What... fifteen hours. You're kidding! I haven't done that since I was a teenager."

"You needed it," Marika said in a mock-scolding tone. "You are here to get better. Would you like to have some breakfast?"

"Actually, I'm starving," John said. "I'm sorry about

all the trouble I've caused you; but, if it's no trouble, I'd love something to eat."

Marika "tsked-tsked" at him and scowled, making him feel that he'd insulted her. There wasn't much more that was important in Greek culture than the obligation they assume for the care of a guest. Marika left her chair, patting John's arm when she passed him, and walked toward the kitchen. He thought again how wondrous Greek hospitality can be.

After John finished eating, Zoë suggested they take a short walk to the beach. They walked at a snail's pace down the narrow street through the village toward the sea. Other than a woman who was sweeping the walk in front of her home, the village seemed deserted. The street descended gradually to the water and John stared at the sea sparkling before him. Marika's food, the sea air, and Zoë at his side all combined to give him a feeling of well being.

At the beach, they rested on a two-foot high wall separating the sand from the street. The beach was quite shallow, extending no more than forty or fifty feet from the wall to the water. This part of the village wrapped around a jade-colored cove three hundred yards wide and perhaps a half-mile's distance from the shore to where the mouth of the cove met the Aegean. The coast curved in a semi-circle to the left. There were houses in that direction that looked down at the water from the tops of steep hills. There is something restful about watching the sea, John thought. He stared at it as though hypnotized, lost in his own thoughts.

Zoë broke the silence first. "Did my father suffer… was he in much pain when you found him?"

Holding Petros Vangelos in his arms, his groans, the difficulty he had breathing, all cycled through John's memory. He knew he couldn't lie to her, but he decided to say only as much as necessary. "Zoë, your father died within seconds after I first found him. He couldn't have been in pain for very long." His answer clearly did not satisfy her. She looked skeptical—arched eyebrows and an almost challenging look in her eyes.

"Your father was very brave," he added, "and his last thoughts were for his family."

"That's all my father ever thought about—his family. He worked hard his entire life so my brothers and I could get the formal education he never had."

John nodded his understanding. "With his last breath he said, 'My family' and 'My life.' He also spoke a couple of words I didn't understand."

"The Inspector mentioned that you gave him my father's wallet and a map."

"It seemed he wanted me to look in his pockets and in his boot," John said. "I had no idea the paper I pulled from your father's boot was a map until I returned to my hotel room that night. I wish I still had a copy of the map to show you. On my way to Christo's office the next morning, after I found your father, I had a copy of the map made for your family. Unfortunately, Christo now has the original *and* the copy."

"Can you remember the words my father spoke that you did not understand?"

"Actually, I do recall the first one. 'Pythagorio'… like the name of the town. The other word meant nothing to me and still doesn't. It reminded me of a wine I used to drink when I lived in Greece back in the seventies. It was called *Pallini*. Except your father said *'palin'*… no, no, *'evpalin,'* or something like that."

Zoë had been staring out to sea again while John talked. But she abruptly turned toward him now. "You're sure that's what he said?"

"As sure as I can be. Why? Does it mean something to you?"

"It just may, John. But I need more information. Can you recall anything about the map?"

"Now that was strange," he said. "The map had no street names, no identifying marks indicating a village or building, no scale, no nothing. But there were three small circles on the map that formed the corners of a right triangle. The three circles were on land. There was a fourth circle that lay out to sea. There was nothing else on the map, except for some gibberish written on the back."

"What gibberish?" she asked.

"I can't recall all of the words, but they sounded like a nursery rhyme. At least that's what Christo thought they were."

"Interesting," she replied.

"What are you thinking?"

"I don't know what I'm thinking, but as soon as I figure it out, I'll tell you. You said Christo has the map. I think maybe I should call on the Inspector."

"When do you want to do that?" John asked. "I'd like to join you."

"I don't think it's a good idea for you to be overdoing things. Besides, you're supposed to be hiding out. Why don't you stay here in Mytilini? I'll come back here after I meet with Christo and tell you what I learn."

"Like hell you're going to leave me here. This business has become very personal for me. I'm in it until the end. Besides, the men who attacked me are probably long gone."

She smiled her glorious smile. "I would welcome the company. I'll pick you up here at eight in the morning."

Despite the fact he felt much better than he had the previous day, the walk back up to the taverna sapped his energy. He spent the next hour in Pericles' hammock, alternately sleeping, thinking about the Vangelos map, and trying to figure out what was so important about it that someone would try to kill him for it. And had murdered Zoë's father for it. Assuming it was the map they were after.

CHAPTER TWENTY-FOUR

May 1

B y 8:00 p.m., John felt rested and stronger. He found the taverna busy with local customers and drifted into the kitchen. "Need a hand?" he asked.

Marika gave him a confused look. Pericles laughed and explained the American colloquialism to her. "Oh, I understand," she said, then gave John a grateful look and pointed at a wooden table where a large bowl sat filled with lettuce and several smaller bowls holding olives, capers, tomatoes, cucumbers, and *feta* cheese. "Do you think you could make two *horiatiki* salads?" she asked.

"I've eaten enough of them. I should be able to whip up something pretty close to the real thing."

Marika smiled. "I hope this 'whip up' is a good thing."

John laughed and reminded himself that he would have to be careful with American slang around her. Her English was good, but not that good.

While he worked on the salads, and Pericles made

frenetic round trips from kitchen to dining room, John once again thanked Marika for putting him up in her home.

"It is no trouble," she answered. "We have enjoyed having you visit us. Besides, we would do anything for Christo."

"Have you been friends for long?"

"Just since Pericles returned to Samos from the United States." She said this with a far away look in her eyes and seemed to suddenly lose herself in her own thoughts. John had the feeling she'd retreated into the past, and there was something in her look that told him it was a troubling past. Pericles entered the kitchen at that moment and must have noticed the storm cloud that had become his wife's expression.

"Tee trekhee?" he said as he snatched two platters off the serving counter.

Marika shook her head as though to clear it of its sudden fog, and smiled at her husband. *"Teepota, agapee mou,"* she said. "Nothing, my love. I was just day thinking," she said in English.

Pericles spun around and moved toward the door to the dining room, casting a toothy grin at Marika. "Day dreaming, my sweet," he said. "Not day thinking."

"I must try better to understand these American sayings," she said, grimacing at John. "I do not want Pericles to think I am stupid."

John had seen the way Pericles looked at Marika, the way he treated her. The furthest thought from Pericles' mind about his wife had to do with her being stupid. It was obvious he adored the woman. John shot a surreptitious glance at Marika to see if the gray mood that had come over her had passed. At least her color was back and she seemed to be quietly humming to herself. He'd already decided not to pursue any further the subject of the Vlacopoulos' relationship with Christo, when Marika abruptly looked at him and caught his furtive glance. There was a flinty look to her eyes now and John thought she had gone from depressed to angry.

Marika brushed her arm across her forehead, rearranging a few errant strands of hair. "I want you to know what it means to have Christo for a friend," she said.

"You don't need to—"

She waved a hand at him, stopping him. She took a deep breath, her chest heaving, then falling. "Shortly after we opened the taverna—it was our first summer—two men broke into our house just as the sun was coming up. They entered through the back door and, before we could even get out of bed, they were upon us. Pericles struggled with one man while the other one held me. The man who Pericles fought must have been thirty years younger than my husband and was very powerful. But Pericles was...." She gave John an anguished look. "Conquesting him?"

"Beating him," John said.

"Yes, beating him," Marika said with a smile. "But the second man ran over and hit Pericles in the back of his head with a pipe. Then the other one began kicking him."

Marika's eyes began to water and her voice broke. "The man kicked him and kicked him. I screamed at him, begging him to stop. But, even after Pericles was unconscious, he still kicked him until I thought he had killed him. Then he turned on me. He demanded cash. I told him we had very little money. We had just opened, and all our money was either in the bank or had been invested in the taverna.

"This made him very angry. My English was not so good then and he spoke with a very rough British accent. He got even angrier when I could not understand everything he said. But he said one thing that I understood very well. He said to the man holding me, 'Well, we're not leaving here empty-handed.' Then he walked over to me and ripped my nightgown off. I was so scared and ashamed."

Marika's chin trembled and she wiped her eyes with her apron. "He hit me in the face and the two men tied my hands and feet to the bed posts. Then the one who had kicked Pericles got... got on top of me. That is when Christo came into the room. Both of the men were looking at me, so I saw Christo walk in before they did."

Pericles suddenly rushed into the kitchen. "I need three more orders of the *kalamaria* and two more salads." He looked somewhat quizzically at John, still working on two salad bowls. "You're going to have to speed up if you want a job around here," he said. He spooned *feta* cheese on top of each salad, grabbed them from in front of John, and raced toward the door again. He looked over his shoulder, smiled at John, and said, "Not so much lettuce, and go easy on the capers."

The interruption cleared the air of some of the tension caused by Marika's story. John didn't have the heart or the nerve to ask her to continue—even though he was dying to hear what happened after Christo entered the bedroom. For the next couple of hours, Pericles ran back and forth between the dining room and the kitchen, placing orders and picking up plates and bowls. John felt good to be helping his hosts.

"Looks like we're about done for the evening," Pericles finally said. "The Stavrogiannis want some coffee, and old man Arvatis wants a Metaxa. That should be about it," he said, walking up behind Marika and rubbing her shoulders. She leaned back against him and moaned with relief.

John felt suddenly melancholy. He couldn't remember one time when someone could have seen Sonya and him together and have gotten the same impression of deep mutual affection he got from watching Marika and Pericles.

After Pericles left to take the coffees and brandy out to the dining room, Marika, busying herself with cleanup, said, "I think I'd better finish my story, otherwise you will not be able to sleep tonight." She chuckled and gave John a wink.

Not wanting to appear too anxious, but nevertheless bursting with curiosity, he said, "Only if it has a happy ending."

"You can be the judge of that," she said. Christo shot one man in the leg. When the man started screaming, Christo walked over and clubbed him on the head with his pistol. Then he dragged the other one—this giant man— off the bed and threw him on the floor. I do not know how he did it--the man seemed twice as big as Christo." She coughed an embarrassed laugh. "Almost everyone I know is twice as big as Christo." She gave John an apologetic look and blushed. "But size made no difference," she continued. "The second man began begging Christo not to shoot him. You know what Christo did?" Marika put her finger to her lips and showed John how Christo had said, "Shh," to tell the man to be quiet. "Then," she said, "Christo shot him in the leg, too.

"After covering me with a blanket and untying me from the bed, Christo helped Pericles get up from the floor. He put him in bed while I dressed. He used the telephone to call the hospital and the local policeman. He ordered the policeman to get two men he trusted and come to the taverna. When they arrived, Christo told them to take the two criminals to a spot in the forest and to hold them there until he joined them.

"Christo drove Pericles and me to the hospital in Vathi. He told the doctor there that two men had broken into our home and attacked my husband. He didn't mention they had tried to rape me and he never said another word about the criminals."

Marika paused. By that time John was dying to find out what had happened to the two Brits. "Were the two men put in prison?" he asked.

"I have no idea what happened to those men," she said in a tone that indicated she couldn't have cared less about what had happened to them. "I have heard rumors, but nothing certain. As far as the public is concerned, the men who beat up Pericles escaped. The story of the attack was in all the newspapers and the police received a lot of criticism for never bringing them to trial."

"What did the rumors say?"

"Now that is a completely other story. Some people believe Christo returned to the location in the forest and joined the constable and his two deputies. From there they supposedly dragged the men to the edge of a cliff overlooking the Aegean, castrated them, and tossed them into the sea."

The shock of the ending must have shown on his face. Marika continued cleaning up while she watched him. Her face was a stone mask. She seemed to be waiting for him to say something. When he couldn't figure out anything appropriate to say, she said, "John, you have to understand that this is Greece, not the United States. The concept of an eye for an eye runs deep in our veins. And there is something I have not told you. Those two Englishmen were travelling on motorcycles. They had left a trail of victims behind them on two other islands before they arrived on Samos. They had already raped at least two women and had murdered one of the women's husbands.

"A report had gone to the police station in Vathi that two foreigners had robbed a gas station and been seen travelling toward Mytilini on motorcycles. Christo had come here to investigate and had spotted the motorcycles parked outside. If he had not come here, Pericles and I could have been killed. And if the rumor about what happened to the two men is true, I could not be happier."

John knew it would be unproductive to debate the concept of crime and appropriate punishment. The cultural void between Marika and him was too wide. But it still shocked him to hear a woman talk so calmly and unemotionally about revenge and violence. Castration and murder.

He just nodded his head when Marika asked, "Now you understand why we would do anything for Christo."

CHAPTER TWENTY-FIVE

May 2

After Zoë picked up John the next morning, he tried to discover why she seemed so exercised about seeing the map, but she wouldn't tell him, other than to say, "First, I have to see it."

So he changed the subject and asked about her family.

"My mother is very upset," she said. "But she has plenty of support. My younger brother, Pavlos, who is in the air force, has taken a week's leave, and my older brother Nick's wife, Ariana, has been a saint. She cooks and cleans and holds my mother's hand and never complains. But Nick is having a tough time. He worked day in and day out on the boat with our father. Every day he goes to work, he will feel my father's absence. Inside he's raging. He needs a target for his anger. With no known suspects, no arrests, it eats at him."

At the police station, John asked for Christo and learned he was in a meeting outside the building. The desk sergeant didn't know when he would return. He suggested they come back in thirty minutes.

They left the station and stopped on the sidewalk by the entrance.

"This may not be a good idea," Zoë said. "What if those men are still here?"

"It's daytime. What can happen?"

She made that hunched-shouldered, open-palmed gesture so common to Mediterranean people. "All right, if you say so."

John had second thoughts. He pointed at his head. "Even with the bandages gone, this lump and the bald spot where they shaved my scalp make me stand out."

Zoë looked over John's shoulder at a sign overhanging the doorway of a shop down the street. A mischievous look came over her face and she winked at John. "Wait here," she said.

John watched Zoë race down the street. Two minutes later, she reappeared with a small paper bag. A minute later, she led a beret-clad, sunglassed John down the sidewalk. "Very rakish," she said, giggling at the look on John's face. "Don't look so uncomfortable. You look like a French tourist. *Oui, oui, tres chic,*" she said.

John took Zoë's arm in his and guided her across the street to the quay.

It was a beautiful, bright day with just a hint of a cool breeze that barely stirred the leaves of trees lining the raised walkway separating Vathi harbor from the city's main street. The bay was calm and the morning sun glistened on the water's surface. Shopkeepers moving displays out to the sidewalks and a few fishermen hawking their early-morning catch to local housewives provided the only activity across from the quay.

Zoë asked, "Have you heard about the *volta?*"

"No, tell me about it," John said.

"The *volta* is the name given to the act of strolling along this seaside walkway at night. There are rules associated with it. Most evenings you will find entire families slowly walking along here. They will never overtake a group walking in front of them, and when they pass a family going in the opposite direction for the first time they don't acknowledge one another. The next time they pass one another they barely nod. But the third time they may stop to talk. I believe the custom is borrowed from the Italians who call it the *passeggiata,* and I think it has more to do with showing off new clothes than anything else." She laughed. "The rules of the *volta* vary from island to island. In some places only the women take part, as though it's their answer to the male-dominated *kafeneios.* The men have their coffee shops, the women the *volta.*"

"So," John said, "if you and I had never met before, and one night we were walking toward each other with our families along this promenade, I would have had to pass you by at least twice before we could talk?"

"That's right! But you can be sure the first two times you passed I would have encouraged you with my eyes." She smiled, batted her eyelashes at him, and coquettishly tossed her head.

"If I had seen you during the *volta,* I might have been afraid to talk to you and could have walked right past you even on the third pass," John told her. "I'm really a very shy person, you know?" He turned away for a moment to hide his smile.

Looking up at him when he turned back to her, she replied, "Then I would have said something to you. After all, I'm a modern woman."

"Wouldn't your family have been horrified? That's scandalous behavior for a good Greek girl."

"Of course," she responded. "But they would have kept their mouths shut."

"Why's that?" John asked.

"Because they would have been glad I had finally found a man—even a *xenos*. I am thirty-seven you know. A very old maid by Greek standards. No longer a girl. My family would have thought that only a foreigner would be silly enough to be interested in a woman so far past her prime."

"Now that I think about it," John said, barely suppressing a grin, "maybe I wouldn't have stopped to talk with you after all. I'd probably keep an eye open for someone younger—someone who hasn't been on the shelf for so long."

A look of mock anger crossed her face and just as suddenly disappeared. "You're terrible."

John smiled at her. He knew his face had reddened; he could feel the heat. "The truth is I'm nervous as hell," he said. "I've been trying to figure out how to tell you that I'd like to get to know you better. You know, after this"—he waved his hands in front of his chest, showing his frustration over not knowing what words to say—"this whole thing is over. I know this isn't the right time to bring this up, what with your father's death and all. I'm sorry, I...."

Zoë gazed at John with her electric green eyes. She

moved closer to him, stood on her tiptoes, and kissed his cheek. Then she wrapped her arms around his chest and hugged him. It was a hug that a friend would give a friend, not a lover's hug, but it held promise for John and his heart seemed to soar.

She released him and stepped back. "My goodness, John," she said, "you're blushing."

He placed his palms against his cheeks. "It appears so," he said, smiling. Then he turned serious. "I regret the circumstances of our meeting, but I'm very happy we did meet."

"Sometimes good things come from bad experiences."

"You know if we stand here much longer your reputation will be destroyed."

She looked back at him and laughed softly, the sound that reminded him of wind chimes. "This is a very traditional island, John. I destroyed my reputation when I went to work in Athens. A good Greek girl does not move out of her parents' home until she marries. So don't worry about my reputation, worry about your own. I'm already a fallen woman in the eyes of my own people."

"Maybe we'd better check to see if Christo is back," he said.

They turned around and began walking back up the promenade. When they arrived at a spot across from the station, John saw Christo drive up to the curb on the other side of the street. He looked very upset as he slammed his car door.

"Christo," John called out. Then he and Zoë walked down from the quay to the street and crossed over to join

Christo. "What's the matter?" John asked. "You look like someone just bit off a hunk of your posterior."

"That's exactly what happened," he said, a chagrined look on his face. "The governor wanted to know what I was doing about capturing the killers." Then Christo's complexion reddened. "What the hell are you doing in town?" He waved an arm around, looked left, then right, and continued, "The men who attacked you could have seen you by now, wandering around Vathi like some damn tourist. They could be anywhere. You're supposed to be in hiding." He didn't wait for a reply, but grabbed John's arm, spun him around, and hurried him into the police building.

In his office, Panagoulakos cleared off two chairs, tossing the piles of papers toward a spot on the floor not already covered by documents. He slammed the office door closed. John was amazed the door's glass window didn't shatter.

Christo collapsed into his chair, sighing deeply. He cleared his throat. "Okay. Now tell me why you two are in Vathi. You must realize how dangerous it could be?"

"I want to see my father's map," Zoë said. "Maybe it will tell me something that could help you."

Without a moment's hesitation, Christo went to his file cabinet and unlocked the top drawer. He spread the map out across several piles of papers on his desk. Zoë turned pale. John assumed it was due to the dark splotches of dried blood showing on the paper. But she seemed to get past the bloodstains and began studying the map's few details. She carefully flipped it over and read the words on the back. John could see tears welling in her eyes. She quickly blotted them away with her fingers and, after a moment, explained that her father used to teach his children by making up rhymes that would help them remember their lessons. "But I don't recall this one," she said.

"Could the words have a double meaning?" John asked.

"I can't think what that could be. Maybe my father was just being sentimental. Who knows?"

She breathed deeply and then asked Christo if he had a map of Samos and a ruler. He provided her with both. Zoë began to measure the distances between several sets of locations on the eastern side of the island. Then she carefully measured the distance between two of the circles on her father's crudely drawn map. Back and forth she went, up and down the east coast of Samos, taking measurements on both maps, calculating differences in scale, keeping a tally of her results on a handy note pad. She kept up a steady stream of conversation with herself. Finally, after about twenty minutes, she drew a dot on the official map of Samos.

She sat back in her chair and rubbed her face, muttering something neither Christo nor John could make out.

"What was that?" John asked.

Zoë removed her hands from her face and stared out at the sea through the office window. "I said, *'Katapliktiko! Then to pistevo.'*"

Christo responded with impatience. "What's amazing? What don't you believe?"

"I could be totally wrong," she told him.

Then she turned to John. "Tell me again exactly what my father said to you before he died."

"'Boot' and then 'Map.' He also spoke two words I didn't understand at the time: *'Pythagorio'* and *'Evpalin.'* Finally, he said, 'My family' and 'My life.'"

"Yes, yes. I understand," she said impatiently, her hands moving in front of her face. "But, tell me what my father said to you in Greek, not in English. Don't translate what he said. Say it in Greek."

"The whole thing, or just his last few words?"

"Just what he said at the very end."

"He said, *'Ee zoë mou.'*"

"John, you translated that as 'My life,' which, of course, is literally correct. But it also means 'My Zoë.' Me. You see, he wanted you to find his family, and me in particular." She jumped to her feet as though she'd been shocked. Moving around the cramped office, stepping over papers and avoiding chairs, she ripped off a rapid fire litany about her theory. "My career in archaeology grew out of my father's interest in Greek history. He used to take my brothers and me to archaeological sites on Samos and other islands when we were just kids. He was always telling us stories about our Greek ancestors. We explored Chios, Limnos, Lesbos, and many others. My brothers tired of the long trips in the small boat my father had back then and soon stopped going along on those excursions. But, for me, they continued to be adventures—explorations of Greece's past—that became more enjoyable with each passing year."

Christo broke into her story. "What's any of this got to do with the map?"

"Wait," she said. She paused, collecting her thoughts. "The trips with my father opened the ancient world for me. At an early age I made up my mind that my life's work would have something to do with archaeology and history. I have seen the remains of some amazing architectural and engineering feats, many of which were accomplished with the most primitive tools and techniques. But the wonders of my home island are still the ones that fascinate me most."

She paused again, took a deep breath.

"Christo, do you remember when you were a high school student and the teachers would take you on field trips to ancient sites?"

"Sure," he said. "The only thing I liked about those trips was sometimes Sophia Loutrakis and I could intentionally get lost together."

"Sophia Loutrakis aside," Zoë said, "what was your favorite site to visit?"

"Oh, that's easy," Christo said. "The tunnel going through Mount Kastri—the Evpalini Tunnel." He stopped talking and stared at Zoë, incredulous. "Son of a Turkish mule! The Evpalini Tunnel! That's what your father was talking about."

"That's right, Christo. And guess which ancient site was my favorite one to visit with my father." She rewarded them with her sparkling smile. "He knew I was the one person who could decipher the circles on the map. I think I've done so; but, until we precisely match the fourth circle on my father's map with a spot in the Aegean, we won't be able to figure out what he really had in mind."

"Where's this tunnel?" John asked.

"Quite near Pythagorio. When my father said 'Pythagorio,' he was trying to help you zero in on the area of Samos drawn on the map. His map could have depicted some part of almost any island in the Aegean. Without those words he spoke to you, John, this would do his killers—or us—absolutely no good. So, you see they must have tried to force him to turn over the map, and he resisted. That's why he got shot. But he somehow escaped from them. He must have put some distance between himself and his killers. After all, he knew the streets of Samos better than they probably did."

"That makes sense," Christo interjected. "We backtracked a trail of blood from where John found your father to a spot one hundred fifty meters away. It followed a winding path through back streets and alleys."

Zoë seemed to be thinking about Christo's comment. "I know my calculations are rough, but I believe the first circle on my father's map depicts the top of Mount Kastri. The second circle appears to lie directly on the site of the ancient mole—the old seawall in Pythagorio Harbor. By measuring the distance between those two circles on my father's map, then measuring the distance between the peak of Mount Kastri and the mole on your official Samos map, I developed a scale for my father's map. The third circle is over the Heraion—the site of the old temple. The only reason I can figure out why those three locations are shown on the map is that my father used them as reference points I might recognize. They form a perfect right triangle. If you draw a straight line through these two circles, Mount Kastri and the mole"—she laid the ruler along the line she'd drawn on the official Samos map—"it connects to this circle a little more than a half-mile out to sea, just beyond the entrance of Pythagorio Harbor. That fourth circle must be the key to something my father found."

"And to something someone was willing to murder him over," John said.

"So where do we go from here?" Christo asked.

Zoë shrugged. "Have either of you ever scuba dived?"

Christo shook his head.

"I'm certified," John said.

CHAPTER TWENTY–SIX

May 2

John and Zoë arranged for the scuba equipment at a dive shop in Vathi. Zoë knew exactly what they needed. Petros had schooled her well. She told the shop owner she would call later with instructions as to when he should deliver their equipment to the harbor.

After finalizing arrangements with the shopkeeper, they walked back to Christo's office. It was now 1:00 p.m. The Inspector led them to a restaurant named *La Calma*, where they sat on a terrace built over the water and watched a fisherman on the beach repair his nets. After ordering a round of beers, broiled fish, and French fries, Zoë provided a history lesson about Samos. She had not gotten very far into her story before John noticed that even Christo, a native of Samos, was impressed.

"Samos has been called the Island of the Blessed, or the Blessed Island," Zoë said. "Unlike many Greek islands, which have been deforested, Samos has a relatively lush landscape—forests, clear springs, and wildflowers. In fact, Homer called Samos *'Hydrele,'* the watery place.

"Our island is the closest to Turkey of all the larger Greek islands—we're less than two miles from the Turkish mainland," she said. "Various foreign empires have ruled Samos over the centuries. In 499 BC, Samians revolted against the Persians, and later fought with Athens. During t he Peloponnesian War, 431 to 404 BC, the Samians did an about face and allied themselves with Athens.

"Even farther back, in 535 BC, the town of Pythagorio fell to the tyrant Polycrates, who used his fleet to raid ships and settlements in the Aegean until he was captured by the Persians and crucified in 522 BC. His short time in power resulted in what Herodotus claimed were 'three of the greatest building and engineering feats in the Greek world.' These included the ancient harbor mole, the Evpalinio tunnel, and the Heraion—the Temple of Hera. When I think about Polycrates' vision, it makes me wish I could have known the man. Of course, he was probably one mean bastard."

"The same three sites on your father's map," John interjected.

"Correct," Zoë said. "The Heraion was the largest temple ever built in Greece. It had 133 columns and was one of the Seven Wonders of the ancient world. Unfortunately, fire destroyed it in 525 BC. The ancient mole protected the harbor at Pythagorio. A modern jetty now replaces it.

"As I mentioned in Christo's office, the third of Polycrates' miracles, the Evpalinio Tunnel, is my favorite— probably because it's the only one of the three still intact.

The tunnel is an underground aqueduct constructed with primitive tools and without the assistance of sophisticated measuring instruments. On Polycrates' orders, Evpalinos of Megara, a hydraulics engineer, put two teams of slaves from Lesbos to work. The teams started digging on opposite sides of Mount Kastri, and fifteen years later they came together in the middle of the mountain, just a few feet off center from each other.

"The story about the island's past would not be complete without mentioning that the armies of the Ottoman Empire conquered Samos in 1550 AD. It became part of Greece again after the Balkan Wars, 1912 to 1913."

While Zoë and Christo finished their meals, John studied the map. He tried to attack Zoë's theory about the fourth circle being the key to her father's death. It didn't make sense. He knew he was being silly, but he didn't feel there was any symmetry between the three points of the right triangle and the fourth circle resting out at sea. But he couldn't come up with anything better.

Christo had been quieter than usual during lunch. "What's on your mind?" John asked.

"Tell me what you're planning to do," Christo said. "I'm investigating a murder and an attempted murder, and I can't have you two interfering with my investigation or tampering with evidence."

"What evidence?" Zoë asked, a rough edge to her voice. "What do you mean 'tampering with evidence?' "

"Your father's map is evidence and, by extension, so is whatever is lying at the bottom of the sea within the fourth circle"—he pointed at the map.

"Now that's a stretch if I ever heard one," John said. "Next you'll be claiming any fish we find should be confiscated as evidence."

Christo gave John an icy look. "What if I told you I was worried about you and I would feel more comfortable keeping both of you within eyesight?"

"That I can buy," John retorted, a smile creasing his face. "So why don't you come along with us?"

Christo eyed John and Zoë skeptically, then waved off John's suggestion. "How do you know that where you'll be diving isn't several hundred feet down?"

"We *don't* know that at this point," Zoë said. "We'll just have to wait and see. If it's too deep for scuba gear, then we'll have to approach the problem differently. Maybe a JIM suit."

John nodded in agreement, but he was not nearly as confident as Zoë seemed about their mission. The memory of a bullet whizzing by his ear and the pain of having been cold-cocked still lingered in his mind. He moved his hand toward his head, but stopped himself. He'd become aware that he had developed the habit, every time he felt the least bit nervous or uncertain, of running his hand over the bald spot where his head had been stitched. And the damned stitches were itching like crazy. There was no way in hell he would allow Zoë to go off on her own, but that didn't change the fact that he kept hearing this little voice inside saying, "Dumb ass! Don't be stupid. You've seen too many men killed or wounded as a result of taking stupid risks." Her mention of using a JIM suit in case they found themselves in deep water just exacerbated his nervousness. His experience did not include deepwater diving.

Zoë excused herself to use the restroom, which gave John a chance to talk privately with Christo. "You know, my friend, I'd feel a great deal more confident about this little excursion if you came along."

"I cannot get away from the office now," Christo said. "I need to continue the investigations into Vangelos' murder and the attack on you."

Zoë returned to the table and the three of them walked back to the police station. When Christo went into the building, Zoë and John retrieved her car from across the street. On the drive back to Mytilini, Zoë explained that she needed to find her brother, Nick. "We're going to need his boat and his help," she said.

"How can you be so sure your brother will want to get involved with some hare-brained scheme?" John asked. She snapped her gaze toward him and glared. "Whoa, hear me out," John said. "You have to admit your theory about the meaning of the markings on the map is pretty thin."

Her face softened. Then she rocked her head back and forth as though she were considering his point. "You could be right," she said. "But, in the absence of any other theory, it's the best one we have." Then she smiled and said, "And as far as my brother getting involved is concerned, I know my brother. And, more importantly, he knows me. He knows I wouldn't ask for his help unless it was important. Besides, I'm his little sister and he adores me."

"A bit manipulative, are we not?" John asked, smiling back at her.

Zoë shot him a wry grin. "I don't look at it that way."

"Let's hope your brother doesn't either. I guess I'd better go back to Mytilini and pack a change of clothes for our upcoming adventure at sea. How about you?"

"My clothes are in the trunk of the car," she said. "Before seeing the map, I was planning to return to Athens."

John realized that his disappointment must have shown on his face.

She looked at him sympathetically. "My dear John, I do have a job in Athens and I've been away for eight days already."

"I know, I know. But who would I get to drive me around if you left?"

She looked at John and laughed. "I'll miss you, too."

CHAPTER TWENTY–SEVEN

May 3–5

Zoë called *Taverna Bacchus* the next morning—Thursday—to let John know that her brother would not return to Kokkari until Sunday. He'd taken his boat to the south coast of Crete looking for bass.

Disappointed to learn she had to fly to Athens to take care of business there, John agreed to meet her on Saturday for some swimming and sunbathing. He spent the intervening time resting and lending a hand in the taverna.

By the time Zoë showed up two days later, he felt as though he was about ninety-five percent recovered from the concussion and subsequent infection. She picked him up early Saturday.

"I want to show you something special," she said. But all the prodding in the world couldn't get her to divulge what it was.

She drove on the main road that meandered around the island. It alternated between being enclosed within the shadows from trees on both sides, to paralleling the coast with breathtaking views of the Aegean. In the middle of a hairpin turn Zoë suddenly braked and the car slid to a stop on a thin strip of gravel.

She got out from behind the wheel and walked to the rear of the car. John followed to see what she was up to. She opened the trunk and rummaged through her suitcase. Zoë held up a bathing suit in one hand and a towel in the other. "Well, aren't you going to join me?" Then she hurried away, down a narrow path he hadn't noticed before.

John grabbed his swimsuit and a towel from his knapsack in the backseat and ran down the path after Zoë. She was nowhere in sight. The path appeared to be one of those strange occurrences of nature, where, for some whimsical reason, the wind, the rain, and the sea conspire to create something usable by man. The base of the path was smoothed rock, as though millions of gallons of sea water had pounded away at it for thousands of years. It literally hung along the side of the cliff, and John had to slow his pace for fear of falling onto the boulder-strewn shore below. He came to a fork in the path, where a left turn appeared to branch off away from the shore. He continued straight, following the path that overlooked the sea. After about a hundred yards, having to circumnavigate three boulders that stood like sentries beside the path, narrowing its width by half, John caught up with Zoë. On the right, the sea crashed against Cyclops-sized rocks sixty feet below. Spray exploded straight up into the air off the rocks and spattered their feet. The Aegean expanse led to the Turkish coast.

"Spectacular!" he said.

"As you Americans say, 'You ain't seen nothing yet.'"
"Perched on the narrow trail, she took his hand and led
him around yet another car-sized boulder. "Look!" she
declared

John saw they were at the brink of a horseshoe-
shaped cove. Within its sheltering stone walls, emerald-
green waves lapped against a pebbled beach.

"This is my favorite beach," Zoë said. "Few Samians
even know it exists, and, thank God, tourists never find
it. Those Samians who do discover it find the prospect
of the climb down slightly forbidding. You're the only
person I've ever brought here, so I expect you to be
suitably impressed."

"Impressed is not the word," John said. "I'm awed.
But how do we get down to the beach?"

"Ah, but that's the secret. You promise you'll never
tell a soul about this place?"

"Cross my heart," he said, drawing an "X" on his
chest with his finger.

Zoë squeezed through a narrow break in the rock
wall beside them. John followed; glad he wasn't bigger
than he was. They took a trail where it descended across
the arc of the cliffs until they reached a place where the
drop to the beach was only about fifteen feet. A series
of cracks and depressions in the rock wall served as steps
and handholds for their descent. John went down first.
After he reached the beach, he turned to look across the
pebbled surface toward the water. The spot was beautiful,
especially with the early morning sun—a fireball rising
over the Turkish coast—now bathing the shore. The

water beyond seemed to be aflame. John looked back up at Zoë. The sight of her—long, dark hair ruffled by the slight breeze, eyes sparkling in the sunlight, radiant smile—took his breath away.

"I don't know which is more beautiful," he said. "This spot, or you."

Zoë laughed, tossing her head back. Then she gave him a look of mock anger. "What do you mean, you don't know which is more beautiful?" She tossed their bathing suits and towels down at him and began to climb down, jumping the last few feet to the beach. John caught her in his arms.

"I must have lost my head there for a moment," he said. "Of course, you're more beautiful."

"That's better," she laughed, kissing his cheek.

As she pulled back, their eyes met and time seemed to stop for him. He pulled her to him and they held each other as though their lives depended on it. Then she looked up at him. Their lips came together as though they'd had years of practice together. He could feel his heart pounding when he broke off the kiss, still hungrily holding on to her. He felt himself shaking like a teenager, his heart hammering in his chest.

"If we continue like this," he said, "I don't think I'm going to be able to stop."

She gave him the look he'd seen a couple times before—the one that said, "What are you, some kind of idiot?" And then she whispered, "Who's asking you to stop?"

He felt his face go hot and knew he was blushing like a kid.

She smiled and put a hand on his cheek. Then she turned and moved thirty yards to the far side of the beach, to a patch of sand no bigger than a small rowboat, surrounded by an almost perfect oval of pebbles. John dropped the bathing suits and towels from under his arm onto the sand, then embraced Zoë. The scent of her hair made him lightheaded, excited. The feel of her firm body elevated his pulse even more. He kicked off his deck shoes, flinging them against the stone wall of the cove.

Zoë placed her hands on John's chest and pushed back from him. She began unbuttoning his shirt. He shrugged out of it before she had finished and popped the bottom button.

She giggled, then intensity came to her eyes and her breathing changed while she rubbed his chest. She stepped forward and kissed his neck, his shoulders, his chest. The touch of her lips sent chills up his spine and he shivered as though he were cold.

John pulled her blouse from where it was tucked into her jeans. She stretched her arms and he lifted it above her head. The swell of her breasts rose above her brassier. He bent down and kissed the top of one, then the other. He felt as though his insides were melting. He unhooked her bra and stared dumbstruck at the beauty of her lush breasts. Her dark-pink nipples were erect, pointing upward, as though inviting—no, begging for—his touch. He took one between a finger and thumb and lightly pressed it, and she moaned. It started as a submissive whimper, but grew into a feral, demanding sound.

Zoë reached for his belt buckle, but apparently her hands wouldn't do her brain's bidding. John took her hands away and released the buckle. She pulled his khakis down and he stepped out of them. Then he helped her with her jeans. She had a strong, athletic body. He felt a thousand butterflies churning in his gut while he ran his hands over her face, her shoulders, her arms, her back. Then he knelt in the sand in front of her and kissed her stomach. She jerked as though he'd touched her with an ice cube. He gripped the sides of her bikini underpants and slid them down her legs.

John stood and admired her. Graceful neck, full breasts, flat stomach, tight buttocks and legs. She was his fantasy. His insides screamed with his need for her. He shed his shorts. They embraced, fiercely. Their lips and tongues clashed. He couldn't get enough of her. She clasped her arms around his neck and hooked her legs around his waist. John's hands swept over every part of her while she clung to him.

"I want you," she said. "Please! Now!"

Slowly kneeling, then lowering Zoë to the sand, John knelt beside her. She was so beautiful. Her skin seemed to glow under the sun's rays and her hair shone lustrously, lying fan-like on the sand. But it was her eyes that mesmerized him. There was a sensuality showing in them that further raised his heart rate and made him start trembling again with almost uncontrollable ecstasy. Zoë's touch was electric.

He'd never wanted a woman as badly as he ached for Zoë at that moment. And he'd never wanted to please one more. He knelt between her legs.

She lifted her hips and pressed against him. When he moved inside her, she cried out and he felt her shudder as though a shock wave had gone through her. She dropped her hips to the sand and reached her arms to him. John put his weight on her and she clung to him. She kissed him as though she wanted to devour him. They moved in a rolling, wave-like rhythm. Suddenly, she arched her head back and cried out, "John, John, John," and he was suddenly lost in his feelings for her. He was aware of their cries echoing off the high stone walls, but of not much else.

They held each other as though they would never let go. Her every touch, every kiss made him tingle. John heard the waves lapping at the edge of the shore and, at some point, the cadence of the waves matched the slower pace of his heart rate. Finally, Zoë sat up, wrapping her arms around her knees. She stared up at the sheer walls around them.

"You know," she said, "this place is like an amphitheater. Perhaps we have been entertaining the gods on Mount Olympus, as Aphrodite and Ares once did. Do you think they enjoyed the show?"

"Maybe they even learned something," John said.

"Aren't you the arrogant one," she laughed.

"You were visualizing an audience of Zeus and Hera on Mount Olympus," he told her. "I imagined a satellite passing over us, taking pictures."

"Oh my God," she joked, tossing her head, running her hands through her hair. "I hope my hair wasn't a mess."

Before he could respond, she jumped up, gingerly ran across the twenty feet of pebbled beach to the shoreline and, like a water nymph, dove into the sea.

John followed and waded into the surf. When the water reached his knees he dove in. The bottom dropped off steeply, the sea floor plummeting about twenty feet, pebbles soon giving way to sand.

It took him a few seconds to spot Zoë, all the way on the bottom, working something loose from between several rocks. After surfacing momentarily to fill his lungs with air, he tried to kick down to join her, but could only make it halfway before he had to retreat to the surface. While he gasped for air, Zoë swam up beside him and rolled on her back, floating like a sea otter. She had a sponge balanced on her belly. Drops of water on her breasts twinkled in the sunlight. "My God," John said. "You must have been down there almost two minutes."

"Oh, that's nothing," she declared. "I'm just a little out of shape. My brothers and I used to dive for sponges with my father all the time. I've been under water for two-and-a-half to three minutes many times."

With that, she tossed the sponge at John, giggled, turned on her stomach, and dove again. This time he decided to just wait for her. The water was cool but comfortable. He bobbed in the sea, turning slightly with the waves until facing the beach and the cliffs enclosing it. He wondered what it would be like to spend every day like this.

A sudden movement caught his eye. From his spot twenty-five yards out from the beach, he saw a flash of brilliance, like sunlight caroming off glass. He could have sworn he'd seen someone—just a person's head--standing near where they'd left Zoë's rental car. He backstroked farther out from the shore until he could see the top of the car. The butterflies erupted in his stomach again, but this time it wasn't passion that caused them. There were two men standing between Zoë's car and a second vehicle. They appeared to be looking inside Zoë's rental car, then they started down the path he and Zoë had followed. John was pretty sure neither had seen him yet, but they wouldn't miss him once they reached the horseshoe of cliffs enclosing the little beach.

CHAPTER TWENTY-EIGHT

May 5

John slipped beneath the surface and kicked with all his might toward the bottom. Zoë rose to meet him. He grabbed her arm, pointed upward, and made a "let your fingers do the walking" sign. She seemed to get the message and started swimming under water on a course parallel to the shore.

He followed her and, after about thirty seconds, his lungs about to explode, they rose to the surface. John was already worn out. Because the beach was so narrow, the short swim had taken them beyond the cliff at one edge of the beach. He had to fight with all his remaining strength to avoid being thrown up against the rock wall by the waves.

"What is it?" Zoë asked, breathing heavily while she treaded water.

"I saw two men standing by your car," John wheezed.

"Probably tourists."

"Maybe, maybe not, but with all that's happened, why take chances. These guys could be trouble." The words rapidly burst from his mouth while he tried to keep his head above water.

"What can we do? Because of the cliffs, there's no other place to get out of the water for at least a mile in either direction."

John looked left and right and saw she was correct. He'd expended a lot of energy and he knew he would be in real trouble if they tried to stay afloat much longer. "Look," he said, "let's swim to the edge of the wall and see if we can get to our things under the overhang without being seen."

She looked where John pointed and nodded.

John followed Zoë, churning through the waves, making it to shore on pure adrenaline, shaking from the effort. Carefully they crawled out of the water and plastered themselves against the side of the wall. Fortunately, the overhang shielded them from view from directly above, where the two men were now apparently standing. John heard voices—German voices.

They reached their clothes and dressed quickly.

John pointed upward with his index finger, as though Zoë had not already figured out where the men were. She nodded to let him know she understood.

"I think we can get out of here without them catching us," she said in a hushed voice. "But if they have guns…." She didn't finish her thought, but only shrugged.

"What do you have in mind?" he whispered.

"I know this area well. Better than they do." she said. "From the direction of their voices, those men took the path around the top of the stone wall and are right above us. They missed the path that comes down here to the beach. Once they see where we are, they'll still have to go all the way around the other side to get to us. I think we can climb back up before they can reach us. Then all we'll have to do is outrun them the rest of the way to the car."

John thought her use of the words "All we'll have to do…" was the height of optimism. But if they stayed where they were, the men would eventually find them. "I'm ready if you are," he said, with much more confidence than he felt.

"Let's go then!"

She raced across the beach with John in hot pursuit.

They'd barely broken out from under the shadow of the wall when one of the men above shouted, *"Achtung, Josef!"*

While Zoë climbed, John looked over his shoulder and saw the men start to run toward the rim of the cliff, toward the base of the horseshoe. They were powerfully built, like weightlifters, but they appeared to be moving with a fluidity of motion that was surprising considering their bulk.

As Zoë had hoped, she and John reached the top of the wall and raced to the fork in the path before the two men could catch them. But the men were moving fast and John had doubts he and Zoë could outrun them to the car.

He again looked back over his shoulder. The men were maybe twenty yards behind. But, just when he was about to turn his head back toward the road, he saw the lead man try to rush around a large boulder, appear to lose his balance, and crash to the stone path. John heard a muffled "oomph" and then a loud string of what sounded like curses. The fallen man apparently blocked the narrow path, slowing down his companion, and giving John and Zoë the few seconds they needed to reach the car.

Zoë jumped into the car and screamed, "Get in—quick!" But John, tired of running away, angry about what had happened to Petros and to him, decided it was time for some sort of offense. While Zoë revved the engine of the Toyota and continued yelling at him, he pulled his Swiss Army knife from his pants pocket and selected the punch blade. He ran to the Peugeot parked directly behind them and stuck the blade into the right front tire. Air started hissing from the tiny hole he'd punched in the tire, then suddenly stopped.

He looked back down along the path. The man who had fallen was limping. But his pal was coming up fast—brandishing a pistol. He pointed it at them and fired. One shot, then two more. He was, thank God, still too far away to get off an accurate shot, at least while he was running. John jumped into the Toyota and Zoë threw the car into gear and punched the gas. The rear wheels momentarily spun in place, shooting a spray of gravel at the Peugeot, before they caught the macadam. She negotiated a wild U-turn and tromped on the accelerator, sending the Toyota hurtling down the road toward Vathi. The acceleration slammed John's door shut.

While Zoë concentrated on driving, John turned and looked back. The guy with the pistol stood on the edge of the road waving his gun. But he was looking back down the path, maybe yelling at his partner to hurry. Then the

Toyota took the first curve in the road and he lost sight of the gunman.

Zoë yelled at John above the noise of the roaring engine and squealing tires. "What were you doing back there?"

"Punching a hole in one of their tires," he yelled back, settling into his seat.

"Didn't do much good, did it?" she shouted, an edge of panic in her voice.

"What…?"

"They're right behind us."

"Oh shit!" John groaned. "They must have non-deflating tires."

They careened around the switchback curves, barely keeping all four wheels on the pavement, the more powerful Peugeot now only ten yards back. While they swept in the wrong lane around another tight turn, Zoë screamed.

A small truck was coming at them. Zoë jerked the wheel to the right, but they sideswiped the truck with a sickening screech of metal against metal. John thought for a moment they would crash into the rock wall or catapult off the road into the sea.

But Zoë gunned the engine of the fishtailing car and suddenly they were once again rocketing along.

"*O Theos mou*," Zoë exclaimed, "I thought they'd killed you when I heard the gunshots."

"Now that I think about it, he may have been trying to get us to stop. I think these guys want us alive—at least for now."

Their pursuers had obviously made it past the truck.

The Peugeot was now close behind them again, barely six feet off their rear bumper. The men had to be aware they had only a short distance to stop John and Zoë before risking crowds of witnesses—they were only a couple of miles from Vathi.

John ducked at the noise of popping sounds. Gunshots! The shots came at regular three-second intervals, as though the gunman was carefully aiming his weapon. One of his rounds ricocheted off the paving and splattered into the rock wall just to John's right. Was he shooting at their tires?

John looked back. It was unreal watching their pursuers from just a few yards away, almost like watching a movie. The driver was blond, the other dark-haired. The Peugeot seemed too small to hold their bulk. Their expressions were grim, determined. They had the square-jawed, crew cut appearance of paramilitary types.

He started to turn back to the front, when he saw something on the car floor between the seats. "What's this tin can back here?" he yelled, feeling the heft of the metal container.

"It's olive oil my mother gave me to take back to Athens. Why?"

A plan materialized in his mind. He grabbed the large can, placed it on his lap, and cranked the sunroof open. He unscrewed the cap on the tin and then shoved himself up head and shoulders through the open roof of the car. He was betting his life on the guess that their pursuers wanted them alive. Balancing precariously while Zoë took the curves in the road at speed, he raised the tin above his head and began to shake the oil out. The slipstream carried the liquid back and splashed it against the Peugeot's hood and windshield. John's hands, arms, and face became slick with the olive oil. He saw the Peugeot's windshield wipers make several rapid swipes, smearing the yellow liquid over the car's glass.

The driver and passenger stuck their heads out the windows. They no longer had any visibility through the windshield. John tossed the tin at them. It smashed into their windshield, spiderwebbing the safety glass. John saw the driver duck.

John heard the shrieking of brakes and rubber against macadam when the other driver hit his brakes and the Peugeot skidded to a halt at the very edge of the cliff. One front wheel hung over the precipice.

Dropping back into his seat, he yelled at Zoë to slow down. She didn't respond. Her concentration on the road ahead was complete. He placed a hand over one of hers on the steering wheel. "Zoë," he said, "everything's all right. You can slow down now."

She peered into the rearview mirror.

"We're okay," John said. "Pull over."

She found a spot where the shoulder was wide enough and from where their pursuers were no longer in sight. Zoë leaned over toward John and burrowed her head into his chest. He could feel her shaking. He kept saying over and over that everything was all right, and, after a couple of minutes, she began to calm down.

Putting a hand under her chin, he lifted her face so he could see her eyes. He kissed her forehead and then her lips.

"When I see your mother," John told her, "I'm going

to give her the biggest hug she's ever had. Magic olive oil, that's what it is. It saved our lives."

Zoë began to laugh. Then her laughter became a little hysterical. And, finally, it turned to sobbing. While John held her, he noticed a small golden shrine by the roadside about forty feet away. He knew that Greek families placed these shrines near the spots where loved ones have been killed in automobile accidents. Because of the Greeks' devil-may-care driving style, these shrines had popped up all over the country. He stared at that memorial. How close we came on this winding road to earning one of our own, he thought.

CHAPTER TWENTY-NINE

May 5

Hans tried to keep his hands steady while he dialed the Zurich telephone number. Even when he had good news to deliver, there was something about the banker that made him feel as though he was in a fog-shrouded graveyard at night, pursued by a pack of wolves. The fact that he was working for that psychopathic bitch, Theo Burger, but was feeding information to Leidner, only made him more nervous. God forbid Burger discovered his duplicity. He breathed deeply and thought, Today I have some good news and some bad news.

"*Was!*" was all the voice said at the other end of the line.

"*Mein Herr,*" Hans said, his voice breaking. He cleared his throat and tried again. "*Mein Herr,* we have found the man. An American."

"And the map?" Leidner barked. "What about the map?"

Hans breathed out slowly. "We believe he had it. We

searched his room. It wasn't there. We know he met with a police Inspector the night . . . of the fisherman's death. If he had the map, he probably gave it to the cop."

"What do you mean, 'probably?' You don't know?"

Hans decided telling Leidner about his attacking Hammond in the Soula Hotel and nearly killing him would not be a good idea. This assignment had been botched from the beginning. Hans felt a visceral hatred toward the American. It was Hammond, he thought, who had caused him to look so bad to his employers. He would make the man pay. "He's in the company of the police Inspector and the fisherman's daughter. We're working on it."

Leidner didn't respond at first. Hans could hear tapping on the other end of the line, as though the man was banging a pen against the telephone mouthpiece. Finally the man spoke, a timbre to his voice that made him seem to be growling. "What is this American's name?"

"Hammond. John Hammond."

"Who is he?"

"Just a tourist, we think. He must have been on his way to his hotel when he ran into Vangelos."

"Huh!" Leidner snorted. "That is Mr. Hammond's bad luck." Then his voice turned calm. "No witnesses, Hans." Pause. "AND I WANT THAT MAP!"

CHAPTER THIRTY

May 5

"That's it!" Christo yelled, his arms windmilling. "That's the last time you two are going to be without protection until I find out what the hell is going on and find the bastards behind these attacks."

Within minutes of John and Zoë's arrival at the police station in Vathi, Christo had dispatched a patrol car to look for the Peugeot and its occupants. Soon a police officer poked his head into the office. John picked up enough of the officer's verbal report to learn that another officer had just radioed in that he'd found the Peugeot, but it was empty. No sign of either of the men.

Christo cursed. "Tell him to check the car's registration and call it in. Then I want you to call Customs and every hotel on the island and see if you can obtain information about these men. And send all available officers to search the area around the abandoned car." Christo paused, then added, "I want every man on Samos with a German passport questioned."

But the two men who had chased them might have decided to cut their losses and already be off the island, John thought.

John had recognized the men during the car chase. They were the same ones who'd put him in the hospital. Probably the ones who'd killed Petros. But how had they located Zoë and him at that secluded beach? And, if they *had* stayed, when would they show up again?

He also thought about their upcoming dive. One thing bothered him: How could they accurately pinpoint the location of the fourth circle on Petros' map? Then he had an idea. He asked Christo if he would call his contact at the military base near Pythagorio and see if the Army had a special piece of equipment.

"You don't want much, do you?" Christo said in response.

"Don't worry. I'll be careful with it, assuming the Army will lend it to you."

That night, Christo put John and Zoë into a hotel on Gagou Beach, just outside of Vathi. He stationed cops at the entrance to the hotel's two hundred-yard-long driveway and on the beach behind the hotel. Because the police contingent on Samos was small, he called on the Army for two soldiers to guard the lobby and two more outside the hotel's rear exit.

John slipped into Zoë's room shortly after checking in. They lay together in bed with him cradling her in his arms. Like two spoons, they nestled together that night, drawing comfort from one another. In the first light of dawn, John opened his eyes and quietly got out of bed. He looked down at Zoë and felt his breath catch in his chest. He realized that she already meant more to him than any other woman ever had.

Christo came to the hotel at 7:00 that morning and drove them to the dock in Vathi. Zoë pointed out her brother's boat. "That's the *Penelope,* at the end of the dock."

A man stood on the dock next to a large fishing boat. It was the man John had seen on the seawall below the Vangelos home more than a week earlier. It seemed like an eternity had passed since then. Zoë ran toward the man, while John remained at the car with Christo.

"Nice lady, nice family," Christo said with no inflection.

Zoë brought her brother over to them and made the introductions. Nicolaos Vangelos made a special point of thanking John for being with his father at the end. His English was almost as good as Zoë's and Christo's, but John's Greek was coming back. He replied in Greek, giving Zoë's brother his condolences on the loss of his father.

In English, Nicolaos thanked John and told him to call him Nick. John wondered, though, if Zoë's brother would be thanking him if he knew he'd become his sister's lover.

The owner of the dive shop arrived in a van. He unloaded the equipment Zoë had ordered and helped Nick carry it aboard the *Penelope.* John started to walk over to help, but Christo signaled him to hold back.

"You see that man over by the Customs Office?" Christo said.

John looked where Christo pointed and saw a man

in his late twenties dressed in jeans and a black T-shirt. He wore a black, short-billed Greek fisherman's cap. John nodded.

"He's one of my best marksmen, A former Greek Army Special Forces member. I'm sending him along with you. At the slightest sign of trouble he has orders to shoot." Christo then waved the man over to him.

"Stefanos Zantsos meet Mr. John Hammond."

They shook hands and then Christo told the young officer to put his bag on board the *Penelope*.

After Zantsos walked away, Christo opened his car trunk, revealing a small athletic bag, a large plastic tube, and an olive-drab metal box with military markings. He lifted the small gym bag and slung it over John's shoulder. Then he handed over the plastic tube and the metal box. John was loaded down like a pack mule.

"I put a nine millimeter pistol in the bag," he said. "If anyone ever asks where you got it, say you bought it on the black market from someone who looked Turkish. This is not the United States where anyone can own a firearm. You're breaking the law by having one in your possession and I'm breaking the law giving it to you. I only hope you won't need it. You can return it to me when you return from your little cruise."

"Thank you, Christo," John said, "but I doubt I'm going to need a pistol. I mean, we're going out less than a mile. Hell, you'll be able to watch us from shore with a pair of binoculars."

"Yes," he responded, "but then so can the bad guys. Be alert, my friend. I don't know the purpose of the game we're involved in here, but I do know it's a dangerous one.

Keep the pistol where it will be safe and out of view, but keep it handy."

"What's in the tube, Christo? A bazooka?"

"Don't be a smart ass," he said. "It's the coastal charts you asked for. And the metal box contains the range finder you wanted. Don't lose any of this stuff—especially that range finder. It would take ten years salary to replace it."

CHAPTER THIRTY-ONE

May 5

Josef groaned as he shifted in the front passenger seat.

"Your ankle bothering you?" Hans asked.

Josef grunted.

Hans chuckled. "If you weren't such a klutz." Then Hans laughed. "You really took a fall when you fell over that boulder."

"Fuck you! At least I don't look as though I've been in the ring with Mike Tyson." Then Josef slapped his thigh and cursed. "Sonofabitch! I can't believe I didn't think of this before."

Hans, a bandage on his forehead, one of his eyes blackened from hitting the steering wheel during the chase in the Peugeot, stared at Josef from behind the wheel of the new car they'd rented under assumed names and false ID. He gave Josef a querulous look, but waited for his partner to continue.

"The wife! Vangelos' widow! Maybe she's got a copy of the map… or knows something about the boat."

Hans tapped out a beat on the steering wheel with his fingers, thinking about Josef's comment. "We need to follow Hammond. The old woman probably doesn't know a thing. It's Hammond we need to stay with." Hans knew Josef still harbored irrational anger at Hammond. The man had knocked him down when they'd surprised him in his hotel room. Josef hadn't expected it. Hans hadn't let him forget it.

Josef shrugged. "Maybe so, but there's no harm in finding out. We'll follow this"—he paused and looked through his binoculars at the fishing boat docked at the pier—"*Penelope* until it drops anchor. Then we should go have a friendly visit with the old woman. We can't do anything about Hammond and the rest of his crew until after dark anyway."

CHAPTER THIRTY-TWO

May 6

Diesel fumes darkened the air. The *Penelope's* engine noise sounded like a ton of nuts and bolts being dropped on a steel floor. Just when John was about to question the reasonableness of going out on a boat that sounded as though it was in the midst of its death throes, he heard the engine noise smooth out.

The 50-foot *Penelope* was a typical Greek fishing boat. Twelve-foot long metal arms rose from the deck on each side of the boat. Zoë explained they were motor-powered booms used to lower and raise the fishing nets. A larger boom rose fifteen feet above the deck and then turned at a right angle into a twelve-foot horizontal extension. This was used to raise large sponge harvests off the sea floor.

Nick Vangelos piloted the boat out of the harbor and into the Aegean. It took twenty minutes to skirt the headland protecting Vathi Harbor and an hour longer to begin the turn around the eastern end of the island on their clockwise course to Pythagorio. John thought he might have been able to enjoy the water and the view of the mountainous island if he hadn't been so damned worried about when the men who had chased them might show up again.

Zoë and John joined Nick in the wheelhouse, while Officer Zantsos remained on the main deck. The cop was already looking a little green around the gills.

"All right, little sister," Nick said. "What are we doing and why am I involved?"

Zoë told Nick everything that had happened to them in the past week. When she got to the part about John getting knocked on the head and spending time in the hospital, Nick gave him a sympathetic look and patted his shoulder. When Zoë told how John had used their mother's olive oil during the car chase, Nick laughed and slapped John on the back with bruising enthusiasm.

John got the impression that Zoë, who spoke to her brother in rapid-fire Greek that John couldn't always keep up with, must have embellished his role in all of this. After she had finished, Nick looked at him with serious respect, shook his fist at him, and shouted, "Good job, John, you got balls."

Balls, John thought. I'm so nervous about what the hell might happen next that I think my testicles have shriveled to BBs.

Zoë spread out the copy of her father's map on the boat's instrument panel and pointed out the landmarks identified by four small circles, three on land, and one at sea.

"That's just outside the entrance to Pythagorio Harbor," Nick said. "It's not so good for fishing, but Papa and I used to go there to find sponges along the reef. It's not too deep."

John asked Nick if he knew anything about the map or what his father might have been up to.

Nick's face reddened. Then he sighed and closed his eyes. When he re-opened his eyes, he looked at John and then at Zoë. "I know Papa had been coming to this side of the island, not with this boat but in a smaller one with an outboard motor. I thought it was nostalgia—Papa reverting to the simpler days of the past. He had been mentioning recently that these big boats had taken the soul out of fishing." Nick abruptly stopped and looked away. He swallowed and shook his head. "A few weeks ago, just before his sixty-fifth birthday, I started teasing Papa about being as old as the gods. I reminded him we owned a big boat just like the ones he was criticizing, and he shouldn't be so old-fashioned. He said he still wished things had not changed so much."

Nick's face seemed to have gone gray and his eyes were moist.

Zoë touched her brother's arm while he gripped the spokes of the boat's wooden wheel so tightly his knuckles went white. "You don't think he went back to the old Pythagorio sponge beds to dive, do you?" she asked.

"I don't know, Zoë. But you know how stubborn and proud Papa was. It wouldn't surprise me if he had. To show me he could still do it."

"Can you imagine a man his age taking a small boat all the way around the island?" Zoë said. "That must have taken hours. And then diving alone in the sea. Incredible!"

Zoë and John walked out onto the deck, leaving Nick alone to deal with his grief. They joined Zantsos in the bow and watched sea spray splash against the prow while the *Penelope* plunged forward through the Aegean. The young cop's color had gone grayish green.

CHAPTER THIRTY-THREE

May 6

Hans stood in the motor launch's bow and directed binoculars at the fishing boat plowing through the water a kilometer ahead. He saw activity up in the boat's wheelhouse, but couldn't make out who was there. He sat back down and looked at Josef. "Keep this distance. I don't want them to get suspicious."

"What's the plan?" Josef asked, a scowl showing on his face. "I still say we should find Vangelos' widow."

"Enough," Hans said. "As soon as they drop anchor, we'll go back to shore, drive to the Vangelos house, and talk to the old woman. Then we'll wait until it's dark and come back here, after they've gone to sleep. They'll probably have a lookout, but we can cut the engines and try to drift into the side of the boat. But, even if they hear us, we're dealing with amateurs."

Josef nodded. "That woman on the boat is good looking," he said, a lascivious grin on his face. "After we take care of the men, maybe we can have a little fun."

Hans looked back at his partner and smiled. He'd had the same thought. "A little relaxation would be nice, wouldn't it?"

Josef rubbed his crotch, then reached in his pocket for a coin. "I'll flip you for who goes first."

CHAPTER THIRTY-FOUR

May 6

They had barely arrived in Pythagorio Harbor when Zantsos weakly called to John, raising his radio set in the air. "Inspector Panagoulakos is holding for you," he said.

"What's up, Christo?" John said into the radio.

"I've been happier, my friend," Christo responded.

He told John he'd learned the two men who had chased after Zoë and him were probably Swiss, rather than German. A clerk at one of the island's hotels had provided names for men who fit John's description of them. After further checking, Christo had determined they were travelling with falsified Swiss passports.

"John, we know we're dealing with professionals," he said. "They've just disappeared. Maybe they stole a car or took a boat, although none has been reported missing. Which could mean they didn't have to steal one, or they used another set of false documents. They may have accomplices. We have no way of knowing if they're aware of your location, but nothing would surprise me at this point. So be careful out there."

When John told Zoë and Nick about the possible Swiss connection and that Christo thought the men were professionals, Nick's face darkened and anger shone in his eyes. The need for revenge was obviously fermenting inside.

"I don't care if these men are professional killers," he spat. "I won't rest until they are dead."

John knew the appetite for payback ran deep in the Greek culture. In mythology and literature, it was a common theme. John felt suddenly uncomfortable being on the same boat with someone who reminded him of a ticking time bomb.

Nick anchored the *Penelope* a hundred yards offshore in Pythagorio Harbor, just when the wind suddenly picked up, kicking up waves that tossed the boat around. Nick set them all to work securing the boat. Outside the harbor walls, whitecaps danced on the Aegean. There would be no diving that day. So they raided the coolers for food and lounged on the rocking deck. Zoë and John each had a beer with their sandwiches, but they could not cajole Zantsos into drinking anything but water.

Nick was a wholly different story. He was highly agitated and wouldn't sit down for more than a minute at a time. He paced the deck, guzzling one beer after another. By 8:00 p.m., Nick was three sheets to the wind. The drunker he got, the meaner he got. He began to joke about Zantsos' seasickness and tried to get Zoë and John to bet how long it would be before the cop barfed again. The sicker Zantsos became, the more protective of him Zoë became. She applied a damp cloth to the cop's forehead and scolded Nick. Once Zantsos started to throw up again, he spent the next hour bent over the side of the boat, dry heaving.

By the time the wind and waves subsided and the stars were out in all their glory, Nick had passed out in a deck chair, the young policeman had finally fallen asleep—from pure exhaustion—on a mat in the wheelhouse, and Zoë had retired to the captain's quarters at the stern end of the boat. John half-carried, half-dragged Nick below to one of the bunks in the crew's quarters on the bow side, then lay down on the other bunk.

CHAPTER THIRTY-FIVE

May 6

The two Swiss parked their car at the bottom of the road to the Vangelos house. They walked up the driveway until it turned to face the front door, then they stalked through the brush, approaching the darkened house from the side.

Hans crept up to an open window, its shutters propped open and secured by hooks fixed to the outside walls. He looked inside. It was dark and quiet. "Let's go around to the front door and see if it's locked," he whispered.

At the front, Hans grasped the door handle and put his thumb on the latch. Carefully, slowly, he pressed down and felt the lever on the other side of the door lift. No one probably ever locked their doors on Samos. He pushed inward and the door opened easily, creaking slightly. Open, unshuttered windows on both sides of the house allowed moonlight to cast a yellow glow on the interior. Hans stepped inside, looked over his shoulder at Josef, and pointed toward the open doorway at the far side of what appeared to be the living room. He led the way across the room.

They were on Layla Vangelos in seconds. Hans' hand smothered her screams. The two men gagged her and bound her hand and foot to a straight-backed wooden chair. They closed the shutters in the bedroom and turned on the lamp beside the bed.

Josef asked the woman if she spoke German. She shook her head, eyes wide with fright. She made whimpering sounds.

"English?" Hans asked.

Layla nodded.

"Good!" he said. Dragging another chair over, Hans sat down directly in front of the old woman and removed the gag. "You answer my questions and you will live. If I think you are lying to me, or holding back information, I will slit your throat." With that, he pulled a knife from his pocket, released its six-inch blade, and held it in front of Layla's face.

"Vat do you know about a boat called za *Sabiya?*"

Her eyes squinted in a confused look and she shook her head several times.

Hans pointed the tip of the knife blade at the spot between Layla's eyes and hissed, "Don't you dare lie to me!"

Layla's face became animated—her eyes widened, her head turned left then right—and she moaned, "Unh, unh."

Hans continued. "Ver did your husband find za boat?"

Again she appeared confused.

Hans had a gut feeling the old woman knew nothing about the boat. Her reactions were too genuine, uncontrived. He decided he'd ask one more question, then give it up and return to where the *Penelope* was moored.

"Tell me about za map your husband made."

Again Layla shook her head, but this time Hans detected something in her eyes. She'd blinked. She knew something.

He put the blade of the knife against her forehead and sliced across her brow, opening a wound that bled profusely over her eyebrows, into her eyes, down her nose, and over her cheeks. The blood flowed down her neck and over her chest. She moaned, then her eyes rolled up, and she sagged forward in the chair.

Josef put a hand against the side of her neck. *"Scheiss!"* he said, "I can't find a pulse." He placed his hand over her heart. Nothing. "I think she's dead," he declared. "She's no use to us now. Let's get out of here."

Hans rose from his chair and followed Josef toward the front of the house. When he passed a credenza sitting against a living room wall, he noticed several framed photographs arrayed across its surface. He scooped up one with the faces of the old fisherman and his wife and three other adults.

CHAPTER THIRTY-SIX

May 6

Nick Vangelos' wife, Ariana, loved her mother-in-law, Layla, like her own mother. Since Petros had been murdered, she'd been particularly concerned about Layla's welfare. Only fifty meters separated their two houses and she made a point of dropping by several times a day. When her day was done—the children put to bed and the dinner dishes washed and put away—Ariana and Nick would spend time together talking about their days. But before she went to bed, Ariana always walked across to her mother-in-law's house to make sure all was well.

Tonight, in the distance, Ariana saw a sliver of light peeking from the bedroom shutters of Layla's house. The light surprised her. It was well past the old woman's bedtime. If Layla wasn't asleep by 8:00, then there must be something wrong. Ariana's heart did a flip-flop. *I hope she remembered to take her medicine,* she thought. The pills were the only thing that kept her arrhythmia in check. She untied her apron and tossed it on the kitchen counter. She quickly checked on her two children. They were sleeping soundly. Then she hurried from the house and ran across to Layla's house.

The front door was ajar. Nobody locked their doors on Samos, but it was strange the door wasn't closed. Ariana flipped on the light switch inside the door and illuminated the front rooms. Nothing. She called out, "Mama!" No response. Quickly moving to Layla's bedroom, she gasped, her hands covering her mouth, at the sight of her mother-in-law, bound and bloody. The old woman's face appeared blue.

CHAPTER THIRTY-SEVEN

May 7

Nick snored like a rhinoceros. The boat creaked while it rocked. Although the wind had dropped, it still made whistling sounds when it blew through the boat's rigging. John got only fitful sleep that night. When he did drift off, his old dream kept repeating itself. As always, he woke up with the memory of the wide, startled eyes of the little man in black pajamas staring at him and the .45 pistol he'd leveled at the spot between the little man's eyes.

It was after he was awakened again by the dream that he thought he heard something. The steady beat of rain hammered on the deck. But that wasn't it. A motor. In his half-sleep state, the sound didn't really register until it stopped. The sudden silence alarmed him. He was already on his feet when he heard a thud and felt a slight jolt that could have been another boat bumping against the *Penelope's* hull. He shook Nick, but in his sodden condition Nick was good for nothing more than ballast.

John pulled on a pair of shorts and a tee shirt, and slipped into his deck shoes.

He crept up the ladder to the main deck. When he reached the top step, he heard a grunt of exertion from the windward side of the boat, near the bow and the anchor chain. Someone was boarding the *Penelope*.

He'd left Christo's pistol under his bunk—still in the bag the Inspector had handed to him back on the Vathi dock. The shortest distance to a weapon was up eight more steps to the wheelhouse, where the policeman had collapsed. Zantsos might still be incapacitated from seasickness, but he had a pistol and an automatic rifle. John started to climb to the wheelhouse, the rain drenching him. But he only reached the fourth step before a flashlight beam froze him to the spot.

In a growling whisper, a man ordered him to come back down to the main deck. The voice sounded German—or maybe Swiss-German, if Christo's information was correct—and he spoke with the authority that comes with being armed. John backed down the steps and slowly turned to face him.

"Zo, *Herr* Hammond, ve haf been after you for a vile, no?" he rasped, aiming the flashlight at John's eyes. Because of the light, John couldn't see more than the outline of the man's shape. A second man, off to his left, scrambled over the side of the *Penelope*. He limped to stand beside the man with the flashlight and whispered, "*Sehr gute*, Hans."

The man holding the light quietly answered, "*Ja, Josef, wir haben unser Fisch.*" They both laughed and then one said something in German to the other, who began to walk with a pronounced limp toward the captain's quarters at the stern, where Zoë slept.

"Mr. Hammond, I think you should relax," Hans said. "I vood not vant to shoot you before ve haf a little talk." He let the light fall slightly away from John, and when John's eyes adjusted he could see the man held a pistol in his right hand, aimed at John's chest.

John strained to detect any sounds coming from the stern. Occasionally, he saw the beam of a second flashlight, sweeping over the breadth of the deck. When Josef returned, he looked at Hans and said, *"Niemand!"*

No one! John thought. Where the hell was Zoë? The two men seemed confused, as though they'd expected to find Zoë on board. Josef, the one who'd searched the stern, now appeared agitated, swinging his arms around, raising his voice at Hans. Hans hissed back at Josef, causing him to shut up.

Then Josef stormed away and went below deck to the crew's cabin. John heard him shout and assumed he'd discovered Nick. John guessed Josef would have no more success than John had earlier in getting Nick out of the rack. Josef came back up to the main deck and said, humor evident in his tone, *"Ein Mann unter Der Deck ist betrunkentot."*

John had trouble following the brief conversations between the two men. He understood just enough German to know that Josef had found Nick passed out below, but why hadn't he found Zoë?

Then Hans began to climb up to the wheelhouse. Josef now held a pistol trained on John's chest. Hans was about to enter the wheelhouse when a gunshot shattered the night. It sounded like a thunderclap. John flinched and ducked. A spray of liquid showered onto him. Josef raised the beam of his flashlight toward the wheelhouse.

With the flashlight beam off him, John dove headfirst down the short staircase that led below deck. The sound of a gun being fired roared behind him. He heard the smack of a bullet smash into the bulkhead. Then something heavy slammed into the deck. Another shot pierced the night.

John lunged through the small cabin—even the gunfire hadn't awakened the besotted Nick—and reached under his bunk. He opened Christo's bag and grabbed the 9mm, released the safety, chambered a round. Then he carefully climbed back up the steps. A body blocked the hatchway. It was the one named Hans, with a gaping hole in his head. He'd just managed to shove the body aside with one hand when Josef slammed his flashlight down on John's gun hand. The pistol clattered down the stairs and skittered out of reach.

"All right, asshole," Josef screamed. "Komm out on zis deck. I haf had enough of your games. I vant zat map you took from za old Greek or I am going to start shooting you in places zat vill not kill you, but vill make you vish you vas det."

John did as ordered, while worrying about what had become of Zoë. He stared at the armed man and said, "What map?"

The man stepped forward, grinned, and then shot his fist at John. The blow landed square in the middle of John's chest and knocked him to the deck.

John felt as though he'd been hit with a baseball bat.

He wheezed while trying to get air back into his lungs.

The armed man gripped John's shirt and tugged him up off the deck. He poked his pistol painfully into John's stomach while he pulled John to him. "Listen to me, you dumbass. You haf three seconds to show me za map, or I vill kill you and your drunken friend below."

Eye to eye with the man, John had no doubt the man meant what he said.

Angling for time, for an opening to escape, he told him the map was in the wheelhouse. The man waved his pistol in the direction of the wheelhouse ladder.

John's foot slipped on the rain-slick surface of the ladder's first step. The slip earned John a painful poke in the back. As he climbed up there, feeling Josef's pistol jabbing at his butt, he tried to put the sequence of shots together. The first shot must have killed Hans. But who had fired it—Zoë, Zantsos? Josef had fired the second shot at him—the one that embedded itself in the bulkhead. So who had fired the third shot? The limp body of Zantsos lying just outside the wheelhouse door answered his question. Zantsos must have shot Hans. Then Josef shot him.

Other than Nick passed out on the lower deck, Josef must have been convinced John was now the only living creature on the *Penelope*. Josef's concentration centered on John, and John knew that once Josef had his hands on the map, Nick and he would be dead.

As soon as they entered the wheelhouse Josef saw the map and Zoë's notes and calculations on the navigation counter. He shoved John roughly toward a corner. John lost his balance and fell. Josef ordered him to roll over and lie on his belly. Now apparently satisfied John was no threat, he shined his flashlight on the map.

Out of the corner of his eye, John watched him scan the document, then exclaim, "*Endlich!* Finally I haf vat ve vere sent to get." Josef tapped the map with the muzzle of his pistol, then turned to look at John. The killer was framed in the wheelhouse door; the eerie light from the flashlight filled the tiny room with a mournful glow. Josef looked ecstatic. John had not the slightest doubt he was about to die.

Josef smiled and said in a dead calm voice, "*Gehen Sie zum Teufel.* Now you die." He aimed the pistol at John's head.

John's concentration on the bore of the gun barrel almost made his eyes cross. He could think of nothing else to say but "Fuck you!"

Josef laughed and resteadied his aim. Then John heard him cough—almost as though he'd had the wind knocked out of him. Josef lurched forward, dropped the flashlight, and then reached up behind his back with his left arm as though to scratch an itch between his shoulder blades. His gun hand dropped, though he still gripped the pistol.

He began to turn slowly toward the wheelhouse door, all the while futilely trying to reach that spot on his back. John got up from the floor and took two quick steps towards the man, who stumbled directly into the beam of the fallen flashlight. A metal rod protruded from his back.

John grabbed the gun from Josef's hand when the killer awkwardly turned to face him. A large, barbed spear point stuck out from his chest.

Josef lowered his gaze. An incredulous look came over his face, his eyes wide, mouth gaping. Then he collapsed to the deck.

John heard movement outside the open wheelhouse and pointed the pistol, ready to fire.

Zoë's head cleared the top of the steps and then she stood outside the doorway—dripping wet in T-shirt and bikini underpants. She gripped an empty spear gun in one hand and grimly surveyed the results of her handiwork.

Zoë looked twenty years younger than she was— like a waif caught in a rainstorm. Her eyes were open wide with wonder—and fear. Rain fell off her head and streamed down her face. John moved to her and gently removed the weapon from her hand and dropped it to the deck. They embraced. Her body shivered against his. Tears rolled down her cheeks. But, at the same time, there was a determined look in her eyes. Her lips were compressed in an angry line. They stood in each other's arms for a moment, then Zoë pushed away and stepped inside the wheelhouse. She lit two battery powered lanterns hanging from hooks in the ceiling. John knelt beside Zantsos, rolled him over on his back. The cop's shirt was drenched in blood, as was the deck around him, and John could see an entry wound over his heart. Zantsos' eyes were open in a fixed, unseeing stare. John stood and entered the wheelhouse.

Josef was still alive. His breathing was shallow and erratic, his eyes glazed over with pain. In a hoarse whisper he said, "Take it out!"

The spear had entered his back near his left kidney and must have punctured one of his lungs on the way through his chest. There was very little bleeding except around the exit wound. John told Josef he would extract the spear on the condition he answer a few questions. The man grunted.

"Why did you kill Petros Vangelos?"

In a pain-filled voice, pausing often, he said, "Hans and I... sent to Greece... to find...vat za old man knew about... *Sabiya*. Ven ve found zat out...ve had orders... kill him. Please... take it out."

John ignored his plea. "Who's *Sabiya?*"

"Cargo boat... chartered to Leidner... Fritz Leidner. Sank in storm off *Samos*... 1945. Vangelos... found boat. Contacted Turk... Maritime Office... salvage rights."

John could tell from Josef's weakening speech that the man was fading fast.

"Who's Leidner?"

"Rich... powerful man," Josef said. "Vill nefer quit... until he finds za *Sabiya*."

"Why is this boat so important?"

"Don't know," he gasped. It took a minute for him to finish answering. "Vas ever ist on... zat boat, Leidner ..."

Every word he spoke was etched with pain, and his voice became ever more strained, his breathing more labored.

"How did you track us down?" John asked.

Despite the pain, the murderer looked at him and leered as best he could. His lips curled up, then a trickle of blood flowed from the corner of his mouth. "Your credit card... za dive shop. Za shop owner... told us he vas... delivering equipment... Ve vatched you...followed you along za coast."

The gaps between words were becoming even longer.

Each time he coughed, more blood oozed from his mouth. Then, unexpectedly, his voice took on strength. "I curse the day I met Fritz Leidner," he said—and then he died.

◼

A sound outside the wheelhouse caught John's attention. Holding Josef's pistol, he pushed Zoë behind him and stepped through the door. The rain had stopped and the moon peeked from behind dark clouds. Nick was sprawled on the main deck, apparently having tripped over Hans' body. He was cursing—and moaning, too. When he saw John staring down at him, he yelled, "What the hell happened? There's a dead man on my boat!"

Zoë then stepped from behind John, and Nick saw her in the glare of moonlight. "Look at you," he said, his words slurred. "Dressed in your underwear!" Then he looked back at John and said, "My God, John, is that blood on you?"

Nick had slept through all the action and didn't have a scratch on him—or a clue about what had happened.

Zoë stood with her hands on her hips and fire in her eyes and laughed. It only took a moment for John to join in. Like two crazies, they laughed and laughed, in the midst of the carnage. Nick showed them the palms of both his hands—the Greek equivalent of giving someone the finger twice—ran over to the boat's rail, and threw up into the sea.

While Zoë went below to get dressed, John used Zantsos' radio to call the Vathi police station. The officer on duty took his name and promised to call Inspector

Panagoulakos at his home. Ten minutes later, just before 5 a.m., the radio squawked and Christo's voice broke the quiet that had once again settled over them. John quickly briefed him. Christo said he would get out to the *Penelope* as fast as he could.

When Zoë returned, the three of them walked to the stern—as far from the bodies as possible. John looked at Zoë. "I was scared to death when one of the killer's went back here. I thought he would find you for sure. Where were you hiding?"

"Underwater," Zoë said.

"What do you mean *underwater?*" Nick asked. "How long could you have been underwater?"

John knew the answer to that question before Zoë responded.

"When I heard the boat motor, then strange voices, I sneaked out of my cabin and came up to the main deck. The door here opens aft—no one forward on the boat could see me. I crept toward the bow until I saw a man aiming a pistol at John. I know enough German to understand that the man with the gun was ordering the other one to search the boat. There was no place aboard I could hide, so I slipped over the side and dived deep enough to clear the keel. It took about a minute-and-a-half to reach the other side of the *Penelope* and to find the boat the two men came in."

It was too dark to see the expression on Nick's face, but John detected admiration in the tone of his voice. "You swam under the *Penelope* in the pitch-black water and—while still underwater--found the killers' boat?"

"Akrivo!" she replied. "Exactly!" she added in

English.

"*Katapliktiko!*" That's amazing! he said, while he turned to face the deck lights.

John now saw wonder showing on Nick's face. "What happened next?" he said. "Did you hear the shots that killed Zantsos and the guy named Hans?"

"The shooting must have happened while I was swimming under the boat. I don't know what I would have done if I'd heard shots." She wrapped her arms around herself as though suddenly chilled. "When I surfaced next to the killers' boat, I heard one of them ordering John to climb the steps to the wheelhouse. He sounded very angry. So I shinnied up the anchor line and dropped over the rail onto the deck. I crouched down and walked around to the bottom of the steps, and that's when I remembered we'd stored the scuba gear along the bulkhead. The speargun and a rack of four spears were lying right on top of the rest of the stuff. I almost tripped on the body lying at the foot of the steps, but managed to step over him instead. I went up the ladder as quietly as I could, until I could aim the speargun at the wheelhouse doorway. I heard the man say he was going to kill John. He had his back toward me. I fired."

CHAPTER THIRTY-EIGHT

May 7

Christo arrived with the sunrise. The three bodies rested where they fell. The sun illuminated the *Penelope's* bloodstained decks, accentuating every gory detail of death.

Christo brought three policemen with him, along with a man from the Greek Coast Guard Office of Investigation. All of the policemen seemed to seethe with anger about Zantsos' murder. The Inspector ordered one of the cops to get headquarters in Athens on the phone. John pieced together enough of the conversation to determine that Christo was asking his superiors in Athens for reinforcements. After terminating the phone call, Christo broke off from the other policemen and joined John, Zoë, and Nick.

Christo's skin color was paler than usual and he looked as though he'd aged ten years since he'd come aboard the *Penelope.* He sighed deeply when he took a seat.

"I'm sorry about Zantsos," John said. "He was very brave."

Christo nodded and said in a subdued voice, "That poor young man. One more wife I have to bring bad news to." Then he looked at Zoë and Nick. "I've got more bad news," he said.

Nick gave a nervous laugh. "What else? Isn't this enough?" He swung an arm in an arc, taking in the *Penelope's* deck.

Christo's Adam's apple bobbed up and down. He looked first at Zoë, then at Nick. It's your mother. She's …"

Nick's face went crimson. Zoë's hands came together and pressed against her chest; her chin began to tremble. Neither one said a word. They just stared at Christo, waiting for him to finish.

"She's in the hospital. Her heart. Nick, your wife found her in her house late last night and resuscitated her. But she's in bad shape."

Nick finally found his voice, tears streaming down his face. "She's had heart problems for years. Papa being killed must have been too much for her after all."

Christo looked over at John, then turned back to Nick. "She'd been attacked, Nick. Someone tied her up and took a knife to her face."

CHAPTER THIRTY-NINE

May 7

Fritz Leidner prided himself on his self-control. He could instill fear, even terror in others with a mere firming of his mouth and a glare. But there was so much at stake. His reputation, his wealth could disappear. He had to find the *Sabiya* before anyone else did. His screams echoed off the boardroom walls. Pacing the length of the room, pausing to stare out at the city of Zurich—his power base—and then walking back across the carpeted floor, he glared at the woman standing at parade rest inside the door.

"You told me your men were reliable. We haven't heard a thing from them in over twenty-four hours. What's going on, Theo?"

The woman stood statue-like. *"Ich wiss nicht, Herr Leidner."*

"I pay you to know, Theo. Do I need to remind you of that?"

"Nein, mein Herr. I shall take care of it immediately. I

will fly to Samos first thing in the morning and take over this… investigation myself."

Leidner stopped in mid-stride and fixed his gaze on the woman's eyes. He pointed a long finger at her. "Investigation, my ass," he said. "Your people have made a mess of a very simple problem. It's time *I* took charge. You find out where this John Hammond is. Then book us both on a flight." He turned again toward the bank of plate glass windows, then suddenly spun around. "And arrange for more men to join us. It appears we will not be able to rely on the two men you already sent to Samos."

CHAPTER FORTY

May 7

Christo ordered one patrolman to remain on board, then he and the others left the *Penelope* on the Coast Guard launch. Christo drove Nick, Zoë, and John from the dock to the Vathi Hospital where Layla Vangelos was in intensive care. While Nick and Zoë went in to see their mother, John and Christo found the waiting room.

"Do you think you could track down information on this boat... the *Sabiya?*" John asked.

"Maybe. If it ever entered a Greek port we might be able to come up with something. But don't be surprised if I find nothing. After all, more than fifty years have passed since this *Sabiya* was supposed to have sunk."

⬚

An hour later, Nick and Zoë joined John and Christo in the waiting room.

"How is she?" John asked, wanting to put his arms

around Zoë to comfort her. But he didn't believe Nick would be able to handle the implications of his embracing Zoë on top of everything else that had occurred.

"Stable," Zoë said. Her voice broke. "She looks so weak, so old."

Nick hugged his sister, all the while looking over the top of her head at John and Christo. The anger showing in his eyes made John shudder.

"You realize this isn't the end of it," John said. "Sooner or later there will be more men sent after us."

Nick nodded his head in agreement. "Why don't you and Zoë stay ashore? I'll go out and finish cleaning up the *Penelope,*" he said. "Get a meal and a good night's sleep and come back out to the boat in the morning?"

"It would probably be a good idea for you to get some rest, too," John said.

"I need to keep busy," Nick said.

"I'll drive you all back to Pythagorio," Christo offered.

"Good!" Nick said. "Then John and Zoë can get rooms at a hotel there while I go back out to the boat."

"I'll send a guard to watch the lobby," Christo said.

Nick laid a hand on John's shoulder. "You take care of my sister."

▯

John and Zoë watched Nick pilot a dinghy out from the dock, then they turned away from the water and started toward a hotel facing the harbor. John thought Zoë looked as though she'd run a marathon. He felt like she looked. It was only mid-morning, but all he could think about were clean sheets and a soft mattress.

While Zoë continued across the quay to the hotel to secure a room, he stopped at a taverna and picked up bottles of water. Then he joined her in the hotel lobby.

Leaning against each other, they plodded up three flights of stairs to their room.

While Zoë used the bathroom, John kicked off his shoes and lay down on the double bed to wait his turn. That was the last thing he remembered until late that night when music drifting up from one of the many seafront restaurants awakened him.

John started at the sound, momentarily confused about where he was. He heard breathing and looked at Zoë sleeping soundly next to him. He carefully slipped out of bed and tiptoed to the bathroom. The thought of a shower and a shave seemed almost erotic. The hot, harsh drumming of the water against his skin felt even better than he'd anticipated.

After toweling himself dry, he moved back to the bed and crawled in next to Zoë. She made a humming-like sound and pressed against him.

They lay together and didn't move. Her head was buried in his shoulder and he held her as though he didn't dare let her go. As though he couldn't take the chance of her disappearing. He knew she was real; but he felt that she was too good to be true. And the feeling swept through him that, like a wraith, she might disappear into thin air.

Suddenly, she spoke into the curve of his neck. "I keep thinking about that man on the boat. How he was about to shoot you," Zoë said. "I can't imagine life without you, John."

CHAPTER FORTY-ONE

May 7–8

John knew he should be relieved about the deaths of the two killers. He guessed their boss, Fritz Leidner, did not yet know what had happened to the two men. But Leidner could have others on Samos hunting for the map. His instincts told him it would only be a matter of time before they became targets again.

He and Zoë walked down the stairs from their room to the hotel lobby. An uniformed policeman got up from a chair in the lobby. John waved at him. He tipped his head in response. Good old Christo, he thought.

It was a cool, cloudy night. The tavernas along the edge of the bay were doing only a modest business—their waiters stationed out front, vying with one another to attract the few tourists strolling along the quay. John and Zoë picked the least crowded taverna and took seats farthest from the entrance. It was after ten, so they decided to eat a light meal—*avgo limono* (egg and lemon) soup and a *horiatiki* salad and then try to get a few more hours sleep before returning to the *Penelope*. The police officer from the hotel lobby now stood about ten yards from the front of the restaurant.

They sat at the table for over an hour, talking about their families, educations, interests, and goals. He was fascinated, but not surprised, to learn she'd received her Doctorate in Archaeology from Oxford University, and had been the head of the Department of Antiquities at the University of Athens for the past three years.

"My father had only a few years of formal schooling," Zoë explained. "But he taught himself by reading books he borrowed from the library and from everyone he knew on the island. People joked about how he always had his nose in a book. Some people thought Papa couldn't really read, that the books were only for show. They had no idea Papa was anything other than an uneducated fisherman." John saw a flash of anger cross her eyes, her face redden. But the moment quickly passed.

Zoë's eyes suddenly went round. She looked surprised, stopped talking, and put her right hand over her heart while she stared over John's shoulder. John turned in his chair. She giggled at his reaction. "It's nothing," she said, "Just a thought." He turned back and she put her hands on his.

"There has to be something significant about what my father wrote on the back of the map."

"I thought you and Christo were in agreement that it was nothing but children's rhymes."

"Up to this moment, I did think that. But now I'm wondering if there may be another explanation. You see, my father read history, archaeology, literature, mythology, medicine—everything. But his favorite subject was mathematics—perhaps because the mathematician Pythagoras came from Samos. Papa taught me the Pythagorean Theorem before I was eleven years old."

"So?"

"Part of what he wrote was, 'Remember, Pythagoras is our friend.' Let's return to the room and look at the map. Maybe we can come up with something."

John nodded, but didn't feel optimistic. Petros Vangelos' words on the map seemed to John like the babbling of an old man. Even the drawing could be the result of some far out fantasy.

He realized the skepticism he felt must have shown on his face. Zoë's enthusiastic expression changed. John quickly stood and took her hand. He forced a smile. "Come on, let's go to the room. Perhaps you're right. We've got nothing to lose by trying."

In their room, Zoë laid the map out and re-read what her father had written on the back. Then she flipped it over and studied the drawing.

She drew a crude copy of the map on another piece of paper and tried drawing lines between the circles in a variety of ways, but nothing seemed to solve the puzzle. They worked on it for two hours, until they could barely keep their eyes open. Finally, John refolded the map and placed it in his knapsack. Zoë phoned the front desk to request a wake up call, and then they undressed, curled next to each other on the bed, and almost instantly fell asleep.

It seemed only a few minutes had passed before John's old dream shocked him awake. His heart rate had nearly settled down to normal when the telephone shocked him anew. He couldn't believe it was already 4:30 a.m.

He gently rubbed Zoë's back and felt his heart swell when she rolled over and smiled as though nothing could have made her happier than waking to the sight of him.

CHAPTER FORTY-TWO

May 8–9

John and Zoë, driven by the policeman Christo had assigned to them, visited Layla in the Vathi hospital at 6:00 that morning. Layla was awake and considerably more alert than on the previous day. Although still weak and in intensive care, the doctor told them he was cautiously optimistic.

After being driven back to Pythagorio by the policeman, they all took a motor-powered dinghy back to the *Penelope*.

The policeman climbed aboard first. John followed Zoë up the ladder and watched brother and sister embrace. With one of his arms draped over his sister's shoulder, Nick said, "Well, you two look rested."

John decided to respond indirectly. "We visited your mother. She's doing much better."

Nick's face lit up. "That's great news."

Then John changed the subject. "We went over your father's map again last night. Zoë thinks the words he wrote on the back have some hidden meaning. But we haven't been able to figure it out. Maybe you'd have better luck."

"I'll try, but first we need to move the boat out to the fourth circle on Papa's map. I want to see if there is anything down there, before anyone else tries to kill us."

Nick asked Zoë to make breakfast. He spoke to her in a way that made it clear cooking was woman's work. John expected some sort of outburst from her, and his expression must have telegraphed his expectations. But she just smiled at him and said quietly so that Nick couldn't hear, "Every time I return home it's as if I go back in time. But I'd rather cook than clean blood and guts off the deck."

When they were under way, Zoë brought hot coffee and rolls up to the wheelhouse. While they ate, they rehashed everything that had happened during the past ten days and tried to make sense of it all. But all they had by way of explanation was Josef's dying declaration.

One thing kept gnawing at John: If there was valuable cargo on the *Sabiya*, why hadn't this mysterious Fritz Leidner just negotiated with Vangelos? Why kill him?

The distance to the fourth circle on Petros' map was only about one point one miles from shore, a half-a-mile outside the harbor entrance. They "guesstimated" the location and anchored. According to their interpretation of the map, they had to be lined up with the tip of the mole and the top of Mount Kastri. The hard part was determining the proper distance from the mole to the fourth circle. That's what the range finder Christo had borrowed from the Greek Army was for.

John gave a short course of instruction to Nick on the use of the range finder. "This is an optical device," he said. "It determines the distance from a reference point to a distant object." He showed him how to line up the range finder on the two reference points—the mole and Mt. Kastri—and then how to make the appropriate calculations to determine distance.

Never in his life did John contemplate having to use a range finder again after leaving the military, and he said a silent thanks to the instructors at Fort Sill. It took him nearly an hour to get comfortable again with the equipment.

According to the map, they needed to be at a spot that lined up through the mole and the top of Mt. Kastri. According to his calculations, the *Penelope* lay one hundred and thirty-seven meters too far out.

Zoë raised the anchor again and Nick repositioned the boat. As best as John could figure, they were now right on top of the spot indicated by the map's fourth circle.

They couldn't have asked for a better day. By the time they'd fixed their location, the sun sat directly overhead and the sky was absolutely clear. To make things even better, the Aegean was smooth as glass.

John helped Zoë check the tanks, masks, weight belts, buoyancy control devices, and regulators. Satisfied everything was in working order, they suited up and were just about ready to enter the water, when Nick brought one of the Coast Guard charts over and spread it out on the deck.

"It looks like we're about fifty to sixty meters from

the end of the reef, which comes out at an angle from the harbor," Nick said. "The top of the reef is only two fathoms below the surface—about four meters. But the depth at the bottom of the reef is closer to ten fathoms, or about nineteen meters. There's a gap of nearly sixty meters across between the end of the reef and the other side of the harbor entrance—and the depth in the gap is over forty-five meters, which allows almost any ship to pass into the harbor. If there is a boat below us, it must have missed that gap and struck the reef." Then as an afterthought, he said, "But how in the world could a ship have been on the bottom below us here without being detected? Papa and I alone must have dived this area a hundred times."

No one had an answer for Nick.

After studying the chart, Zoë and John—in their flippers—slapped their way across the deck to the side of the boat, sat on the rail, and backflipped into the sea.

The sun overhead, the relatively shallow depth of the water—about sixty feet—and the white sand on the bottom combined to make visibility extraordinarily good. A rainbow of creatures swam around them. Two bright-blue fish darted in front of John's face mask, while an array of yellow, pink, and gray fish watched them from about ten feet away. Jet-black sea urchins studded the reef and John saw a tiny octopus jet away from its hiding place between two large rocks.

They didn't need to dive all the way to the sea floor. If there was a boat down there they would surely be able to see it from almost any point below the surface. John thought about Nick's question. If a boat had sunk here over fifty years ago, why hadn't others discovered it by now?

He let Zoë set the pace. For thirty-five minutes they criss-crossed a large area of the sea floor, always orienting themselves on the Penelope's keel. The sand at the bottom looked undisturbed and they saw no wreck, not even any bits of debris that might have come from a boat that had ripped its hull on the reef. With twenty minutes of air left in his air tank, John signaled Zoë it was time to surface. He could see disappointment on her face through her mask, but like all good divers she followed her diving partner's lead and began to move upward. They ascended slowly and reached the surface with plenty of air to spare.

Nick climbed down the *Penelope's* ladder, grabbed their tanks, and passed them to the policeman on deck. John and Zoë tossed their flippers over the rail and then followed Nick into the boat. John was disappointed too that they hadn't found anything. But Zoë seemed disconsolate.

"I hope we're more successful the next time," she said. "I would hate to think someone murdered my father over a patch of empty sand."

They dove again later that day and early the following morning, each time moving farther from the *Penelope*. But the results were the same--no wreck. John guessed that even fifty years of storms roiling the bottom would not have been enough to completely bury a large boat beneath the sand.

Back on the *Penelope,* John voiced his doubts about the accuracy of Petros' map. But neither Zoë nor Nick would listen.

"There's nothing wrong with my father's map," Zoë insisted. "We're just reading it incorrectly."

"Yeah," John said, "but how in God's name could the measurements on your father's map be accurate? It's not as if there are mileage markers in the sea."

"I don't know exactly how Papa would have done it," Nick said, sounding angry. "But I assure you every one of the marks on this map was put there for a reason. When taken together, they will tell a story. We just haven't deciphered it yet."

"Did you two ever consider that perhaps your father just plain made a mistake? Hell, maybe he was playing a joke on you." John regretted the words as soon as they'd escaped his lips, but the frustration he felt needed a release.

Zoë and Nick glared at him. He braced himself, anticipating one or both of them to respond. But then he had a sudden flash of insight. He almost shouted, Archimedes-like, "Eureka!"

CHAPTER FORTY-THREE

May 9

John moved across the deck to his backpack, took out the copy of the map, and spread it out on an equipment locker.

"I think your father *was* playing a joke on someone," he said to Zoë. "But that someone wasn't you. I believe he drew the map so only you would have a chance of solving the riddle. I'd guess the fourth circle your father drew on his map is nothing more than a false clue. A red herring." John saw the confusion on Nick's face, but he waved him off, preempting the question. He didn't want to get bogged down explaining *red herring*. His Greek wasn't *that* good. "I'll bet the fourth circle's only significance," he continued, "is that it lies at sea. I think your father wanted to tell you your objective is under water, but it's up to you to determine exactly where. Leidner's hired assassin confirmed that. Your father made an inquiry about salvage rights." John hesitated a moment, wanting to be sure he put enough conviction in his tone. "I think the essence of your father's message is what he wrote on the back of the map."

They stared at him as though he had a screw loose.

"That nursery rhyme, or whatever it is?" Nick said.

John nodded, then turned to Zoë. "Do you remember when we were in Christo's office and you said the lines connecting Mount Kastri, the mole, and the Temple of Hera—the Heraion—formed a right triangle?"

"Of course! But all three of those sites are on land. You said a minute ago our objective is under water."

"That's right! But hold on a moment longer. The rhyme about triangles and rectangles your father made up has to do with bisecting a rectangle to create two triangles and combining two triangles to form a rectangle. Is that correct?"

They both nodded.

"Okay. So what do we have so far? One right triangle and no rectangle. Right?"

"Yes," Zoë said.

"So what!" Nick blurted impatiently.

John ignored Nick's outburst. "Now take the rest of the words your father wrote on the back of the map: 'Pythagoras is our friend.' What was Pythagoras most famous for?"

"The Pythagorean Theorem," Nick answered. "Every high school kid in the world knows that—'a squared plus b squared equals c squared.' "

"That's right, Nick. And that may be the key. The triangle formed by the three sites on the map is only half the picture! Your father wanted you to add another triangle to the one on the map."

"Huh?" Nick said.

"According to Zoë's calculations," John continued, consulting the measurements Zoë had written on the copy of the map, "we know the distance between Mount Kastri and the mole is 1.1 miles, and the distance from the mole to the Heraion is 3.6 miles. Although you didn't measure the distance from Mount Kastri to the Heraion before, using the Pythagorean Theorem we can quickly figure it out."

On a piece of paper John drew his own map. First, he laid out the same diagram Petros had drawn on his map. Then he added another triangle to the map, creating a rectangle:

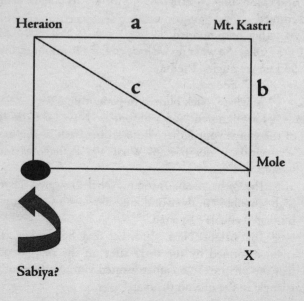

"We say in America, X marks the spot. But, in this case, X doesn't mark the spot. The X is the red herring I referred to before. The *Sabiya* may be at the right angle of the other triangle, where I drew the large black dot." He tapped the spot on the map with his pencil. "Remember what your father said: 'When you marry two triangles, you get a rectangle.' That's part of the clue."

"Son of a bitch!" Nick shouted. "Didn't I tell you Papa knew what he was doing?"

Zoë looked at John with a sparkle in her eyes.

John held up both hands. "Whoa, wait a minute, you two. Let's not get carried away. This is just a theory. We won't know until we dive at the location I drew on the map."

He could see that his warning about getting carried away was lost on them.

❒

They took the dinghy back into Pythagorio. Nick needed to restock supplies. John and Zoë strolled around town, their police escort shadowing their every step.

"You think we could dump our friend back there?" John said, joking with Zoë.

Zoë laughed. "I don't think that would be a good idea. Christo's already angry enough with us for going off on our own the other day." Then she seemed to realize that John was teasing her.

She looked up at him and smiled. "I was very proud of you back on the boat," she said.

❒

Despite the happiness showing on her face, John could see Zoë was exhausted. Between the stress of the past few days and the physical toll three dives had taken, she looked spent. There were dark circles around her eyes and her skin had become pallid, instead of her normally healthy ruddy tone. They reversed direction and walked back to the hotel where they had spent the night a couple days earlier. He took two rooms this time and made sure Zoë was tucked into bed. Then he sat down at a table in her room, removed his drawing from his backpack, and opened it. He alternated between studying the map and checking on Zoë. Only a couple of minutes passed before her breathing settled into the slow rhythm of sleep. Continuing to watch her for a few more minutes, he marveled at how quickly they had connected with one another. Connected, hell! he thought. It was way beyond that!

He left her then and went to his room, leaving the adjoining door open. He used the telephone in the room to call the police station in Vathi.

Christo was eager to learn the results of their diving and was disappointed they'd come up empty-handed.

"I have a plan that's too complicated to go over on the phone," John told him. "Do you think you could meet us here in Pythagorio at eight tonight? We can all get together for dinner."

"I can be there at eight," Christo said, "but why don't you and I meet at seven—just the two of us," Christo said. "I've made progress since we last talked, and have received some information on Fritz Leidner and the bank he owns, *Banque Securité de Swisse.*"

"I noticed a taverna one block up from the quay, at the corner of the street that runs up the hill to the north. It's called *Dionysos*. We can meet there," John suggested.

John replaced the receiver and stretched out on his bed. He tried to nap, but he couldn't get comfortable and was too wired to sleep, anyway. A plan was developing in his head and he needed to put it into action. He checked in on Zoë again, then quietly left her room.

John took the stairs to the lobby and approached the reception desk. He remembered from years ago that the Greeks knew how to make things happen and just about every hotel desk clerk in the country could arrange for anything you wanted. He hoped that spirit and skill were still alive and well.

Using his Greek, which had become less rusty with each passing day, he told the clerk he needed a boat, diving equipment, and a long list of supplies. He offered to pay him two hundred dollars to arrange for these things, and for not telling anyone for whom he was working. John knew from the smile on the clerk's face he could count on the man's assistance and discretion.

John then told the policeman in the lobby he was going out for a couple hours and that he should watch out for Ms. Vangelos. His leaving the hotel alone seemed to make the young officer extremely nervous. The cop protested, but he was in a quandary—either stay with John and leave Zoë alone, or stay in the hotel and protect Zoë, and let John leave. John watched the cop seem to wrestle with himself over his choices, then firmly told the young man to stay in the hotel, and quickly left the lobby.

John looked left and right, searching the street for anyone who seemed out of place. It looked safe. He walked a block from the hotel to a row of shops and found a Greek National Bank branch office. He realized anyone watching him would have thought he had a serious nervous disorder the way he kept jerking his head around to see if he was being followed. It crossed his mind that he did have a nervous disorder. But after the past two weeks he had an excuse for being paranoid. He cashed five thousand euros in travelers checks and, using one of his credit cards, got a five hundred euro cash advance, as well.

John had thought this out. He used his credit card because the assassin named Josef had said they'd traced him to Vathi through the credit card he'd used at the dive shop. This time he was intentionally laying a trail of breadcrumbs for Leidner to follow. He wanted the bastard to know his general location, but not what he was up to. And he wanted Leidner to know he was still in Pythagorio, to lure him here. To get him off his home turf in Switzerland and onto Greek soil. It was time to go on the offensive.

At exactly four o'clock, he returned to the hotel. After stopping at the front desk to request a six-thirty wake up call and waving to the policeman, he climbed to his room, checked on Zoë, then flopped down on the bed and slept like a baby.

CHAPTER FORTY-FOUR

May 9

Fritz Leidner had not wanted to spend part of his sixth decade dealing with this bullshit. His life had been charmed up to now. Sure he'd worried about the possibility of someone discovering the *Sabiya,* but when there had been no word about the boat for so many years, he thought he was home free. But now that damned boat could be the end of it all—his wealth, his reputation, his place in Swiss society.

He pushed off the arms of his chair and stared at the three hired guns he'd brought with him from Zurich. The two men, Peter and Tomas, were tall, burly mercenary types, with rippling muscles, military haircuts, and sculpted jaws and cheekbones. The third person was Theo Burger. Peter and Tomas worked for her, as did the two men, Hans and Josef, whom she had sent to Samos earlier to find Vangelos, and who had disappeared. He stared at the three of them lined up in front of him on the yacht deck.

"I will say this only once. Your compatriots, Hans and Josef, failed." He made a point of glaring at Theo when he said this. "They did not get the map. They did not discover the boat's location. I assume you will be more successful."

Theo Burger answered for all of them. *"Ja, mein Herr."*

"This Hammond fellow is still on Samos. Apparently, he's working with Vangelos' daughter. Find them!" he ordered, a cruel edge in his voice.

◻

Theo led the way down the stairs to the motor launch. She and the two men took the launch to shore and got in the black Mercedes they'd rented at the airport.

"Drive to Pythagorio, Peter," she said. "That's the logical place for Hammond to be hiding."

"You know, he and the Vangelos woman could be anywhere by now," Tomas interjected, impatience in his voice.

"Yes," Theo responded, "and they could be in Pythagorio right now, too. We have to start somewhere. Unless you'd like to go back and tell *Herr* Leidner that you think you're wasting your time."

CHAPTER FORTY-FIVE

May 9

Christo met John on the sidewalk outside the *Dionysos Taverna.* Christo had a cigarette in one hand and a set of worry beads in the other. They entered the taverna. It was too early for the restaurant's Greek patrons to be out for their evening meal, so they had the place all to themselves.

"So, what have you found out about this man Leidner?" John asked, after a waiter served their drink order.

Leaning forward, elbows on the table, Christo lowered his voice. "We requested information from Interpol on Leidner and learned that he is the principal stockholder of *Banque Securité de Swisse.* But Interpol has absolutely nothing on either the man or his bank. I then called a contact with Swiss Intelligence. Again, nothing. As far as I can tell, Fritz Leidner is just another law-abiding Swiss banker."

"So, you've got nothing," John said, disappointment

heavy in his voice. "I thought you said—"

"Well, not quite nothing. I called our embassy in Bern, Switzerland, and talked to the son of a friend of mine. He's the Greek Commercial Attaché there. He made calls to some of his banker friends and even called Leidner's office on the pretext of making an appointment with him to discuss the possibility of Leidner's bank opening a branch in Athens. He gathered a couple bits of information. For example, Leidner inherited the bank from his father, Friederich Leidner. The old man had a reputation for being tough, to the point of being ruthless. He was not well liked by his contemporaries. The son has never worked anywhere else but at the bank. Fritz Leidner is fifty-five years old now and has a son of his own who works in the bank. Leidner apparently had a reputation for being a rebel in his younger days, but today he's a respected part of the banking community."

Christo paused to sip his drink and then continued. "One member of the Zurich banking community even dropped a hint that the elder Leidner may have been involved with the Germans during World War Two."

"The Nazis?" John said. "You've got to be kidding me."

Christo shrugged. "It could have been just sour grapes from a competitor."

Christo's face suddenly sagged. "My contact at our embassy can be very charming. When he talked to Leidner's secretary this morning, he learned her boss left late last night on a business trip. Would you like to guess where he traveled to?"

John felt a chill run down his spine. He knew exactly

what Christo would say: Greece. "Don't build up the suspense," he said.

"The sonofabitch is in Greece. I called Olympic Airlines. They told me an 'F. Leidner' had booked a seat from Zurich to Athens on a noon flight today. He connected there with a flight to Samos. He's already on the island."

"Oh, Jesus," John said. "Leidner is a step ahead of us."

"The agent at Olympic told me there were three other persons with Swiss passports on that flight from Athens"—here Christo consulted his notebook—"Peter Muther, Tomas Burkett, and Theo Burger."

"It ought to have been a pretty simple job to intercept this foursome at the Samos Airport," John said.

"Yes, it would have been, if I'd been alerted in time. I didn't get the call from our attaché until after the plane had already landed," he said, with a hangdog look. "We missed them at the airport. I ordered a search of all of the hotels in Vathi and in Pythagorio, but nothing has turned up yet. They could be staying at any one of a hundred hotels, or in a private residence, or on a boat. By this time, Leidner must know he has a problem here. He must be worried he hasn't heard from the two men who died on Nick's boat, and is probably bringing in reinforcements. The other three Swiss passengers on the Olympic flight are more than likely his men. We've released no information about the death of those two killers. Whatever is going on, it must be damn important for Leidner to put himself on the ground here with his troops."

"I have to tell you I'm more than a little worried," John said. "Zoë's at great risk here."

Christo gave him a knowing look. "I understand, my friend. And I assure you I'm taking every precaution within my authority to keep Zoë, Nick and you safe. I've got officers on the way here from Athens. I just don't have enough men on Samos to get the job done. I need the three of you to stay put so I can effectively protect you."

John didn't want to get into an argument with Christo at that moment. There was no way he was going to sit around like a sacrificial goat.

"Did you come up with anything on the *Sabiya?*" John asked.

"Oh, now that's another story," Christo said. "I contacted the Greek Maritime Office in Athens and asked if they had records back to the end of the war. They did. He found a file about the *Sabiya.* But there was nothing in it more current than from 1940." Again Christo consulted his notebook. "The boat was fifty-eight meters long, a little over nine meters wide, and had a draught of three-and-a-half meters. It was constructed in 1934. That's really all the information I got. If they come up with anything else, the director will call me."

"Did the guy at the Maritime Office know anything about the boat's owner or who it might have been chartered to?" John asked.

"He did say the owner and the captain were one and the same—some Turk by the name of Mehmet Arkoun.

John reflected on all Christo had told him, then shared his theory about the words Petros Vangelos had written on the back of his map.

Christo eyed him skeptically, and shrugged. He didn't appear to buy what John was selling.

Just before eight o'clock, John suggested they start back to the hotel to join up with Zoë and Nick.

"Are you getting to know Zoë's brother well?" Christo asked when they were halfway to the hotel.

"We've spent an awful lot of time together over the last few days," John said.

Christo had a mischievous smile on his face again. "You say that as if you resent his presence."

John started to pretend he didn't understand Christo's point, but decided to give his friend his due. "You've known from the very beginning the effect Zoë has had on me. How could you tell?"

"Other than the look on your face whenever she's around, a look I usually only see on love-struck teenagers, and other than the fact you could have left Samos and gotten away from this madness of death, maps, and sunken ships, I really didn't have a clue."

John laughed. "That obvious?"

"Yes, since the first time I saw you looking at her. And you know what? I'm thrilled for you. So what are you going to do about it?"

"Whatever she'll let me do about it, Christo."

Wanting to change the subject, John asked, "When is Athens going to send in the additional men you requested?"

Christo momentarily looked confused, and then said, "Oh, you were eavesdropping when I called from Nick Vangelos' boat."

John nodded.

Christo shook his head. "I don't understand," he said. "They know me well enough to realize that I would never ask for help if I didn't think it was absolutely necessary. The Chief told me that his boss at the Ministry of Public Order vetoed my request."

They turned the corner at the bottom of the hill and John saw commotion around the hotel entrance, where Nick and the cop from the lobby paced outside, both obviously agitated. They rushed over to them.

"Zoë went out about thirty minutes ago," Nick shouted. "She asked the desk clerk for directions to a drugstore. She told him she would be right back and asked him to tell Panos here." He jabbed a thumb at the policeman. "She took off while Panos was taking a piss."

The young policeman dropped his head and stared at his shoes.

From the look John saw Christo shoot at the policeman, he guessed the cop would pay a heavy price for his bladder's poor timing.

"I arrived here just a few minutes after Zoë had walked out," Nick continued. "It took me five minutes to find the drugstore. She'd already been there, according to the store's clerk, and when she left she got into a car with several people. When I asked him if they'd forced her into the car, he told me he hadn't been paying close enough attention."

CHAPTER FORTY-SIX

May 9

"You idiot!" Theo Burger shouted from the back seat of the black Mercedes. "I told you to stay below the speed limit."

"I—"

"Shut up!" she hissed at Peter. "Pull over and get out. Talk to the cop. Try to keep him from getting too close to the car."

The police car's roof lights flashed through the back window of the Mercedes. Theo ground her teeth at the aggravating, monotonous sound of the siren. She hoped the chloroform they used on the Vangelos woman was enough to keep her quiet for another ten minutes.

Peter stepped out onto the road. He walked back past the rear of the vehicle, intercepting the Greek policeman by the front of the police cruiser.

Theo wanted to turn around in the back seat and stare at the cop. It was dark outside, but with the police car's highlights shining on the Mercedes she knew the cop would see her. She needed to remain calm. It's just another traffic stop, she told herself.

Tomas, seated in the front passenger seat, had half-turned toward her. "If the cop moves in our direction, kill him," Theo ordered. She then lowered the right rear window and listened to the conversation going on between Peter and the policeman. It sounded as though the cop spoke no German. Peter, she knew, spoke no Greek. "What's going on back there?" she whispered to Tomas.

Tomas shifted further in his seat. He peered at the sideview mirror and said nothing for a moment. Then he turned and met Theo's gaze. "Peter's doing a lot of hand waving and the cop seems to be getting agitated. Peter just pulled out his wallet and is trying to hand money to the guy."

Smart move, Theo thought. She knew that money greased the bureaucratic wheels in Greece. She assumed it would do the same with the police. "Did the cop take the money?" she asked.

Suddenly, hammering sounds came from the Mercedes' trunk, rocking the vehicle.

"Oh shit!" Tomas exclaimed, now twisted around and staring through the rear window. "The cop just put his hand on his pistol and is yelling something."

"Too bad!" Theo said, when the angry sounds of the policeman's voice carried to her. She cocked her head at Tomas. "Take care of it," she said. While Tomas opened the passenger door and stepped out, Theo turned. She saw the policeman look at Tomas, who had his hands in his pockets. She saw the bulge Tomas' pistol made under his jacket where it was wedged in the waistband at the back of his trousers. Tomas walked to the cop's right side, removing his hands from his pockets. She saw Peter shift his position more to the cop's left. The cop glanced from one man to the other, apparently trying to keep an eye on both men. He continued shouting. His pistol was now halfway out of the holster on his utility belt.

Theo twisted around, now facing the front of the Mercedes. She lifted herself off the backseat, reached over the front seat, and leaned her hand on the horn. While she did so, she looked back over her shoulder and saw the cop jerk his head toward the Mercedes. In that instant, Tomas removed the pistol from his waistband, aimed it at the policeman's head, and pulled the trigger. A crimson-red spray blew out of the side of the cop's skull, hitting Peter, covering him with brain matter, bone fragments, and blood. Theo laughed at the look on Peter's face, highlighted in the glare from the police car's lights. Priceless, she thought.

CHAPTER FORTY-SEVEN

May 9

John felt a devastating sense of loss and a profound anger that threatened his self-control.

Christo laid a calming hand on his arm, then did the same to Nick. "All right, let's approach the situation as unemotionally as possible," he said. "We won't be doing Zoë any good unless we keep our wits about us. Nick, where's this drugstore?"

They marched a hundred yards down the street to the tiny shop. Christo told them to wait outside while he talked to the clerk. After five minutes of conversation, during which the clerk looked like a Dutch windmill with his arms flying above and around his head, Christo returned.

"He described Zoë exactly, so I have no doubt he saw her get into a car. He said there were at least one person in the car and another two who got in after Zoë. He wasn't sure if she was forced into the car. He didn't have a very good view out to the street because of the shop's display racks. He couldn't describe the car except that it was black."

Without waiting for any response from them, Christo pulled a telephone from a pouch on his hip. He dialed a number and ordered all available police officers to report to the hotel lobby where John and Zoë had rooms. He also ordered a search of the entire island for a black car containing three Swiss males and a Greek female. After a pause, while he appeared to be listening, Christo said, "Make immediate inquiries at every car rental agency on the island concerning vehicles rented to anyone with a Swiss passport. And set up roadblocks every mile for ten miles on the Samos Highway north and south of Pythagorio."

The policeman on the other end of the line must have balked because Christo raised his voice for the first time during the entire conversation and yelled something. John caught enough of the diatribe to understand what Christo said: "Then get your fat-assed relatives, your inbred children, and your dead grandfather to do it! They've kidnapped a Greek woman and they may kill her."

Christo set up a command post in the hotel lobby, explaining that the Pythagorio station was too small. If the men who had taken Zoë were going to contact anyone, he added, they would probably try to call John. These men wanted the map, and, as far as they knew, John was the way to it.

It was no stretch for John, either, to figure that the men who had Zoë wanted the map. He would turn over a thousand maps to get her back.

Nick and John tried to make themselves useful. Nick used the police radio to broadcast a plea on the Greek fishermen's frequency to boats in the area to keep an eye out for his sister. John ordered meals from the hotel's kitchen for all of them, including the entire contingent of fifteen policemen and citizen volunteers. But mostly John and Nick sat, paced, cursed, and paced some more.

The sight of so many cops in one location caused quite a stir among the local populace, many of whom were standing around outside the hotel entrance. Rumors circulated through the group of locals that someone had gotten caught smuggling. It didn't take long for the word of a kidnapping to work its way through the crowd. The shocked reactions on the locals' faces—hands covering mouths, women crying, men cursing—spoke volumes about how unaccustomed the Samians were to violent crime.

John had conceived a plan to try to trap Leidner. He knew it had been risky—even crazy. He had wanted to lure Leidner to Samos. The sonofabitch had been a step ahead of him, however. He'd been on his way to Samos even before John had used his credit card. But he was desperate now that Zoë had been kidnapped. He went over his entire plan in his head one more time, scrutinizing it for flaws and danger points. It was full of both. A plan fabricated out of worry and anger, and about to be implemented out of desperation.

He had the copy of Petros' map on him. But Zoë knew its every detail by heart. The only thing that would keep her alive was her value to them as a bargaining chip—Zoë for the map. If she divulged what she knew about the map, they would no longer need to find a copy. Once they proved up what she told them, she would become expendable.

But they didn't know the map was itself an intricate puzzle. Without help from Zoë, Nick, Christo or him they would never be able to understand the hidden meaning of Petros' inscription—the rhyme that John felt more and more was the key to the map.

It was time to put the rest of his plan in motion. He crossed the room to the communications table where Nick was working the radio. "Nick," he asked, "how much do you estimate the *Penelope* is worth?" John asked him.

The look on Nick's face showed his surprise at John's question. His brow furrowed, eyes narrowed. It was obvious he found the question inappropriate, in bad taste.

John met Nick's gaze. "This has to do with your sister. I have a good reason for asking."

Finally he said, "Two hundred fifty thousand American dollars."

"Fine! I want to buy it."

"You wouldn't make much of a fisherman," he snorted, turning back to the radio.

"It's immaterial what I want to use it for. Will you sell it to me?"

"Sure!" Nick said, sarcastically. "You have that kind of money?" His tone told John that Nick didn't believe he could pay his price and that Nick didn't really want to discuss selling his boat at a time like this.

Christo had continually been on either the telephone or the police radio. John assumed his men were providing him with status reports. Judging by his reactions, the reports had been routine. But, just as John handed the IOU over to Nick, he happened to look over at Christo—and this time his face had turned red and he excitedly waved his free arm at John, while he spoke into the radio handset.

John and Nick rushed over to Christo and listened while he barked orders into the radio. Christo's color had gone from red to white. John's heart thumped in his chest. The look on the Inspector's face told him it was bad news. Please let Zoë be okay, he silently prayed.

"Set up a perimeter around the cars and question everyone in the area," Christo shouted. "Find out if anyone saw or heard anything, or where the occupants went. Get someone out there to check for fingerprints."

Christo turned the volume down on the radio. "We think we've found the car the pharmacist saw Zoë taken away in," he said. "It's parked near an out-of-the-way taverna about halfway between Pythagorio and the Heraion. There's a dock across from the taverna used by fishing boats and small private yachts. One of my men questioned the restaurant owner, who saw three or four people—including two women—leave the car about 45 minutes ago and board a high-powered recreational fishing boat. My man identified the rental car company from a decal on the car's windshield. The company said the car had been rented to a Helmut Grüne."

"That's not one of the names of the three people travelling with Leidner," John said.

"No," Christo said, "but it could be an alias. It makes sense that they would try to cover their tracks."

"Did you say that a witness saw two women?" Nick asked.

"That's right."

"I thought the pharmacist saw three men with Zoë."

"He *thought* he saw three men. He wasn't really sure about their gender."

"In other words," Nick interjected, "we can't be sure it's the right car."

Christo gave Nick a cold-eyed look, then softened his gaze and nodded.

"So, we may be dealing with at least two men and one woman," John said. "Plus Leidner. Or, the people this witness saw aren't the same ones who have Zoë."

Christo just shrugged. Nick stalked off. He looked as though he were ready to explode.

"Did you say 'cars' plural," John said.

Christo's eyes narrowed and John felt a current of uneasiness run through him. He'd never seen the Greek cop look as he now did. There had been anger in the set of his jaw, the flaring of his nostrils, the ice in his eyes when he'd learned of Zantsos' death. But this was different. There was a visceral hatred showing in the turn of Christo's mouth. His eyes blazed. But, at the same time, there seemed to be an unbearable sadness about him.

"About one kilometer this side of where we found the black Mercedes, on the coast road, my men found the body of a young police officer. He'd been executed. One shot to the temple. His car was parked by the side of the road, its engine and flashers still on. His body had been dragged into a ditch. He may have stopped the people who kidnapped Zoë."

"I'm so sorry, Christo," John said.

"So am I," Christo said. "That young man was my sister's only child."

Nick fastwalked over to Christo. "They've taken my sister out on the water," he exclaimed. "How the hell are we ever going to find her? By now they could be anywhere on any one of a hundred or more islands. They could even be in Turkey."

"Yeah, but where they are is irrelevant," John said. "They want the map. They don't have a chance of getting it if we don't get Zoë back." John wanted to believe his own words, but he knew if they forced Zoë to talk, they would never see her again.

The desolate look John saw in Nick's eyes told him that what John had just said offered no consolation.

While Christo took care of various logistical matters, John talked with the hotel desk clerk. He learned the man had already arranged everything John had requested earlier. Then he gave John directions to where the rented boat was docked, gave him an invoice covering the cost of the boat and equipment, and gratefully took the money.

In order to put his plan into effect, John needed Christo's assistance. He pulled Christo aside. "I want to use the *Penelope* as a decoy, but I need something from you."

"What you need to do," Christo said, "is stay right here where I can protect you."

John breathed out a heavy sigh. "Look, Christo. Things are out of control. The only way we're going to get Zoë back alive is to give her kidnappers the map. They could care less about me at this point."

Christo glared at John; but, after a moment, he seemed to realize that John made sense. "So, what do you want from me?"

"Explosives."

CHAPTER FORTY-EIGHT

May 9

"Ach, can't they stop that woman's screaming? Stuff a rag in her mouth."

Theo Burger rose from the chair opposite Fritz Leidner. "I'll take care of it, *mein Herr.*" She walked from the lounge area on the rented yacht's rear deck, along the rail, descended a staircase, and disappeared below.

Leidner lifted his glass from the table in front of him and sipped the cognac. He reflected on the fortunate turn of events. Theo's seeing the woman leave the hotel had been purely fortuitous. Theo had recognized her from the photograph Hans had taken from Layla Vangelos' house and sent to Zurich before his disappearance. Theo and two of her men had followed Zoë Vangelos to the pharmacy, snatched her off the street, and brought her to where the yacht had been moored. Leidner cocked his head to try to pick up any sounds coming from below deck. Nothing. Theo had handled the situation.

He thought how much he would enjoy watching

what the men were doing to the woman. But it would be undignified for mere employees to see him display emotion. He would have to be satisfied with looking at her after the others were finished. If she knew anything, he was confident the two men below would force it out of her.

Leidner watched Theo cross the deck toward him. She was a stunning creature. Tall, blue eyed, and cropped blonde hair. It amazed him that her mannish haircut only seemed to make her more beautiful, setting off her high cheekbones and perfect nose. A real Nordic beauty. He felt a stirring in his groin. Even when he was pissed off at Theo, the sight of her was enough to excite him. And, of course, looking at her while remembering the night she stabbed his father to death, only made his sexual reaction even more intense. She met his gaze and he shuddered. He had a sudden image of a black widow spider. The woman exuded a sense of danger, but that made Leidner's desire heighten to the point he thought he might lose control. He turned away and thought about what Peter and Tomas were doing to the Greek woman below deck. The combination of violence and sex had never failed to excite him, even when he was a young man.

Back to business. He raised his glass in salute. "Thank you, my dear. That screaming was quite grating on the nerves."

Theo tilted her head in acknowledgement. "Perhaps I should make further inquiries about Hans and Josef. It's not natural that we have heard nothing from them."

"Don't bother yourself, *Liebchen*. We must assume they are either in custody or dead. If the authorities have

them, we have nothing to worry about. They will say
nothing. They're professionals. And if they're dead"—he
paused and smiled—"then we truly have nothing to
worry about. *Ja?*"

"*Jawohl, mein Herr.*"

◻

Tomas Burkett stepped back from the bed and wiped
his face with his shirtsleeve. "Turn up the air conditioner,
Peter? I'm sweating like a pig. I thought this Greek bitch
would have snapped like a twig the first time I hit her.
She's tougher than she looks."

"Ah, Tomas, you just don't know how to deal with
the weaker sex," Peter Muther said. "Your methods are
much too brutish. Why not let me try?"

"You think you can do better, have at it," Tomas
said, drying his face with a towel. "This should be fun
to watch."

Peter walked closer to the bed set against the
bulkhead in the yacht's stateroom. He moved almost cat-
like, while he checked the ropes binding Zoë's wrists and
ankles to the head and footboards. "Tsk, tsk," he clucked
while he looked down at her face. One blackened eye had
swollen completely closed. The other eye was unnaturally
wide with her fear and pain. The woman's cheeks were
also swollen and had split open from the pummeling
Tomas had given her. From the grimace on her face, he
could tell she was in great pain. The heavy blows Tomas
had administered to her stomach and chest made Tomas'
gut hurt—not out of sympathy, but out of empathy. He

knew how much agony they must have caused.

"Now, my little *Kookla*," Peter said. "Zat is how you Greeks say "doll," *nein?* You do not look zo beautiful anymore. I can make this stop like zat." He snapped his fingers. "All you haf to do is tell me about za map your fater made. Or tell me ver za *Sabiya* is. Then ve vill let you go. See, very simple."

Zoë mumbled something through the gag the blonde woman had stuffed in her mouth.

"Zo, you vish to talk?" Peter said, shooting a satisfied glance toward Tomas. He reached down and yanked the washcloth from her mouth. The woman tried to speak, but her mouth was apparently too dry. "Get some water!" Peter ordered.

Tomas grabbed a pitcher from a bureau and poured water from it into a glass. He handed the glass to Peter, who bent over, tipped the glass, and poured water into Zoë's mouth. She coughed, spluttering water over her bruised chin and torn, bloody blouse.

"Now, *Kookla*, vat do you haf to tell us?"

Zoë whispered something, but her voice was so low her words were unintelligible.

Peter sat on the side of the bed. "Vat?" he said.

She again said something, but it sounded like gibberish.

Peter glared up at Tomas. "If you've addled her brain, Leidner will feed you to the fish." He turned back to Zoë and lowered his head to her, his ear close to her mouth. "Vat vas zat? Say it again."

Zoë raised her head a couple inches. She whispered sounds that made Peter move even closer. Then she bared her teeth and clamped down on the man's ear. Her head whipped back and forth like a lioness tearing meat from its prey, biting with a fury that severed the man's earlobe. She spat the bloody piece at Peter while he howled and leaped off the bed.

Tomas laughed, "I don't think your method is any more successful than mine."

"Go to hell," Peter shouted. "Sonofabitch!" he screamed. He touched his ear and immediately jerked his hand away. "Look what she did," holding his bloodied fingers toward Tomas. Then he stepped back over to the side of the bed, one hand now holding a handkerchief to his ear. He leaned toward Zoë and said in a cold, quiet tone, "You shall be very sorry you did that." Then with his free hand he slowly began stripping her, watching her one good eye follow each movement. First, the ripping of her blouse, then unsnapping and opening the zipper on her jeans, sliding them down her legs. He tossed the bloodied handkerchief away and jerked her blouse from under her. He then tore her jeans with his hands, as though they were made of tissue paper. The severed halves of the material draped her ankles. When all she had on were her panties and bra, he removed a switchblade knife from his pants pocket, popped the blade, and sliced the fabric of her bra between the two cups. Her breasts fell loose. He stuck the knife blade into the lamp table beside the bed and bent over the side of the bed. Taking one of her nipples between his thumb and index finger, he squeezed as hard as he could, until he could no longer stand the sound of her screams. Then he inserted the washcloth back into her mouth.

Peter turned toward Tomas and pointed a finger at the stateroom door. "Leave us!" he shouted. "I will call you when it's your turn." While Tomas opened the door and walked out into the hall, Peter jerked up on the waistband of her bikini briefs, lifting her lower body off the bed until the band snapped and she bounced back on the bed. She now lay completely naked, struggling against the ropes that held her to the bedposts. Her good eye seemed to bulge and she made several sounds that progressed through a series of octaves, crescendoing into high-pitched moans.

Peter went to the bathroom and found some cotton and tape. He patched up the wound on his ear, then returned to the bedroom. He took his time undressing. He wanted the woman to anticipate the pain and violation. He'd done this before and he knew how fragile a woman could become once she faced the realization of being defiled. He stripped naked, then moved to the foot of the bed where Zoë could get a clear view of him. He massaged his erection and said, "Now ve vill see vat kind of voman you are, my dear."

He circled the bed once, enjoying the way she jerked her head to follow his movements. When he reached the side of the bed, he knelt on the mattress and squeezed her breasts. She thrashed her head back and forth.

"Now, now, *Kookla*," he said. "None of zat vill help." He straddled her and ran his hands over her body. "You are gorgeous, you know zat," he said. "It vould haf been nice to meet under other circumstances. But, it is too late for zat. Far too late."

When Peter was finished with Zoë, he climbed off

the bed, dressed, and then opened the door and shouted, "Tomas, it's your turn." When Tomas appeared at the other end of the corridor, Peter waved him forward. When they passed each other, he said, "Call me when you're through. I should be ready again for her by then."

CHAPTER FORTY-NINE

May 9

C hristo stared at John, open-mouthed, eyes widened to twice their normal size. "I don't think I heard you right. Tell me again."

"I want to use the *Penelope* as a decoy, but I need explosives to make my plan work."

Christo had heard John correctly the first time. "What! Are you crazy?" he shouted. All conversations in the lobby stopped. Everyone turned to look at them. Christo glared toward his men, who immediately averted their eyes.

"Do you have any idea how many laws I've already broken on your behalf?" he complained in a quieter voice. "Borrowed government property and let a foreign civilian use it, loaned you a pistol. Now you want me to provide you with explosives? *Ochi, then tha to kano.* I won't do it!" he said, walking away and out the front door of the hotel.

John followed and joined him on the sidewalk. The

evening breeze had turned cool and scudding clouds laced the sky, first revealing then obscuring a yellow moon. The two of them stood there with their heads turned skyward, as though mesmerized by the brilliance of the moon and the stars. Finally, Christo quietly asked, without turning his head, "What do you want with explosives?"

John explained what he had in mind. Christo didn't react at all for a while. "I'll get you what you request," he said at last, "on the condition you can convince me you know how to use it."

"Christo," John said, "I trained at the U.S. Army's Special Warfare School in all types of demolitions. Hell, I can still make a bomb out of ingredients from under your kitchen sink. I know more about explosives than most terrorists. I assure you I have a profound respect for the stuff and I know how to handle them." He then explained how he planned to set up the charges and detonate them.

"Okay, John. But remember—"

"I know, I know. If I get caught with it on me, I should say I bought it on the black market from some Turk."

The desk clerk cut Christo's laugh short when he came out of the hotel and announced, "There's a man on the telephone asking to be put through to Mr. Hammond's room."

As John ran to the front desk, Christo hurried over to the police communications table and rested a hand on one of the phones connected to the hotel switchboard. He raised the phone receiver at the same time John raised the phone receiver on the front desk.

"This is John Hammond."

"Ah, Mr. Hammond, are you having a good day?"

The voice was clipped, with a trace of an upper class British accent. His accent and obvious arrogance grated on John's nerves. This was it. It had to be Leidner or one of his cronies. This was the call they'd been waiting for. John had a momentary feeling of elation. The fact that they were calling told him they had been unable to get the information they wanted about the map from Zoë. She must still be alive. "Who am I speaking to?" John asked.

"That is unimportant, Mr. Hammond. What is important is that one of your friends is a guest of ours. She has been quite uncooperative, by the way. She must have a very high pain threshold."

"You sonofabitch! When I get my hands—"

"Now, now, Mr. Hammond. Let's not lose our composure. I guarantee that will not help you or your friend. So take a deep breath and listen carefully to what I tell you."

The condescendingly superior tone of the man infuriated John. He looked across the lobby at Christo and took some comfort from the anger showing on the Inspector's face. Nick, who had left the lobby for a time, came back at that moment and stood next to John.

"I'm listening," John said into the phone.

"We have Zoë Vangelos. I believe you have a map you took from her father. I want that map. Unless I get it, you will never see her again."

John didn't believe for an instant that the man would keep his end of the bargain. He couldn't leave a trail of potential witnesses behind. The minute he handed over the map to the man, he would be sealing Zoë's death warrant, and maybe his, too.

"All right," he said, "I'll give you the map. But I pick the location for the trade. Otherwise, it's no deal."

"Fine, Mister Hammond. I see no reason to bicker over any of this. Where would you like to meet?"

He told the man where they'd moored the *Penelope* and to meet him there, at ten in the morning. He would turn over the map once Zoë was safely aboard the boat.

"And how will I be sure you are on this boat?" he demanded.

"You will send one of your men to the boat to meet me before you drop off Zoë," John replied. "He can verify my presence."

"Then why not just give my man the map? He can bring Ms. Vangelos to you. There is no need for us to meet on this *Penelope*."

"Oh, but there is. Without my explanation, you will never be able to decipher the code on the map. Only I have the key to that code," John lied, "and I will give it to you, and no one else. I want to see your face. I want to know who you are, you evil son of a bitch."

The man actually giggled at John's words—as though pleased by the insult.

"Remember, Mr. Hammond, no police," he said. "If I see one policeman, I will execute the lovely Ms. Vangelos. Is that understood?"

"Yes!" John hesitated a moment. The man's willingness to trade for the map made no sense. He had to know—or at least guess—that the police already had the original map. Before they turned over the original to Leidner, they would make copies. So what good would it do him to get the map, when there were copies out there? What was the point of getting the map if John had already deciphered the code, knew how to find the boat, as he had just admitted to the man on the phone? And, the police would be waiting for Leidner if he showed up at the site of the *Sabiya*.

"Leidner, or whoever you are, do you really believe the police will give you the original map and not keep a copy? That they won't track you after we make the trade?"

There was a pause. John guessed his mention of the Leidner name had surprised the caller. Then the man said, "You let me worry about that, Mr. Hammond." Without another word, he hung up the phone and left John listening to the dial tone. John replaced the receiver. He stared at his hands. He had to stick them in his pants pockets to hide how badly they were shaking.

Nick grabbed John's arm and demanded, "How's Zoë?"

"Alive," John said. "But that's all I know." He decided not to mention that the man on the phone had implied that Zoë had been roughed up... or worse.

"Thank God," Nick exclaimed.

John and Nick walked over to Christo. "You heard what he said about no police," John said. "I want your word you will follow his instructions."

He could see Christo was prepared to argue the point. His eyes narrowed and the muscles in his cheeks twitched, but he caught himself when he realized he had little choice. "You have my word," Christo said. "We will not close in until you and Zoë are safe. You realize, don't you, there is a damn good chance the minute he gets his hands on that map, he will kill both of you. I'll arrest him and his men, but that won't be much consolation for you and Zoë."

"I'm not so sure you'll get him. This makes no sense. You heard what I said about copies of the map and the police going after him once the trade was made. He wasn't even fazed. Yeah, I'm convinced he does plan to kill us. But I have no choice. I can't leave Zoë in his hands without at least trying to help her. Do you think you can deliver the explosives and the other gear to the dock by midnight?"

"I'll take care of it," Christo said. "In the meantime, I'm going to ask the Coast Guard to comb the entire eastern coast of the island. Maybe we'll get lucky and find Leidner before your meeting."

John nodded, then turned to Nick while Christo walked away. "I guess I owe you an explanation," John said.

Nick gave John an "I'm waiting" look.

❑

Leidner knew he had exposed himself by coming to Greece; but the stakes were so high, he couldn't risk leaving the problem in others' hands. Hammond's mention of his name had surprised him. He needed to erase the man and all those around him. Then he had to get back to Switzerland as quickly as possible, before the

Greeks figured out what he had been up to and got their hands on him. He thought about the videotapes he had back in Zurich. If worse came to worst they were his ace in the hole. Theo had arranged for some very powerful men to satisfy their sexual fantasies. The senior judge in Switzerland would see to it that Leidner would never be extradited no matter how hard the Greeks tried to make that happen. Otherwise, video proof of his pedophilia would become public.

CHAPTER FIFTY

May 9–10

Christo met Nick and John at the dock in Pythagorio Harbor at midnight.

"Everything you asked for is in these two bags," Christo said, handing them to John.

"Thanks, Christo," John said. "I know you stuck your neck out to get this stuff. If all goes well, we'll see you in the morning."

"Malaka!" he cursed. "You're crazy if you think I'm going to let you two go out to the *Penelope* alone."

John had neither the inclination nor the time to argue with him; besides, he knew he could use Christo's help. The three of them rowed out to the fishing boat like commandos on a night raid.

John led the way up the ladder. Nick started to toss the two bags over the rail. John leaned over the rail and whispered, "Be careful with those. They're full of explosives and blasting caps."

Nick gasped.

By the time Nick and Christo were aboard, John had already begun to lay out the contents of one of the two bags. When Nick turned on his flashlight and saw the dynamite lying in tight bundles on the deck of his beloved *Penelope,* his eyes opened wide.

"Let's get started," John said. "Christo, take three of these dynamite packages. Tape one to the prow, one to the stern, and one under the lid of the cargo hold. Nick, you know the boat better than we do, so I want you to go below to place the remaining bundles. Put them along the spine of the boat and in the engine room. When you two are finished, come back and join me here."

While Christo and Nick went about their tasks, John prepared the detonators. The control box Christo had gotten for him had eight contact points. Each bundle of dynamite would be mated to a detonator that would, in turn, be connected by a wire running to the control box. The electrical impulse that would set the explosions in motion would come from a remote-controlled detonator. John knew this was going to be very dangerous. If he misjudged the amount of dynamite it would take to get the job done, he could wind up killing Zoë and himself. Or, if he used too little explosive, the detonation wouldn't have enough impact on the kidnappers to allow Zoë and him to escape. He wiped the perspiration on his brow with one hand and then swiped his wet hand on his pants.

Christo finished first. When he came back, John followed him to each of the dynamite locations and inserted the detonators into a dab of C-4 explosive he carefully pressed against each bundle of dynamite sticks. He attached a wire to each detonator and ran it back to the control box, being especially careful to make sure the wires were concealed on the undersides of the deck rails. He repeated the same steps with the explosives Nick had placed. The entire process took two hours.

Then they sat on the deck and rested. John used that time to explain to Nick what he wanted him to do when he got back to shore. He told him about the boat and the supplies and equipment he'd arranged for through the hotel desk clerk. He emphasized the importance of locating the spot marked *"Sabiya?"* that he'd drawn in on his version of Petros' map.

"Bullshit!" Nick growled. "I'm not going anywhere. If the bastards who have Zoë are coming here, then this is where I'm going to be."

John knew he had to handle Nick just right. It was vital that things went as planned. While he had Leidner preoccupied, Nick had to find the *Sabiya*.

"Nick, I understand your concern for Zoë, and your desire for revenge, but unless you do what I ask, her life could be forfeit. This guy Leidner isn't going to stop until he finds that sunken boat. Unless we find it first and discover whatever it is about that boat that's worth killing over. Once we disclose the *Sabiya's* secret, Leidner will be done."

"You hope," Nick said.

John nodded and handed his version of the map to Nick, who unfolded it. He ran his finger over the mark John had drawn in about a mile offshore from the Heraion.

"You know this could be nothing but a waste of time," Nick said. "Your idea that my father sent us a clue tied to the Pythagorean Theorem could be totally wrong."

"Yeah, Nick, I know. But maybe I'm right, and maybe now you're not giving your father enough credit. We'll never know unless you're willing to check it out. The hard part of the operation will be using the range finder. Do you think you can do it?"

"Now you're not giving *me* enough credit. Unless you were a terrible teacher, I'll make it work."

"You'd better get moving then. You and Christo need to be well away from this boat before the sun starts to come up and Leidner shows up."

While Christo and Nick started back to shore in the dinghy, John went up into the wheelhouse and started the *Penelope's* engines. Steering the bulky old fishing craft through the gap in the reef, he positioned it as close as possible to where he and Zoë had dived earlier. It was not critical the boat be over the exact location, as long as he anchored close enough to it to convince Leidner it was situated in conjunction with the fourth circle on Petros Vangelos' map. He walked over to the bags Christo had supplied and removed two more items—a 9mm pistol and the original map—the one without the extra triangle, the sucker's map. He hefted the Ruger to get comfortable with its weight and balance. The fifteen round clip made him feel a little less nervous.

Then he tied two of the refilled scuba tanks and two breathing apparatuses to a nylon rope and carefully lowered them over the side of the boat, about three feet below the water's surface. If his plan worked, this would be his ace-in-the-hole—his and Zoë's escape route.

John sat in a corner of the wheelhouse and tried to grab a couple hours sleep. But he was too tense, waiting there on a boat loaded with enough explosives to blow him and the boat to smithereens. He wondered what Zoë's thoughts were at that moment—if she was still alive. The thought of her in pain, or dead, was unbearable. He tried to force himself to concentrate on a variety of different scenarios that might occur when Leidner's man boarded the *Penelope*, but his thoughts kept switching back to Zoë.

CHAPTER FIFTY-ONE

May 10

Leidner sat on the cushioned bench built along the inside of the yacht's stern. He wore knife-sharp gray slacks and a white sweater over a light-blue oxford shirt, looking like just another tourist waiting for the sun to come up. He heard footsteps and turned in the direction of the sound.

Theo stepped up to where Leidner sat. "We are ready, *Herr* Leidner," she said.

"*Sehr gute,* Theo. Bring her to me."

Theo looked back at the two men holding the Greek woman's arms. She waved at them, beckoning them to come forward.

Tomas and Peter dragged Zoë by the arms. They stopped under the beam of a deck light.

"I see you have her dressed and ready to travel," Leidner said, eyeing the Vangelos woman's torn and bloody clothing, and battered features. A momentary smile creased his lips. "It appears she had a rough night."

"Ja, mein Herr," Theo said. She looked disdainfully at the Greek woman. "But there isn't much left of her." She tapped the side of her head with a finger. "You know…she's seems quite out of her head."

"Yes, my dear. But that won't make one bit of difference when we are finished with Mr. Hammond. Sanity is only important to the living." He chuckled, then suddenly changed his tone. "Get her aboard the boat," he snarled.

Tomas dragged Zoë back up the deck to the stairway leading down to a double-decked fishing craft tied to the side of the yacht. A sleek speedboat was also tied to the yacht. He hefted Zoë onto his shoulder and carried her down the steps to the fishing boat. He and Peter laid her on the bench on the lower level, under the canvas canopy.

Theo stood next to Leidner at the yacht's rail and looked down at the two men. Coldly, she said, "Get that map. Then slit Hammond's throat, and"—pointing at Zoë—"her's, too. I want both of them at the bottom of the sea."

Peter climbed to the upper deck, stepped to the fishing boat's controls, and turned the ignition key. The twin inboard engines roared to life, churning the water at the rear of the boat. He backed it away from the yacht, and pushed the throttle forward, guiding the craft southward, toward the *Penelope's* location.

Tomas came over and stood next to Peter. "What the hell did you do to the woman?" he asked. "She seems catatonic."

Peter shrugged. "Nothing that you probably didn't

do," he answered. "You know these Mediterranean types. They get raped and their menfolk turn on them, as though it was all their fault." Peter laughed.

Tomas looked back over his shoulder at Zoë. "That woman's got bigger balls than most men. She never told us a thing. That's the kind of woman I'd love to meet some day. Under different circumstances, of course."

"Bullshit!" Peter said. "A woman like that would make your life a living hell. You need some simpering little trollop who tells you about fifty times a day what a big, brave macho man you are."

Tomas punched Peter on the arm, then walked to the steps leading to the lower deck. "Right as always, Peter. You know me better than I know myself."

CHAPTER FIFTY-TWO

May 10

Zoë lay on the bench, pain searing every nerve ending in her body. Her brain screamed from the agony she felt. But it was the shame she couldn't endure.

She knew she was on a boat, but her eyes were shut and she didn't seem to have the strength to open them. Her head hurt terribly. The motion of the boat when it surged through the water had an almost calming effect on her, however. Since she was a child, the sea had acted as a palliative for her. If she were sick or worried about something, things would always seem better once she boarded a boat and moved over the water. But the effect this time was different. She felt calm, but not better. She couldn't rid herself of the shame. With a sudden clarity of thought, she saw the sea as a way to purify herself.

With great effort, she tried to open her eyes. Something seemed to be sealing her eyelids and she slowly moved a hand and touched her face. She lay a finger on her left eye and immediately jerked it away when an electric shock shot through her. A moan escaped her lips. The eye felt swollen. She tried the other eye, but it seemed to be crusty with something. She pried at the lid and was able to open it no more than a slit.

She slowly rolled from her back to her side, suppressing the cries of pain that movement wanted to rip from her throat. Moving her head first left, then right, she saw through blurred vision a man's back several meters away. She heard two male voices, but she couldn't see the second man. His voice seemed to be coming from above. Getting her elbow underneath her, Zoë propped herself up off the cushioned bench. She gritted her teeth against the pain and pushed herself to a half-sitting position. Then she lowered her legs to the deck. Pushing off the bench, she came to a bent over, standing posture. Testing her legs, she found she could just support herself. She took one tentative step, then another, and staggered to the three-foot-high rail along the rear of the boat. She placed her hands on the top of the rail, lifted one leg over it, and sat—one foot dragging in the boat's wake, the other now planted falteringly on the deck. She guessed the sounds of the wind and the boat's engine had kept the men from hearing her movements.

But then she heard a man's voice shout, "Peter, behind you!" She ignored the voice, said a silent prayer of forgiveness to God for the sin she was about to commit, closed her eyes, and leaned over the side of the boat.

The collision with the water shocked Zoë. Her body convulsed with excruciating pain, but then, while the cool water enveloped her, it acted like a sedative, and she suddenly found peace. She drifted down into the comforting arms of the sea. Her father's face came to her and smiled. Zoë smiled back. *Baba,* she thought, please forgive me. She saw him reach a hand out to her and she extended her fingers to take his hand in her's.

⬛

Tomas dove headfirst off the top deck of the fishing boat, cutting the water like a knife. In the crystal-clear water, he quickly saw the woman sinking toward the sea floor. He knew if he didn't get to her quickly, she would be too deep for him to reach her. He kicked with all the force he could muster and closed the distance between them. Ten meters, then five, then just one more. His lungs were near to bursting. He had only seconds before he would have to reverse direction and kick to the surface.

Then the woman raised one arm, stretching it toward him. He couldn't believe her expression. She was smiling. At peace. He scissored his legs one more time, propelling himself downward, and reached out with his arm toward her hand. Their fingers touched for a brief moment, separated, then touched again. Tomas made a desperate effort to take her hand in his. He gripped her thumb in his fingers and circled her wrist with his other hand. Then, turning back toward the surface, he kicked while he felt the last of the air in his lungs escape through his nostrils.

Clutching the woman in his arms, he slashed at the water with his legs, straining to keep his mouth closed, trying with all his might not to succumb to the urge to breath in. The first rays of dawn were beginning to light the surface of the sea and the outline of the fishing boat was visible off to the left, its propellers turning, the noise of its engines beckoning him to them.

Tomas gulped like a fish when his head broke the surface. He gasped for breath while he turned toward the onrushing boat. The woman felt like a dead weight. She neither moved, nor appeared to be breathing. Leidner will kill me, he thought, while he struggled to stay afloat.

CHAPTER FIFTY-THREE

May 10

Nick located the dive boat John had hired. All the equipment had already been stowed aboard. With the help of a couple of his father's old fisherman friends, Paulus Zacharias and Antonio Karamilas, he took the craft out of the harbor and cruised up the coast until he spotted one of the few still-standing pillars of the Heraion. The massive white column stood like a beacon to the past, clearly visible from the sea. Nick could no longer see the mole at Pythagorio, but he had a clear shot of Mount Kastri, where the Evpalini Tunnel was located.

After cutting the engine, he took the range finder from its box and concentrated on what he'd been shown about its operation. After a frustrating hour, he finally remembered all the steps he needed to go through. He consulted the map John had given him and took measurements with the instrument, until he decided he had a pretty good idea where the black mark on John's map should match up with the location where the *Sabiya* had sunk—assuming John's theory was correct. This process took another two-and-a-half hours.

After moving the dive boat about a mile farther from shore, Nick recomputed the distance with the range finder, backed the boat one hundred meters closer to shore, and then dropped anchor.

"Paulus," Nick said, "Help me get into this dive gear. Antonio, I want you to keep an eye out for anyone coming in this direction." He handed Antonio a shotgun. "Anyone tries to board us, you shoot. Understand?"

Antonio had been a partisan during World War II. Nick knew Antonio had killed many Nazis. The old man's eyes seemed to light up at the possibility of shooting someone again.

"Are you expecting anyone in particular?" Antonio asked. "Turks, maybe?"

Nick couldn't help but smile. "You never know. Remember, shoot first, ask questions later."

"Just like Dirty Harry," the old man said, smiling. "Make my day!" Then Antonio eyes narrowed and he looked serious. "Are we smuggling something?" He beamed and said, "It's been years since I ran booze over to Turkey. Come on, Nick, tell me that's what we're doing here. We're smuggling something to Turkey."

Nick shook his head, patted the old man on the back, and walked over to where Paulus was checking the scuba gear.

"What the hell are we doing, Nick?" the man said. "There's nothing of value out here. The sponges were all harvested years ago and the reef will rip fishing nets to shreds."

Nick hadn't told the two men much of anything. He'd said he wanted to check on something. Both Paulus and Antonio were retired so they had nothing better to do, except maybe sit in some taverna, drink coffee, and argue about politics. So they'd leaped at the chance to take a boat ride. But now Paulus was wondering what Nick was up to. The last thing Nick wanted was for these two men to return to their villages and start talking about the crazy Nick Vangelos and his dreams of sunken ships. The word would be all over the island within twenty-four hours. He'd be branded for life. The local laughing stock.

After donning the scuba equipment, Nick dropped over the side of the boat into the sea. He didn't like diving alone, but he felt he had no alternative. Besides, as far as he knew, his father had found the *Sabiya* while solo diving. If a man his father's age could do it, then he sure as hell ought to be able to.

Swimming in slow, ever-widening circles, Nick looked intently for any signs of wreckage. He couldn't imagine a ship being down here all these years and not having been discovered. Sponge divers had worked the reef for centuries, and they'd continued harvesting sponges from the area during the years since World War Two, up until the sponges petered out a couple years back. Nick was not feeling optimistic.

The reef formed a meandering line that closely paralleled the coast. It extended for about two hundred meters. Nick started at the north end of the coral and rock formation, then swam south along the reef's starboard side. He then turned and swam north along the leeward side. Nothing. He checked the gauge on his breathing apparatus. He'd go for another fifteen minutes, then he'd have to surface.

After returning to the end of the reef, he kicked upward, to try to get another aerial view. Perhaps there was something beyond the reef. Again, he saw nothing but fish, plants, white sand, and the multi-colored reef. Exasperated, he twisted to try to sight the hull of the dive boat. After turning, he noticed the slash of an ancient lava flow in the distance. He knew the black stripe of lava ran from the top of the now-extinct volcano far above the shore, down to the shoreline, and then about a mile out to sea. The lava had never been of any interest to the local fishermen. For some reason—perhaps the sulfur content of the lava—sponges never grew there.

What the hell! Nick thought. He again looked at his air gauge, then set out in the direction of the lava formation.

CHAPTER FIFTY-FOUR

May 10

Peter swung the fishing boat around and bore down on Tomas where he bobbed in the water. He cut the engines and drifted ten feet from his partner and, he now saw, the Greek woman. He tossed a life preserver tied to the end of a rope to Tomas, and when Tomas hooked an arm in it, Peter towed him to the boat. After hefting the woman's limp body on board, he helped Tomas into the boat. While his partner lay on the deck gasping for breath, Peter began giving the woman artificial respiration.

Breathe, he thought while he worked on her. Don't be dead. Peter knew that Leidner's plan wouldn't be worth a damn if they showed up for the meeting with Hammond with a dead Zoë Vangelos. He knew with absolute certainty that Leidner would have Theo Burger kill him and Tomas if they showed up without the map.

Peter blew air into the woman's mouth, then pressed down on her chest. He repeated the process over and over again, until he wanted to collapse from exhaustion.

Sweat dripped off him and his breathing became labored, while the seconds, then the minutes went by. Tomas now knelt beside him, exhorting him to bring her back. Peter wanted to tell him to shut up, but he didn't have the strength. He'd just about decided to give up when the woman's chest heaved and a gush of water poured from her mouth. She coughed spasmodically and didn't stop for well over a minute.

Peter fell away from her, lying on the deck trying to get his breathing back to normal and his heart rate slowed. He looked over at the woman and realized that, although she was now breathing, she was far from well. Her skin looked pallid and she shivered as though she were freezing. Shock, he thought. He watched Tomas lift her from the deck and place her back on the cushioned bench at the stern. Tomas draped a blanket over her, turned to the boat's controls, and pushed the throttle forward.

CHAPTER FIFTY-FIVE

May 10

It was now seven a.m. The sun began its assault on the horizon thirty minutes earlier. It had lit up the edge of the sea and then sent out fiery fingers of light creeping toward the *Penelope*, like molten lava flowing across the surface of the water. John now shaded his eyes with one hand and looked into the rising sun. For a brief moment he thought that only good could come on a day that began with such a spectacular sunrise. But that thought passed almost instantaneously. It was difficult to maintain any sense of optimism as long as Zoë was in Leidner's hands.

John didn't see the double-decked, sport fishing boat coming at him with the sun at its back, like the smart gunfighter in a duel, until he heard the roar of its twin inboard engines. He'd told Leidner 10:00. It was only 7:00.

When the boat came within fifty yards of the *Penelope*, it circled twice. John saw a man on the boat's upper deck eyeballing him. A second man stood by the rail on the lower deck. Then John heard the sport boat's engines cut. Momentum carried it to the *Penelope's* side. John stood outside the wheelhouse, at the top of the stairs that ran down to the main deck. On the spot where Officer Zantsos had died.

A powerfully built man of about thirty came on board the *Penelope.* He had the exaggerated build of a professional wrestler, but the face of an accountant. He peered at John over sunglasses with tiny lenses that, for some reason, made him appear even more sinister, and declared, "You are John Hammond!"

He sounded like a character actor playing a Nazi agent in a World War II movie. John said, "Yes! And who are you?"

"My name is Peter Muther. I have been instructed to get a map from you."

It was a bad sign, John thought, the man giving him his name, unless it was an alias. But if it was his real name, then the obvious conclusion was that the man wasn't worried about John being a witness. Dead men don't testify.

"I don't give a shit what your instructions are, *Herr* Muther," John hissed. "Your boss and I had a deal. He would meet me here and I would hand over the map to him and him alone. But only after I knew Zoë Vangelos was safe. Where is he and where is she?"

Muther looked at John—a vacant, absolutely emotionless stare. "Now, now, Mr. Hammond, zer is no cause for excitement. My boss, as you put it, decided to change za plan a little. He sent me to get za map. And your friend is on my boat. Vy not go over and take a look?"

John went down the stairs to the main deck and walked around the man to the rail. The man on the fishing boat bent, lifted a blanket, and dropped it to the deck. John saw Zoë's battered face. Her features were so distorted he almost didn't recognize her. The man lifted her, holding her from behind. She hung lifelessly in the man's hands. The sight of her face made John's heart ache and bile rose in his throat. Swelling had completely closed her left eye, and her cheeks, chin, and forehead were covered with ugly bruises and raw cuts. The neck of her blood-spattered blouse had been torn and hung off her left shoulder. Her clothes appeared wet, clinging to her form. John couldn't tell if she were still alive.

Zoë's good eye suddenly opened and she appeared to be trying to focus in John's direction. Then she turned as though to hide her face and the movement caused her blouse to slide further down her left arm, exposing more cuts and bruises. But the worst of the bruises were on her breasts. When she began to sag to the deck, the man holding her jerked her upright and slung her over his shoulder. Zoë screamed.

John was about to go to Zoë's aide, when he heard the one named Peter off to his side start to move. John quickly moved away along the rail, pulling the pistol from inside his windbreaker. He pointed the gun at Peter. "Tell your partner to come up on the boat with the woman."

Peter looked at John calmly. "I am sorry, Mr. Hammond, but I cannot do zat. Not as long as you are armed. Now if you gif me zat gun, I vill do as you ask and haf your friend brought aboard. If you do not, I vill tell Tomas to kill her."

John had to get Zoë away from the man guarding her, and he realized the only way to do that was to turn over his pistol. His plan was in shambles. But he still felt there was a chance if he could get Zoë by him. Maybe they could still slip over the side of the boat where he'd tied up the diving gear. But Zoë's condition suddenly defeated him. She was in no shape to go diving. Leidner had trumped his every move. Almost.

John tossed the pistol onto a tarpaulin covering a stack of fishing nets. Peter waved at the second man, who climbed on board the *Penelope*. John approached the man to take Zoë from him. When he touched her arm, she cried out.

Peter shoved John and Zoë toward the center of the deck—John barely able to support her as he stumbled backwards. Both of the men carried holstered weapons. They seemed to be confident that, unarmed, John was no longer a threat.

"Now za map, Mister Hammond," Peter said.

John had hidden the map under the boat's rail, just above where the diving gear was hanging. He gently moved Zoë to the spot, the two Swiss following, pulled the map from under the rail, and handed it over. Peter unfolded it, looked at its markings, and then consulted with his partner.

Then Peter looked back at John. "Vell, Hammond, since you are a great deal more cooperative zen your girlfriend, perhaps you vill explain vat all of zese marks mean." Then he gestured at Zoë. "You know, Hammond, you haf one brave voman zer. She never told us a thing. It's too bad you don't haf za same courage as she does." He laughed. "Hell, she didn't even talk ven ve took turns with her." He grabbed his crotch as though to emphasize the point.

Before John could react, a moan burst from Zoë, and then a banshee-like shriek. She pushed away from John and leaped at Peter with her fingers extended like claws.

She caught him completely by surprise and knocked him to the deck, raking his face with her fingernails, tearing bloody furrows in his cheeks. The other man pulled Zoë off Peter and threw her aside like a rag doll. Her head hit the deck with a sickening thud and she rolled to the rail, curled in a fetal position.

John jumped to the tarpaulin-covered nets and grabbed the pistol while the two men were distracted. They didn't have the time to pull out their own pistols. Leveling his pistol at them, John ordered them to stand by the rail and toss their weapons over the side. They calmly obeyed.

John shook with anger, but was still under control. "What did you plan to do with the two of us after you got the map?" he demanded, his pistol leveled at first one then the other man. He already knew the answer. He just had to hear it from their own mouths, in their superior, guttural tone. He needed to feed his hatred for them until he would be capable of anything.

"You must know zat you ver both going to be killed," Peter said, seemingly unworried, almost gleeful. "Vy then did you gif up your gun?"

"Because, asshole, I have a much larger weapon." He

pulled a small, black box, about the size of a garage door opener, out of a pocket in his windbreaker and showed it to them. "This is a remote control detonator. This entire boat is wired with explosives. Now tell me what your orders are."

Peter seemed to be fixated on the little box in John's hand. He ignored his question. "You ver prepared to blow yourselves up along viss us? Is zat vat you vant us to believe?" He laughed and looked over at his partner. He pointed a finger at John and laughed again.

When John didn't respond, Peter asked his comrade, "Vat do you think, Tomas? Do you think zat Hammond has za guts to make good on his threats?" They both seemed to have recovered from the initial shock of seeing John with the pistol and the detonator in his hands.

The other man laughed and said, "No! Do you?"

John couldn't believe it. They just stood there laughing at him. He felt his rage grow almost to the point of desperation. Then all became calm. His hands no longer shook and he suddenly felt unencumbered by training or ethics. He aimed the pistol, confidently pressed the trigger, and put a 9mm round into Peter's right kneecap. The man crumpled, screaming, to the deck. Zoë, still huddled against the rail, moaned at the sound of the shot, but didn't move. Blood quickly soaked Peter's pant leg and started to pool around him.

"What do you think now, Tomas?" John asked.

Tomas had that deer-in-the-headlights look.

John stared at him with contempt and ordered, "Talk!"

The man became an instant gusher of information.

"Ve ver ordered to kill you both and dump your bodies into za sea. Ve are zen supposed to radio our employer zat ve haf za map and zat ve know ver za sunken boat is."

"But you realized you couldn't kill us until you knew the meaning of the markings on the map?"

"Zat's correct," he answered.

"What's the name of your employer and where is he right now?"

After only a moment's hesitation, Tomas said, "*Herr* Fritz Leidner," confirming what the killer, Josef, had told him in his dying declaration. "He is on a boat about nine kilometers south of here."

"Okay, let's assume you now have the map and you know it will lead you to a sunken ship. What are you supposed to do?"

"Ve are supposed to radio *Herr* Leidner und tell him it is safe for him to join us."

"Why don't we do just that," John said. He felt a surge of satisfaction at the thought of luring Leidner aboard the *Penelope*. He fingered the remote control detonator in his windbreaker pocket,

He ordered Tomas to use his shirt to tie a tourniquet above his friend's knee, and then had him tie Peter to a large metal deck cleat near the bow. He told Tomas to climb down to the sport fishing boat and radio Leidner.

John remained on the *Penelope,* all the while keeping his pistol trained on Tomas, who had turned on the sport fishing boat's radio equipment and now talked into the hand-held transmitter. On the third attempt to raise someone, a voice finally responded.

"*Ja, Tomas, hast du die Karte?*"

"*Sorgsam,* Tomas," John said in a hoarse whisper, warning the man to be careful, "*Ich spreche Deutsche.*" He'd just used up four of the twenty words of German he knew. He hoped his bluff would work.

John could hear both ends of the conversation, and did not have one iota of an idea what the two men said. After Tomas shut down the radio, John ordered him back aboard the *Penelope.* He made him sit next to the anchor chain and then clubbed him on the side of his head with the pistol. He tied him to the anchor chain, and then checked the rope securing the other man. Satisfied they were going nowhere, he grabbed the map the Swiss man had dropped to the deck, folded it and placed it inside his shirt. Then he knelt next to Zoë.

Now conscious and in obvious pain, she moaned when he lifted her shoulders off the deck. He cradled her in his arms and rocked her back and forth. He told her again and again he loved her. Tears flowed silently down her cheeks and dropped onto the arm of his windbreaker. She looked at John with spiritless eyes, a defeated creature. He had to get her off the *Penelope.* Leidner would arrive in a matter of minutes.

John tried to get her to stand, but she couldn't. So he hoisted her to his shoulder, carried her to the rail, climbed down the ladder to the sport fishing boat, and laid her on the bench at its stern.

He covered her with his windbreaker, then retrieved the blanket from the deck and draped it over her. Though the morning had already grown warm, she began to shake. John turned to the boat's control panel—the keys were not in the ignition.

Grabbing the *Penelope's* ladder, he climbed as fast as he could. Peter was passed out where he'd left him tied to the deck cleat. Tomas had recovered from the blow to his head, but still sat where John had tied him up with his hands behind his back. He searched Peter's pockets, but found no key. Then he rushed to Tomas. "Do you have the boat keys?" he demanded.

Tomas gave him an evil grin and said, "Fuck you!"

The sound of a powerful motor caught John's attention. He turned and saw a sleek sport boat, the kind sometimes called a "cigarette boat," pounding the surface of the sea about two miles away and coming straight toward them. He rifled Tomas' pockets and found a set of keys. John had his hand wrapped around them and was starting to pull them from the pocket when suddenly one of Tomas's hands slipped out of the bonds he had loosened. Tomas clubbed him on the side of his head with one of his fists, causing white-hot sparks to flash behind John's eyes.

John's hand came free of Tomas' pocket as he fell backwards. He still gripped the keys. While John struggled to get up off the deck, Tomas ran over to him, and kicked him in the side hard enough to flip him over onto his back. He kicked at John again, but this time John managed to grab Tomas' leg with both arms and knock him off balance. Tomas fell backward and his head struck one of the metal deck cleats. His skull split like a ripe watermelon.

John got to his feet and shook his head, trying to clear it of the fuzziness there. It seemed to help. He saw that the cigarette boat was closing fast on the *Penelope's* starboard side. He would wait until the boat came up against the far side of the *Penelope,* and would then climb down to the smaller sport boat on the *Penelope's* port side and make a run toward shore. He hadn't explained his entire plan to Christo. John wanted Leidner dead. He'd never intended to use the explosives as just a threat. He'd hoped he would be able to use them to kill the Swiss sonofabitch.

CHAPTER FIFTY-SIX

May 10

John heard the cigarette boat's engine noise drop from a thunderous roar to a loud rumbling idle. The powerful boat was coasting to the Penelope's side. John climbed over the rail and vaulted to the deck of the sport fishing boat. There were five keys on the ring he'd pulled from Tomas' pocket. The third key he tried fit the boat's ignition.

Voices carried over the *Penelope's* deck and down to where John stood at the controls of the sport fishing boat. He heard a woman shout, "Peter! Tomas!"

John turned the key in the boat's ignition and the engine roared. He steered the boat directly toward shore. With the *Penelope* still screening them from view, he hoped they would get a good start toward the coast before the occupants of the speedboat could react. And he prayed they could reach the safety of the harbor, where Christo would be waiting with police and Coast Guard personnel, before the occupants of the cigarette boat could recover and overtake them.

He popped the throttle to maximum power and felt the sport fishing boat surge ahead. Two hundred yards separated them from the *Penelope,* the cigarette boat suddenly came around the *Penelope's* bow and started after them. He needed to detonate the explosives now, while the cigarette boat was still within the blast radius. John felt for the detonator he'd placed in his windbreaker pocket. "Shit!" he exclaimed while looking over his shoulder. He'd draped the windbreaker over Zoë.

The cigarette boat followed his wake through the entrance to the harbor. John didn't believe their pursuers could catch them before they reached the shore, but then bullets, like angry hornets, ripped the air all around them and impacted the rear of the fishing boat. Whoever shot at them was using a fully automatic weapon with a high firing rate. And they were not firing warning shots. Apparently, Leidner wanted to cut his losses. Map or no map, he was going to get rid of the players. Maybe he had another way to get a copy of the map. Christo. The thought careened like a ricocheting bullet through John's brain. Leidner would go after Christo next. Leidner would go after anyone and everyone who had touched the map. The realization hit John that Leidner must have many men on Samos. Leidner had declared war, and John and Zoë were only two of his targets.

John knew that if your enemy throws enough bullets at you, sooner or later one of them is going to hit something. A bullet slammed into the control panel of the sport fishing boat, right under his left elbow, and careened on into the boat's electronics. The engine died and smoke billowed from the panel. They drifted to a dead stop in the water, the acrid smell of smoldering electric wires swirling around him.

While he helplessly watched the rapidly approaching cigarette boat, John saw Zoë lift herself up on her elbow and raise her right hand. She held the remote control detonator box. She must have heard him mention the detonator to Tomas and Peter aboard the Penelope.

Everything seemed to happen then in slow motion— Zoë's arm reaching toward the *Penelope*, her finger depressing the detonator, the *Penelope* lifting itself out of the sea.

With the sound of the first explosion, everything returned to real time while dynamite tore the *Penelope* apart, turning her into a rain of debris falling back onto the water—and onto them and the cigarette boat. He rushed down the stairs to the lower deck and leaped over to where Zoë lay. He covered her with his body. Fortunately, only small pieces of debris from the wrecked fishing boat found their way to where their boat now floated in Pythagorio Harbor. John craned his neck to see over the boat's stern and saw that a storm of debris fell on the cigarette boat.

The sounds of the explosions subsided into a momentary quiet quickly filled by the shrill wail of sirens. The morning air was gray with smoke and the distinctive odor of explosives assaulted John's nostrils.

The cigarette boat banked into a turn and raced away. Like cavalry coming to the rescue, two Coast Guard boats sped after it.

John watched with dismay while the powerful speedboat ran for the mouth of the harbor, outdistancing its pursuers. It had gone well beyond the range of the guns on the Coast Guard boats when another explosion rocked the harbor, followed by two more thundering blasts. A tower of flame and black smoke shot skyward along the shore. Then the Coast Guard boats chasing after the speedboat simultaneously erupted, spewing flaming debris in all directions. They'd been sabotaged. The rescue of Zoë had been successful, but only at the expense of more lives. Leidner had out-thought them all. He'd covered his escape.

Then John's heart seemed to lurch in his chest as a helicopter swooped down toward the water. It charged through the smoke from the onshore explosions and flew in the direction the fleeing speedboat had taken. A man sat in the open side door of the helicopter with his legs dangling out. He sat behind what looked to be a .50 caliber machine gun.

Like a spectator at a ballgame, John cheered for the good guys. The helicopter was past the harbor entrance, when he again heard the distinctive sound of automatic weapons.

Black smoke spiraled from the top of the helicopter. Its engine sputtered and the craft began to autorotate. John knew the aircraft and its occupants were lost, that they were going to crash before it actually happened. He'd seen it happen in Vietnam, when Viet Cong groundfire disabled American helicopters. The chopper dropped, then blew apart in a fiery explosion.

CHAPTER FIFTY-SEVEN

May 10

Zoë and John were taken to the Greek Army Hospital. While John watched the nurses place Zoë on a gurney and wheel her away, he tried to imagine a future without her.

A doctor gave him the once over, cleaned up some cuts and abrasions he didn't realize he had, and gave him pills for back pain and to combat infection. He told John he should call him if he saw any evidence of blood in his urine, then walked off to care for another patient.

Zoë had been moved to an examination room down the hall. John dragged a chair from the waiting area and parked himself outside that door and waited... and waited. Over an hour passed before a tall, stout woman with a grim face came out. The dark bags under her eyes attested to a schedule that didn't include much sleep.

"I am Doctor Stavrogianni," she said. "You are Miss Vangelos' friend, is that correct?"

He nodded. "I am more than her friend," he said. "I love her."

"Good!" Dr. Stavrogianni said. She rocked her head back and closed her eyes. Then she kneaded the back of her neck with one hand and let out a long sigh. She seemed to have gathered energy from the slight pause. "She's going to need all the love she can get. Miss Vangelos has been badly abused. Her physical injuries will heal, although I'm worried about the possibility of pneumonia because of the seawater in her lungs. We're working on that now. But it's her mental and emotional condition I'm most concerned about. She's going to need support and understanding. I hesitate telling you what she has been through. But if you're not aware of the problem, you won't be able to help her."

John cut her off. "Are you referring to her being raped?"

The doctor looked at him, surprised. She lowered her voice. "How did you know? She won't even acknowledge the rapes herself. I discovered she had been sexually assaulted when I performed my examination. It's obvious she has been brutally raped and beaten. She screamed at me each time I brought up the subject of rape. Unfortunately, her reaction isn't unexpected. Even with a highly educated woman. It's a legacy of what we call *epithexi andhrismou*—what you might call machismo. If you were a Greek male, I would probably not share any of this with you. I hope you're more enlightened than most Samian men are."

"Doctor, the men who raped Zoë bragged about it to me—in front of her. I love her and I'll do everything in my power to help her recover."

"Wonderful!" she said, resting her hand on John's arm.

"But, Doctor, I'm a little confused. You said Zoë wouldn't admit to having been raped. She heard one of her attackers admit to raping her. She has to be aware I already know."

The doctor hesitated for a moment. "Maybe she just doesn't remember, or she could be intentionally suppressing it. Either way, she is not going to get well until she acknowledges to herself what she experienced."

"I understand," he said. "You can count on my support."

She gave him a tired, but warm smile and walked off.

⬚

Christo found John in Zoë's room, watching her sleep. "How is she?" he whispered.

"Sedated," John said. "I'm told she's going to be out for a long time. You don't have to whisper. She's so drugged you couldn't wake her if you shouted."

This was the first chance John had to talk with Christo since the explosions in Pythagoria Harbor. "How much damage was done by the explosions in town?" he asked.

Christo thanked God, and then explained they had cleared all the buildings prior to the time that Leidner was expected to rendezvous with John on the Penelope. They hadn't wanted to take the chance that stray gunfire might injure someone. "Your meeting with Leidner was going to happen too damn close to shore for comfort. There were no civilian casualties, but we lost eight sailors and five policemen." He clenched his fists and looked out the window in Zoë's room. John could see the anger Christo felt. "If I get my hands on that Swiss bastard...."

After a moment Christo calmed enough to tell John that an entire block of buildings across from the quay had been destroyed.

"You know, Leidner must have more people on Samos," John said.

Christo just nodded.

"Well, let's go into town," Christo finally said. "We can get something to eat. We'll pick up Nick at the hotel. He just called the Vathi police station. They relayed the message that he'll meet us in town. He said he wants to talk to us."

"I don't know," John said. "I shouldn't leave...."

Christo walked forward and laid a hand on John's shoulder. "Come on, my friend. There's nothing you can do for her now. We'll return later; maybe she'll be awake then."

John blew out a deep breath. "Okay," he said, trying to inject some enthusiasm in his voice, despite feeling as low as he'd ever felt. "I can't do anything for Zoë as long as she's drugged up, I guess." Then he brightened a bit. "Did Nick say anything about finding the *Sabiya?*"

"Not a thing. The message I got just said he wanted to meet us. No explanation."

"Nick is crazy enough over Zoë's kidnapping," John said on the drive to town. "When he finds out Zoë was raped, he'll be uncontrollable."

"And you, John?" Christo asked. "How controlled are you?"

He took some time to think about his answer. "The difference between Nick and me is pretty basic," John said. "He'll seek revenge and will do so with passion. And when the job is done he'll feel fulfilled—no self-recrimination, no remorse. The act of revenge would actually be cathartic for him. With me it would be different. If I get the chance, I'll make Leidner suffer. But I'll be left with no feeling of fulfillment. I'll have performed an unrewarding task that'll leave me with nothing but a hollow feeling. I don't come from a culture grounded in revenge. I can seek revenge when I think it's the only alternative, but I don't believe I can feel good about it. Does that make sense to you?"

"Yes, but I don't like any of it. Let me handle the revenge business. You concentrate on helping Zoë get well."

John tried to control his anger, but he was only partially successful. "How the hell are you going to handle anything? You've lost most of your policemen. When are they going to send in reinforcements?"

Christo turned scarlet. He looked as though he wasn't going to say anything, but swallowed and said, "They'll be here tomorrow."

"What changed?" John said.

Still red-faced, Christo said, "An Internal Affairs Investigator somehow learned about phone calls being made between Athens and Zurich by the Deputy Minister of the Ministry of Public Affairs, Dimitris Kostamaris. With all that's been going on here on Samos—the Swiss connection and all that—the investigator checked on the phone number in Zurich. It was the number for *Banque*

Securité de Swisse. Leidner's bank. The Deputy Minister has been on Leidner's payroll for years."

More to himself than to Christo, John wondered aloud, "How the hell did an investigator even think to check phone records of the Deputy Minister?"

Christo smiled at John and said, "The investigator is married to my little sister. I called him the other day and asked him to check on Kostamaris. I couldn't understand why he kept preventing reinforcements being sent here."

John gave Christo a toothy grin, but his expression changed after a few seconds. "I heard what you said about revenge. You're right, of course. But, if I find myself alone with Leidner or any of his men, I can't promise that the first thing I'll do is call you."

They pulled up to the front of the hotel. "Then let's hope you don't find yourself alone with him or any of his men," Christo said.

"Let's hope," John echoed, not convincingly.

CHAPTER FIFTY-EIGHT

May 10

Nick paced the hotel lobby in Pythagorio where the police command post had been established. Like an expectant father in an obstetrics ward, he criss-crossed the ceramic tile floor, worry showing in the set of his jaw, in the way he held his head and shoulders. When he saw John and Christo come in, he rushed over. "Christo," he said, grabbing the Inspector by the arms, "one of your men told me Zoë's in the hospital. How is she? How's my sister?"

"She's fine. She's resting," Christo answered. "She was sound asleep when we left." It was the truth, but not the whole truth—and Nick seemed to know it.

"If she's fine, why is she still in the hospital?" he asked.

John came to Christo's rescue. "Nick, the men who took your sister beat her up. She has cuts and bruises and a few cracked ribs; but, thank God, there are no internal injuries. The doctors have her heavily sedated, so she feels little or no pain. They just want to keep her in the hospital for observation for a day or two."

Christo quickly interjected, his expression showing his torment. "But it wasn't me who rescued Zoë. I failed her again. It was John."

Nick released his hold on Christo and turned to face John. He gathered himself to his full height, his posture suddenly appearing formal. He almost stood at attention. "You have a habit of coming to the rescue of people I love." He then embraced John, the way a brother would hug a brother.

John coughed his embarrassment, his face warming. He patted Nick on the back several times until he stepped back. There were tears in the man's eyes.

Nick took a handkerchief from his pants pocket and wiped his eyes. "I want to go see her. How do I get onto the Army base?"

"Nick," Christo said, "she's resting now. Why not wait until later, after the drugs have worn off? She won't even know you are there for at least several hours. Let's have dinner. I can escort you to the base later."

Nick seemed satisfied with Christo's reasoning. He let out a giant sigh. Like him, John suspected, Nick was struggling to remain calm on the surface, while deep down his insides were churning.

They found a taverna along the quay that was just starting to come to life, and took a table near the front. They ordered beers and, after finishing two each, told the waiter to bring them a bottle of wine. The alcohol seemed to take the edge off John's anger and hunger for revenge against Leidner. He didn't realize how exhausted he was and welcomed the relief the beer and wine gave him. They had just ordered meals when John noticed a cruise ship slowly peek around a headland and move toward the harbor. Nick spied the giant ship a moment after John did and voiced a crude curse involving the Virgin Mary.

Christo scolded Nick. "Remember my friend, without those tourists you wouldn't be able to sell as many fish as you do."

"I know, but sometimes—"

Christo cut him off. "I'll bet you had no problem with these ships coming here when we were younger. You probably entertained many young European women who came to the Greek Islands to get their annual dose of sun and a little romance."

Nick rewarded them with a guilty smile. John felt glad to finally see him relax a little. Up to that moment he'd been so tense it had appeared he might explode. John considered asking Nick whether he'd found anything on his dive. He wanted to barge ahead—take care of business. But he somehow resisted the urge. He took it as a bad sign that Nick hadn't already volunteered any information about his day. The dive had apparently been a bust.

Christo ordered another bottle of Samian wine, and then another after that one. John now felt lightheaded and he could see that Nick and Christo, who had each consumed twice as much as he had, were seemingly without inhibition. The alcohol had loosened them up and they began to regale John with their stories of one youthful adventure after another. Without having ever left Greece, Nick, in particular, had vicariously traveled the world through young female tourists. He spoke of each romantic experience with reverence and respect, rather than salaciousness. Not until their meals were served did Nick change the subject. And he did it in a way that belied any indication he had been drinking. He sounded completely sober.

"I guess you both would like to hear about my day," he said, looking somber. He looked first at John, then at Christo, obviously wanting some sort of response.

"Absolutely!" John said.

"Asfalose!" Christo added.

"After Christo and I left the *Penelope*," Nick said, little expression showing on his face, "after our little dynamite sabotage mission, I followed your instructions. I went to the dock and picked up the boat you hired—the *Aphrodite*. All of the supplies and diving equipment were on board, just as you said they would be. I called a couple of my father's old friends who used to have a fishing boat together and asked them to join me. I figured I would need someone to help with the diving gear and to keep a lookout while I was underwater. I told them I wanted to do some diving, but didn't mention anything about a sunken boat."

Nick seemed to be drawing out the story. John wanted to tell him to cut out all the detail and get to the bottom line, but he controlled his impatience and let Nick carry on with his story.

"Once I arrived at the area you had marked on the map, it took me an hour to recall how to work the range finder. Then it took me even longer to pinpoint the exact spot. The water in that area is deeper than where you and

Zoë dived near Pythagorio, but still shallow enough to use scuba equipment."

"How deep?" John asked.

"About thirty meters. Any deeper and I wouldn't have felt comfortable with the gear we were using. At first I descended about 10 meters to the top of a coral formation that forms a reef that runs parallel to the shoreline. I inspected the length of the reef twice. I have to tell you I was plenty disappointed by the time I finished with the reef. There was no sign of any boat having gone down near there." Nick made a point of looking directly at John. "I must have cursed you out a dozen times for putting me up to such a waste of my time."

John felt a terrible letdown. It seemed Nick was taking an awfully long time to relate a story of failure.

"Then I saw a stretch of lava flow. It appeared to extend all the way to the shoreline in one direction and for another mile out to sea in the other direction—like a bumpy blacktopped road running away from the shore." He paused and then said, "I didn't see a sunken boat. No debris, no nothing. By this time, I was very low on air."

Christo looked disappointed and exclaimed, *"Shit!"* which expressed John's sentiments exactly.

Nick raised both hands as a signal to let him continue.

"I then dropped to just above the top of the lava bed and started exploring both sides of the formation. On one side the lava had frozen into a sort of rolling mass about ten meters high. The other side was a different story. The lava had apparently flowed in a way that caused it to form a sort of cave all along that side. Sand had piled up along the side of the lava flow. Where I first saw it, there was a two meter-high opening at the top of the flow. I swam through the opening and moved along the side of the lava formation, going further from shore. It appeared that the opening in the lava grew larger the farther from shore I swam. I have to tell you it was pitch dark in there. Thank God I had a flashlight."

I swam for about five minutes, and the opening grew to almost 20 meters high and at least 90 meters wide, but it was clogged with sand. It resembled an amphitheater in there, a giant, wide-mouthed underwater cave. The sand had accumulated across the mouth of the cave, obscuring most of the opening, except for a gap at the top."

He paused and met each man's gaze. "The cave was big enough to hide a pretty good-sized boat," he continued.

Nick paused again. "In fact, that's exactly what I found inside that giant cave—a pretty good-sized boat."

Nick started laughing at the surprised looks on their faces, and the more questions they asked and the more excited they became, the more he laughed. Soon, tears flowed down his cheeks and he held his sides in pain.

John reached over the table and slapped Nick on the shoulder. "Congratulations, you sonofabitch," he said. "You couldn't have told us at the beginning that you'd found a boat. You had to drag it out and make us suffer."

"Oh, but it was worth it," Nick roared, slapping the tabletop, knocking over bottles and glasses. "The looks on your faces were priceless."

"Did you see a name on the boat?" Christo asked.

"I couldn't find a name anywhere on the hull," Nick said. "But I did find a life preserver still attached to the ship's rail. Some of the letters had worn away, but I could read a few of them."

He paused again, asked Christo for a pen. John wanted to shake the name out of Nick. Nick wrote several letters on a paper napkin. When he'd finished, he turned the napkin so they could see what he'd written: _ab_ya.

"I'll be damned!" John exclaimed. "You found it! You found the *Sabiya*."

Nick beamed. "Yes, and I found something else. He fished around in his pants pocket and came up with what looked like a military ID—a "dog tag." It hung on the end of a chain. "I found this wrapped around a piece of jagged metal on the bulkhead. It's an old Greek Army name tag." He placed it on the table so John and Christo could read the printing stamped into the one-inch long piece of metal: PETROS VANGELOS.

CHAPTER FIFTY-NINE

May 10

When John, Nick, and Christo entered the wing of private rooms at the military hospital, they ran into Dr. Stavrogianni in the hall outside Zoë's room.

"How's she doing, Doctor?" John asked. "Any improvement?"

She hesitated. When John realized she might be uncomfortable talking in front of two strangers, he introduced Nick and Christo to her.

"We confirmed with x-rays that she has no broken bones, other than three ribs, and no internal injuries," the doctor said. "We gave her antibiotics to reduce the possibility of infection and a less powerful sedative than the last time to help her sleep. But it's the dullness in her eyes that worries me."

Nick didn't wait to hear more. He barged into Zoë's room. John followed him to Zoë's bedside.

She was awake but showed no sign she recognized either of them.

"Kookla mou," Nick said. *"Eesay endoxie?"* Zoë didn't respond, except to roll over, turning away from them. John guessed that, like himself, Nick had noticed that Zoë's eyes lacked sparkle and that her usual smile was absent. No, she wasn't okay. "Must be the sedatives," Nick said.

John knew better.

They tried for an hour to engage Zoë in conversation, with no success. They finally left her in the care of the medical staff and solemnly drove back to Pythagorio. Seeing Zoë had definitely taken the edge off their excitement over finding the *Sabiya.* Halfway to Pythagorio, Christo said, "I've had no word from any of my men regarding Leidner or his people. Whoever was on that speedboat yesterday got away clean. I had the entire southern coast of the island searched, but there was no sign of him or the speedboat. He may have gone to another island. He could be almost anywhere within a hundred kilometers, or more."

"Did anyone notice how many people were on the speedboat?" John asked.

"Two," Christo said. "But we never got close enough to get descriptions."

"Bad luck!" Nick said, almost to himself. He seemed to be only half-listening to their conversation. John assumed his mind was still on Zoë.

"Well, let's go get the *Aphrodite* and dive the wreck," John suggested. "We've got to find whatever it is on the *Sabiya* that has turned Leidner into a killer."

"I'd love to get my hands on that sonofabitch," Christo said. "What bothers me is we have no evidence he's the one behind all this mayhem, other than the admissions of a couple killers who are now dead. This guy Leidner is mighty careful."

This seemed to pull Nick away from his thoughts. He turned in his seat next to Christo, looked at John in the back seat. "The *Aphrodite* and all that equipment has got to be costing you a fortune. Why don't we return it and use the *Penelope?*"

"I guess I forgot to tell you about the *Penelope*," John said. "You remember those explosives you helped me plant on her?"

CHAPTER SIXTY

May 10

Leidner stalked the yacht deck, screaming curses at John Hammond, Petros Vangelos, and Zoë Vangelos. Even his own father, Friederich, and the *Sabiya's* captain, Mehmet Arkoun, dead for over five decades, didn't escape his wrath. He was as angry as he'd ever been. But he was also scared. Things hadn't worked out the way he'd wanted. They'd kidnapped and brutalized Zoë Vangelos, killed most of the police on the island, had shot down a helicopter, and had boobytrapped Greek Coast Guard boats. And he was no closer to having Vangelos' map than he was the day the Turk from the Turkish Maritime Bureau had called him. He shot Theo a vicious, teeth-bared look and shouted, "A tourist and his professor girlfriend have beat you, and four of your well-trained"—he said "well-trained" as though it were a dirty word—"assassins are dead. What other surprises do you have for me?"

Theo said nothing.

Leidner pointed his finger at her. "You know where Hammond and that Greek woman were staying. Go there. He has to be somewhere on this godforsaken island. Find the sonofabitch. I can feel it in my bones. He knows where the *Sabiya* is, and he's going out to her. When you find out where that is, you come back here and pick me up."

"But, *Herr* Leidner, do you think that's wise? The police will surely be protecting him. We should try once more to get the map. You should—"

Leidner cut Theo with a vicious glare. "Don't you dare tell me what I should or should not do. I should have handled this differently from the beginning." He was screaming now, a crazy man whose madness had now gone to an even higher level. "I don't need that map. I don't need that boat. What I need is to destroy the map and everyone who knows about it."

CHAPTER SIXTY-ONE

May 11

After a night at a Pythagorio hotel, John and Nick were scheduled to meet Christo in the lobby at 7:00 a.m. When they went there, the desk clerk told them Inspector Panagoulakos had just called to say he would be late. John and Nick found a place across from the hotel to have breakfast, and from where they could observe the front of the hotel. Christo showed up at 8:30. John thought he looked agitated.

Christo fell into a chair at their table and blew out a gush of air. "The stakes just got raised," he said. "Someone blew up the Vathi Police Station. Took down the entire building, as well as the buildings on either side."

"Anyone hurt?" John asked, not looking forward to Christo's answer.

Christo crossed himself. "It was a miracle. The man on duty had stepped outside to smoke a cigarette. He's got a concussion and his hearing's probably damaged, but other than that, he's fine. But the place was a total loss, including the safe in my office." He looked at Nick. "Your father's map was destroyed, along with everything else in the building."

Nick shook his head. "That's too bad, Christo, but we don't need the map. We know where the *Sabiya* is."

"That's all well and good," Christo said. "But, my real concern is that Leidner has obviously decided to change tactics. The explosions that destroyed the Coast Guard boats and the buildings in Pythagorio Harbor, and now leveled buildings in Vathi tells me the man has adopted a scorched earth policy. He's going to wipe out all evidence of the map. That means each of us is a threat to him. So is Zoë." He hesitated, letting his words sink in, then said, "I called the Ministry of Justice after the explosion. I've asked for more police to be sent over from Athens. The ten men they've already sent here aren't going to be enough. They're sending more men tomorrow."

☐

They took a rowboat out to the *Aphrodite*. The atmosphere on the little boat was almost solemn. Each man seemed lost in his own thoughts. John wasn't surprised they all had fallen into a kind of funk. As though the discovery of the *Sabiya* was somehow anticlimactic. His concern for Zoë weighed heavily on him, and he suspected that Nick had similar thoughts. But, at least she was alive. Leidner and his cronies had done much worse to a dozen policemen and sailors.

Something else bothered John, too. He felt as though there was a hot spot on the back of his neck. As though someone was watching him. He looked around, back at the shoreline, to see if he was imagining it, and saw no one. The fishermen and pleasure boaters were already out to sea. He shook his head several times. He knew he was feeling paranoid, but considered that was a perfectly reasonable way for him to feel, considering all he'd been through over the past week-and-a-half.

John inspected the diving equipment on the *Aphrodite*. There were enough tanks for multiple dives. Everything appeared to be in tip-top shape.

"There are enough provisions on board for two days," Nick advised. He looked at the others. "Are we ready to go?"

Christo dropped off the rail where he'd been sitting and picked up a canvas bag between his feet. He unzipped the bag and removed two pistols. After handing one to each of them, he said, "You see anyone who looks like they came from any country north of Greece, you shoot. Got it?"

"Got it!" they said simultaneously.

CHAPTER SIXTY-TWO

May 11

Theo took a motorboat to Pythagorio Harbor under the cover of darkness. She wished she could have used the cigarette boat, but since the disaster yesterday, it would be a police magnet. Leidner had ordered it scuttled. She made it to a small dock at the end of town and moored the boat to an ancient-looking, rusted metal ring inset in a masonry wall. She found the hotel they'd seen Zoë Vangelos walk out of the afternoon they'd snatched her. The boy behind the reception counter seemed bewitched by her and Theo had no trouble milking him for information. Including learning that Hammond had asked for a 6:00 a.m. wakeup call that morning. He'd told the kid he was going to go fishing. The boy even knew the name of Hammond's boat: *Aphrodite*. He'd arranged to rent the boat for the American. He told Theo that Hammond and another man left the hotel at 7:00 a.m. and ate at a restaurant across the street, where Police Inspector Panagoulakos had joined them. The clerk seemed to want to impress Theo with his awareness and his familiarity with important persons on Samos, such as Panagoulakos. He told her the three men had taken a small skiff out to a fishing boat moored inside the harbor. She'd just missed them.

Theo dropped a twenty euro bill and a million-dollar smile on the kid and checked her watch when she walked outside: 8:45 a.m. She returned to the motorboat and leisurely took it out beyond the harbor mouth. Hiding in a cove a half-mile from the harbor entrance, she sat back against the driver's seat, the boat bobbing in the water, and waited for the dawn. No craft would be able to exit the harbor without her seeing it.

The full ball of the sun rested well above the horizon when the Aphrodite left the harbor. Theo lowered her binoculars and let them hang by the strap around her neck. A sudden burst of visceral hatred consumed her. She would find the *Sabiya,* then kill John Hammond and everyone around him.

She clenched her jaw while she lifted the binoculars to her eyes. Focusing in on the men on the *Aphrodite,* she picked out one she thought might be the American. She dropped the glasses once again and stared out at the small boat and its three-man crew. Killing John Hammond and his friends would be her pleasure. And then she'd go after the Greek bitch.

CHAPTER SIXTY-THREE

May 11

Nick steered the *Aphrodite* to the area where he'd found the Sabiya the day before. The sun was twenty degrees above the horizon. The sea was calm and the sky cloudless. It looked as though it would be a perfect day for diving.

Per Nick's instructions, Christo stood in the bow and looked down at the crystal-clear water, while Nick eased the *Aphrodite* forward. He stood there for ten minutes before he finally raised his arm and shouted, "Stop! It's right ahead."

John ran over and stood by Christo. He looked down and saw the dark scar of the frozen lava flow lying twenty meters away from the prow, below the boat. Thirty yards ahead a rubber buoy that Nick had left yesterday to mark the site bobbed in the sea. By the time Nick yelled at John to drop the anchor, the *Aphrodite* coasted to a stop directly above the lava flow.

"You ready to go?" Nick asked John.

John finished checking the second regulator, made sure the pressure gauges on the tanks were operational, then stood up and smiled at Nick. "You bet!" he said.

Nick and John donned their scuba gear and, leaving Christo on deck, dived the *Sabiya*. They spent twenty minutes exploring the exterior of the boat on their first dive, and then dove again later that morning and spent twenty minutes inside the hull. They were equipped with underwater flashlights, which helped them find their way around the confined, pitch-black innards of the boat.

The stairwells were difficult to negotiate. After shifting some metal lockers aside, they found their way into a short passageway just below the main deck. Because the boat lay on its side, the doors to the cabins were above and below them. They swam to the first of three doors along the passageway. It was open enough to peer down into the cabin. There was nothing but a couple of metal bunks. The doors to the other two rooms, both above their heads, were closed. They tried to open each of them by pushing up against them, but they were either blocked by something inside the rooms, or were sealed shut by years of rust and corrosion.

Sea life had claimed squatter's rights on the wreck. Minute snail and barnacle shells covered its metal surfaces. Fish wandered passageways on what appeared to be aimless routes. They showed curiosity at the humans' intrusion, but no fear.

At the end of the passageway they found a door below them bearing the faded letters of the Turkish word, "KAPTAN."

They tried to force it open, but it wouldn't budge. Nick tapped John on the arm. When he turned to look at him, Nick touched his watch and pointed his arm upward—time to resurface. They slowly rose to the surface—too rapid an ascent could have been dangerous because of the threat of the bends. Christo helped them climb aboard the *Aphrodite* and shuck the scuba gear. He handed each of them a beer.

"I think we should concentrate on getting into the captain's quarters," Nick said. "If there's anything of interest on that boat it's probably there in the ship's log or a cargo manifest. Reading those documents would be the quickest way to discover what cargo the *Sabiya* carried."

"Yeah," John said, "but after it's been under water for fifty years, how in God's name are we going to find anything of value?"

Nick massaged his chin. "You may be right, John, but then why would Leidner be concerned? Most boats of any size are equipped with a waterproof vault or safe that can protect important records such as the log and manifests. Let's hope this one isn't the exception."

"Well, let's also hope, safe or no safe, there's something in the captain's quarters that will explain Leidner's actions," Christo said. "Unless the two old fisherman you took with you are very tight-lipped, it won't be long before word is out all over the island about where you were diving. And Leidner is likely to hear about it."

After a light lunch of tomatoes, cucumbers, bread, and cheese, they went to work planning their afternoon dive. They placed the tools and equipment they needed next to the boat's rail, then discussed how they would break through into the captain's quarters on the *Sabiya*. After two hours rest, Christo helped John and Nick load the tools and equipment—a crowbar, a wedge, an acetylene torch and tank, phosphorous flares, and other items they thought they might need—into a cargo net. John and Nick donned their scuba gear and dropped into the water. While Christo slowly lowered their tools in the net attached to a heavy nylon rope fed through a pulley and hoist, they followed it to the sea bottom. They maneuvered the net into the *Sabiya's* passageway. They then opened the net and arranged its contents on a bulkhead that now served as their floor because of the boat's orientation. They tugged on the line to signal Christo he could retract the net. It had taken them thirty minutes to follow the net, guide it inside the hull, and stack the contents outside the door marked, "KAPTAN." By then, it was time to return to the surface. They left the tools and equipment inside the wreck.

By the time they shucked their gear, stored it, and had a quick bite to eat, the sun had just touched the edge of the western sea. Feeling spent, John said goodnight to his two Greek friends. He went below deck and flopped onto one of the four bunks in a cramped room that also served as the kitchen. He was nearly asleep when Nick came in and took one of the other bunks.

"What's Christo doing?" John asked.

"Cleaning his pistol."

CHAPTER SIXTY-FOUR

May 11

From a mile away, hidden in a three-boat cluster of small fishing boats, Theo surveilled activities aboard Hammond's boat. The fishermen in the boats around her initially seemed transfixed by her presence. But, after fifteen minutes, they ignored her and continued their work.

Theo fixed the location of Hammond's boat. She could see a gigantic white marble column from some ancient ruins on shore, directly behind where the boat was anchored. She had seen two men in scuba gear backflip off the starboard side of the boat just minutes after it arrived at the spot. She watched them return to the boat about a half-hour later. They looked as though they were settled into the location. It was time to go tell Leidner.

[]

"What did you see?" Leidner demanded.

Theo had noticed he no longer referred to her as "my dear." "There are three men on the boat," she said. "Two of them dived the site early this morning. The third stayed on board. He appeared to be alert. Always pacing and looking out to sea."

"He didn't see you?"

"No."

Leidner rose from the desk chair in his stateroom. He paced the carpeted floor, his arms crossed, his back hunched. Theo followed his back and forth course, wondering what the man was thinking.

Finally, he stopped pacing and, standing in front of Theo, said, "We will move the yacht to where Hammond and his friends are diving. It's not uncommon to see luxury vessels in that area. Hopefully, we will not rouse their suspicions. But, if we do, we will have to react to the circumstances."

"Yes, sir," she said, and turned to leave.

Leidner placed a restraining hand on her arm. "That can wait until later," he said, his voice husky. She nodded, took Leidner's hand, and guided him to the stateroom bed. Theo gently pushed him down into a sitting position on the mattress. Then she took a cassette from a cabinet, slipped it in to the TV/VCR unit, and pushed PLAY. Images of a Swiss politician being masochistically punished by a leather-clad Theo appeared on the screen. Then she dropped to her knees, unbuckled Leidner's pants, and helped him slide them over his hips and down his milky-white, almost hairless legs. He stared at the screen as she lowered her head.

CHAPTER SIXTY-FIVE

May 12

Christo's banging around in the kitchen woke John and Nick just before dawn. He looked as though he'd been up all night. His hair was a mess and the bags under his bloodshot eyes were puffy and dark. He made them a breakfast of eggs, ham, and potatoes, which they washed down with thick, black coffee.

"By the way," Christo said, "while you two were sleeping like babies, I got a call from my office. The director of the Hellenic Maritime Office called and left a message. The *Sabiya* and her captain, Mehmet Arkoun, had a terrible history of one bad luck incident after another. It went aground on at least five occasions before it finally sank. The boat's captain was arrested four times for smuggling contraband. The man had a criminal record in Italy, Turkey and Greece. The last information available came from a man in Turkey. Remember, this is based on rumor. During World War II, Mehmet Arkoun may have been working for the Nazis."

"Doing what?" John asked.

"No one was able to discover."

By eight a.m., John and Nick were in their wetsuits, ready to dive. They again followed the cargo net—this time weighted with a one-pound sinker—down to the wreck, then dragged the net through the hull to the corridor outside the captain's quarters.

Nick took a flashlight and a crowbar and inspected the door. John stood close behind him with his own flashlight. Standing on the door, Nick handed John his flashlight and began prying at the door's edges with the crowbar. The sound of the crowbar banging against the door was amplified under water. Nick made a lot of noise, but seemingly not much progress. He'd knocked loose most of the encrustation built up around the outside edges of the door, when suddenly his weight caused it to break free and the heavy metal door swung down on its hinges into the room below. Nick dropped through the opening, along with the tools, the acetylene torch, and the flares. The rotted door hinges held for a moment, but then broke loose and the door followed him down.

John aimed his flashlight through the opening. The door had fallen on top of Nick.

John checked the connections, hoses, and air quantity gauges on Nick's breathing apparatus after dropping into the room. Nick was still breathing and his equipment seemed to be intact and functioning properly. He lifted the door off Nick, rolled him over on his back, and looked at him through his facemask. His eyes were closed. John rapped on his mask, but got no response.

John forced himself to remain calm. The last thing he needed to do was to exhaust his air supply on a surge of adrenaline.

Even with the buoyancy provided by the water, he wasn't confident he'd be able to lift Nick through the opening, a good ten feet above his head. But he had to get him out of there as quickly as possible. They were already at the halfway point of their maximum dive time. Nick's injuries didn't appear to be serious—he saw no evidence of bleeding or broken bones. But he couldn't really check his condition until he got him aboard the *Aphrodite*.

Searching the cabin for something that might help him lift Nick through the opening, he noticed a safe lying in one corner. An old combination-lock affair, with what remained of a pastoral scene painted on its door. The safe stood about three feet high and two feet wide. Six metal strong boxes, each secured by a rusted padlock, lay near the safe. Had they struck the motherlode? Was this what Leidner was after?

CHAPTER SIXTY-SIX

May 12

Christo had a reputation for being one of the toughest cops in Greece. He was indomitable under pressure. But he was first and last a Greek. And when a Greek sees a woman—especially a beautiful woman—in distress, he is congenitally incapable of not coming to her aid.

The sight of the wonderfully tall, bikini-clad blond took Christo's breath away. She stood behind the controls of a streamlined, white yacht and frantically waved an arm out a window at him as her boat approached. Christo could see she was anxious about something.

Standing by the *Aphrodite's* rail, he watched while the woman brought her boat to within twenty meters of the *Aphrodite's* starboard side.

"My husband!" she cried out in accented English. "I think he has had a heart attack. Can you help us?"

Christo watched the yacht's anchor deploy. He could see a man who looked to be in his fifties lying on a deck lounge chair. He felt a slight twinge of suspicion. But then he filled his eyes with the long-legged blonde's curves and angles and her distraught expression, and suppressed whatever his instincts were trying to tell him.

Christo lowered the *Aphrodite's* ladder. He climbed down to the dinghy tied to the boat, he rowed over to the yacht, and ascended the ladder built into the side of the luxury vessel. He moved to where the man lay and pushed up one of the man's eyelids. He had just placed his hand on the man's neck to check for a pulse, when something jabbed the back of his head.

"Stand up," the woman ordered. She had a pistol in her hand.

Christo stood; he felt as stupid as he had ever felt in his entire life.

The woman swept her free hand at Christo's belt and extracted his pistol from its holster.

Christo felt heartsick when he saw the man rise laughing from the bench.

"See, I told you, Theo. The easiest way to a man's heart is through his manhood. Particularly if he is Greek." The man looked at Christo. "You are Greek, are you not?"

Christo glared back.

"Ah, I thought so," the man said. Then his tone changed to one that sounded as though there was gravel in his throat. "We need to get on board his boat." He took Christo's pistol from the woman and climbed down the ladder to the dinghy. The woman poked Christo with her pistol, signaling him to follow the man.

When they were all aboard the *Aphrodite,* the woman backed Christo against the boom and viciously swung her right fist into the side of his face. He dropped like a stone onto the deck.

"Now, asshole, you are going to tell me what your friends have found below."

"Now, now, Theo, my dear," the man said, a mocking tone in his voice. "I am sure our Greek friend will be more than happy to cooperate with us. No need for violence."

"Gamise!" Christo cursed. *"As sto diavolo!"*

The man laughed. "Well, I guess I was wrong." He stepped back and in a voice as calm as though he were telling someone the time, he said, "Shoot him!"

The blonde leveled her pistol at Christo and pulled the trigger.

Christo roared as the bullet tore through his lower leg, ripping a hole in his flesh, shattering his tibia.

The man came over to Christo, carefully stepping around the stream of blood running from his leg and pooling onto the deck. He cruelly grasped Christo's chin. "I suspect you would like to cooperate now."

Christo spat in the man's face.

The man straightened and took a handkerchief from his pants pocket and wiped his face. He sighed as though what he was about to do was difficult for him. Then he spoke to the woman in German.

She stuck the pistol in her belt and pounced on Christo. A foot taller than Christo and in significantly better condition, she pummeled Christo with her fists, then thudded several kicks into his back and side. After tying his hands behind him and binding his feet, she dragged him across the deck, leaving a smudged, bloody trail behind. She tied one end of a rope to the rail. She formed a slip knot at the other end of the rope and looped it over Christo's legs. Then she lifted him—now nearly unconscious—off the deck as a mother might lift a small child and dropped him over the side.

Christo screamed when the rope snapped to a stop. At first he was disoriented. It took several seconds for him to realize where he was and the dire nature of his predicament. He looked up at the boat rail and saw the rope. It was tied around his legs just below his knees. His weight had caused it to tighten mercilessly. Dangling upside-down at the end of the rope, his arms hanging down, his hands brushing the water as it lapped against the side of the boat, Christo cursed himself for his stupidity. His vision blurred. He quickly asked John and Nick to forgive him. Then all went dark.

CHAPTER SIXTY-SEVEN

May 12

John swam back up through the door opening, grabbed the empty cargo net, and carried it back into the captain's quarters. He spread out the net next to Nick and rolled him onto it. He then jerked three times on the cable. He knew each pull on the cable would ring a bell attached to the winch on the *Aphrodite's* deck. Christo's signal to bring it up. The net started to slowly lift out of the cabin. John swam along, while the net lifted Nick. The net had nearly passed through the doorway when it snagged on one of the door hinges. The pull of the winch only made the problem worse. It quickly took up the little bit of slack in the net and caused it to be trapped on the hinge.

Holding onto the doorjamb with one hand, John pulled down on the net with his other arm. He should have pulled on the cable alerting Christo to stop the winch, but he thought it would be quicker to just try to pull the net loose by himself. It took all the energy and strength he could muster to release the net. Just when it slipped from the hinge, he felt something pop and then an excruciating pain shot through his shoulder. He knew what he'd done—it had happened before when he was a high school wrestler. He'd dislocated his right shoulder. A tingling sensation joined the pain running down his arm and into his hand. It felt as though he'd hit his funny bone, except ten times worse. In a matter of seconds, his right arm hung useless. Every time he allowed the water to float that arm away from his side, he felt a shock of pain in his right shoulder. Now he only had one good arm. It was only then he really started to worry.

John followed the net in its slow creep through the passageway and the staircase, managing somehow to prevent it from getting hung up again.

By the time they cleared the *Sabiya* and the cave opening, he was exhausted. He'd been sweating inside his wet suit, and now began to feel chilled. In less than a minute he was downright cold and began shaking. He had to get out of the water and out of the wetsuit as soon as possible.

While the winch continued to slowly lift the net, Nick remained unconscious. John gripped the outside of the net with his good arm, all the while concentrating on Nick's breathing apparatus. Nick could easily have spit it out in his unconscious state.

The net broke the surface. John looked for Christo, to tell him he needed his assistance. But what he saw made his breath catch in his throat. Christo was hanging upside-down from the *Aphrodite's* rail, a rope tied around his legs. His skin ashen. He looked dead.

CHAPTER SIXTY-EIGHT

May 12

Christo's body moved with the motion of the boat as it bobbed in the sea. A blonde Amazon pointed what looked like an Uzi at John. She had the same crewcut hairstyle that Leidner's other enforcers had.

A man operated the winch and hoisted John and Nick over the rail as though they were a fisherman's catch—Nick regaining consciousness and John hanging on with one arm, his flippered feet wedged into the openings in the net. While they dangled high above the deck, John noticed a fifty-foot yacht off the other side of the *Aphrodite*.

He'd been careless, because of his concern about Nick and the pain of his own injury. If he'd been paying attention while they came toward the surface, he would have seen the yacht's hull. He didn't know what he would have done about it, but he felt stupid to have fallen into a trap.

The woman wore tight-fitting leather pants and

a sleeveless T-shirt. A runway model with the eyes of a killer.

The man standing by the winch's controls wore tasseled loafers, linen trousers, and a tweed sport coat. Ready to go grab a bite at Le Cirque after killing them. He released the brake on the winch and unceremoniously dumped them three feet to the deck. Nick groaned when he hit. John landed on his bad arm, and barely suppressed a cry of pain. The net drooped around them, a sagging nylon cage.

"Well, well, what do we have here?" the man said. "It's too big to be a fish, don't you think, Theo?"

"Ich wiss nicht, mein Herr."

"Remove their tanks, my dear," the man said.

John looked up at him as the woman stripped the diving gear from him. "You must be Fritz Leidner," John said.

Hearing his name threw Leidner off balance for a moment, but he quickly recovered. With as much disdain as John had ever seen on a person's face, the man said, "Ah, the fish speaks. I presume you are John Hammond. You have caused me much inconvenience, Mr. Hammond, and for that you will pay a very dear price. But first you are going to tell me how your diving is going. What have you found?"

"Go to hell!"

John had barely completed his retort, when the tall blonde with the machine gun kicked his bad arm, sending hot tentacles of pain into his shoulder.

"Here is the deal, Hammond," the man said. "I am going to ask you a couple of questions. You are going to answer those questions quickly and completely. If you do not, then my lovely companion here is going to make you very sorry. Do we understand each other?"

All John could think about at that moment was the terrible suffering this man had inflicted on Zoë, and how she'd never told them a thing about the map. He rolled to a sitting position. "I understand you quite well, asshole. Screw off."

The woman unloaded on his chest with her size elevens, and John felt a couple of his ribs go. Like a trained dog, she then retreated a step, but kept her eyes on him.

"All right, Hammond. Let us try once more. What have you found?" He pointed down at the deck as though John didn't understand what he was referring to.

It hurt terribly just to breathe. John took in as much air as he could and then slowly, painfully let it out, wrapped around the words, "Shove it, Leidner. You, too, Butch."

That really pissed her off. She kicked at him so hard that when he moved to dodge her foot she lost her balance, only landing a grazing blow to his right side, and falling back against the rail.

She started to come at him again, but Leidner held up a hand and she came to an immediate stop.

Leidner stared at John for a few seconds and then looked over at Nick's prostrate form. "Why don't we do this a different way, my dear," he said. "Go put a bullet in Mister Hammond's friend's brain."

"All right, Leidner, you win," John said.

"I thought so," he said. Then, as calmly and dispassionately as someone might order a sandwich, he told the woman, "Shoot his friend anyway."

"No!" John shouted. "I know where the strongboxes are. If you kill him I will never tell you anything. You'll kill me before I'll do a thing to help you."

Leidner gave Burger the hand signal and she again stopped in her tracks.

"Here's the deal, asshole," John said. "You let me tend to my friend and you pull the man hanging over the side of the boat back up on deck. *Then* I will tell you everything I know."

All he could hope for was a little bit of time.

"Let me make something clear," Leidner said. "I would prefer to get what I want off that shipwreck. But I can accomplish almost as much by killing you and your friends. By disposing of everyone who knows about the *Sabiya*. You are trying my patience, Hammond. I will go along with you for the moment. But the minute I think you are not telling me the truth, I will kill you all. *Now* do we understand each other?"

John nodded, knowing Leidner would eventually kill them all, regardless of how cooperative he might be.

CHAPTER SIXTY-NINE

May 12

Nick had started to come around. John checked his arms and legs and found no obvious breaks. He could see a nasty bump on the back of Nick's head where it had been struck by the metal door. He was still groggy and seemed to be having trouble focusing. John suspected Nick had a bad concussion and he knew he needed medical attention, because a bad one could be fatal. He'd become an expert on concussions since coming to Greece. Of course, it was more likely they would all soon die from multiple Uzi bullet wounds than from concussions or broken limbs. When he'd done as much as he could for Nick, Leidner took the machine gun from the woman and ordered her to tie up Nick.

Once Nick was secured, Leidner told the woman to haul Christo on deck. Even though he was small, and Burger was big and strong, it still amazed John to see her bend over the side of the boat, grab Christo's belt, and hoist him aboard with ease. She dropped him at John's feet and walked over to her boss. Leidner handed the Uzi back to her.

Christo looked as though he'd been run through a meat grinder. He had what appeared to be a bullet wound in his leg, just below the knee. The wound was not bleeding profusely, probably because the rope used to hang him over the side had acted as a tourniquet. And hanging upside down had also slowed the flow of blood to the wound. His breathing was extremely shallow, however. Christo had also been severely beaten, his face swollen and blood-encrusted and both eyes completely closed. John couldn't imagine Leidner having done this. He would never have gotten his hands dirty. But he could hardly imagine a woman doing the damage, either. He'd never encountered the likes of Theo before. He glared at her. She half-smiled and flexed her right biceps at him.

Leidner didn't even bother having Theo tie up Christo. "I have done as you asked, Hammond," Leidner said. "Now you will tell me what I want to know."

John stood, with some effort, and faced him. "All right! We found it. Your old boat is a hundred feet beneath us."

"What did you find on this boat?" he asked.

"We had barely begun to explore it when my friend got hurt."

"Yes! But you said you found strongboxes."

"That's right," John said. "Six strongboxes and a safe, all in the captain's cabin."

Leidner visibly brightened at the mention of the safe. "*Sehr gut,* Herr Hammond. *Sehr gut,* indeed."

Leidner rattled off several sentences in German to Theo and then turned his attention back to John. "This is what you are going to do, Mr. Hammond. You and Theo are going to go for a nice little dive. You will show her exactly where the boat is, and you will take her to the cabin where the safe is located."

"I can't imagine how I'm going to be able to dive with broken ribs and the use of only one arm," John said.

Leidner again looked at John with disdain, stepped closer, and put his hand on top of his injured shoulder. John winced at his touch. Although his lower arm and hand had long since lost all feeling—numb from elbow to fingers—the top of his shoulder hurt like hell. Leidner again said something in German to the woman. She put her gun on the deck, walked around behind John, threw her arms around him, and squeezed him in a rib-crushing bear hug. The pain in his chest was incredible. It took his breath away and immobilized me.

While she had him in her vise-like grip, Leidner grabbed John's right wrist in both hands, pulled his arm straight out to the side and twisted it. John felt a horrendous pain shoot into his shoulder, so bad he forgot about the pain in his ribs. He moaned despite himself. Then he heard a "pop." Almost immediately, his arm started tingling again as feeling returned to it.

"Feeling better, Mr. Hammond?" Leidner asked. "It was merely a shoulder separation. You will be as good as new in a moment or two."

Theo the Amazon released him, cuffed him hard on the back of the head, and pushed him away. She laughed.

Leidner picked up the Uzi. He ordered the woman to inspect the diving equipment. She seemed to know what she was doing. When she finished, she spoke to Leidner. He said, "Gute!" and pointed the Uzi at the middle of John's chest. "Time to go swimming, Mr. Hammond."

John gave Leidner the most determined look he could manage. "I don't think that's a good idea."

Leidner and his Amazon gawked at John as though they couldn't believe what they'd heard. "I do not think you appreciate your situation, Mr. Hammond. Either dive or I will shoot you and your friends."

"No, it's you who doesn't appreciate the situation. I've just been underwater longer than I should have been. My right arm is still almost useless. And, thanks to your girlfriend, I can hardly breathe. If I don't get some rest I'm not going to be any use to you down on that wreck."

"Theo, my dear, if Mr. Hammond does not immediately start putting on his diving equipment, kill both of his friends."

Burger took a pistol from her waistband and placed the muzzle against Nick's temple. Nick's senses had returned enough to realize what was going on. John saw him close his eyes in anticipation of a bullet. John stepped over to where the fresh air tanks were stored.

Burger looked downright disappointed.

CHAPTER SEVENTY

May 12

They were down about fifty feet, with Burger carrying a spear gun pointed at John, when the cargo net—weighted with deep-sea fishing sinkers—slid past them toward the sea floor. John led her along the lava flow and into the cavern where the boat lay. With a movement of the spear gun, she ordered him into the boat.

When they entered the captain's cabin, Theo, dragging the net, she swam to the corner of the room and inspected the strongboxes. Attached to the padlocks on the boxes were metal tags on which appeared the Nazi swastika and a series of numbers. Burger carefully looked at each of the tags.

She removed a lengthy piece of rope with carabiners at each end from her belt and attached one end to the handle of one of the strongboxes. She then ran the rope through the handles of two of the other strongboxes. Now that she had three of the boxes linked together, she handed the other end of the rope to John and pointed the spear gun at him. He was getting pretty good at reading her signals. He hooked the carabiner end of the rope to the end of the cargo-net cable. Then Theo tugged on the cable three times. They swam up through the doorway and waited, while the rope grew taut with the weight of the strongboxes. John heard the clang of metal against metal when the strongboxes started to move upward.

The rope rubbed hard against the side of the doorway while the strongboxes continued their inexorable climb. When the first box approached the hatch, Burger poked John in the back and pointed down. He guessed she wanted him to prevent the box from hanging up on the edge. John eased it through the opening and did the same for the other two boxes when they came within reach. Then they followed the boxes while they slid along the passageway.

When the boxes reached the staircase, he had to scramble to keep them from wedging against the steps. Just as soon as he'd free one, a second would get hung up on a step. Swimming back and forth along the staircase to shepherd those boxes took its toll. His ribs felt as though someone had stuck a knife in them. His breathing became labored. His shoulder still gave him a great deal of trouble. But every time he showed any sign of slowing, Burger prodded him with the spear gun.

The strongboxes finally cleared the staircase and scraped through another hatchway to the main deck. The cargo cable slowly raised them toward the surface. John watched while the boxes danced lazily at the end of their tether and wondered if the winch and boom were strong enough to hold the load.

John waited with Burger next to the *Sabiya,* slowly swimming in a circle like two underwater predators waiting for unsuspecting prey. The pain eased slightly in his side and he was able to catch his breath. But his eyesight was growing fuzzy—one of the first signs he'd been at depth for too long.

The cable soon returned. Its weighted end hit the bottom and sent up a little puff of sand that immediately resettled. They reentered the *Sabiya,* with John dragging the cargo cable along while she, his work partner and captor, trailed behind with the spear gun.

This time he knew the routine. They dropped into the captain's cabin and roped up the remaining three strongboxes as before, attaching them to the cargo cable. After that, using more pointing and prodding with the spear gun, Burger directed him to wrestle the heavy safe into the cargo net which she'd again carried into the cabin. With the safe in the net, John reconnected the net to the cable.

She yanked on the cable three times. But instead of directing John to follow the boxes and the safe through the hatch as she had before, she gestured that he should stay in the room. When he started to swim up toward the doorway, she blocked him with the spear gun. The spear point penetrated his dive suit and about an inch of his right pectoral.

He fell backwards and, when he groped to steady himself, he felt a cylinder about the size of a large tooth paste tube beneath him. It was one of the phosphorous flares Nick and he had brought down with them. He slipped it into the back of his weight belt. The wound in his chest was more irritating than painful, but it had started to send a rosy plume of blood into the water.

Burger alternately watched him and gazed up at the dangling safe and strongboxes while they inched toward the doorway.

She looked up once again, just when the cargo net got hung up on the hinges. She moved forward, as though to swim to the net, but stopped. Taking advantage of this distraction, John kicked toward her, churning the water with his flippers. He operated now almost solely on adrenaline. Exertion, injuries, and too much time underwater were taking a heavy toll on his reserves. He knew this could be his last chance.

She must have sensed him coming. She looked back, swinging the spear gun toward his chest, but she was a fraction of a second too late. The shaft of the spear gun bumped against his left arm just when she squeezed the trigger. He heard the whoosh of the weapon ejecting its projectile and then the spear clanging into a bulkhead.

Burger dropped the now-useless spear gun and grabbed for John's breathing tube. She yanked it from his mouth and air bubbles exploded all around them. The woman was powerful and he was half-incapacitated. They struggled, trying to throw the other off balance. John grabbed her upper arms, her hands gripped his neck. He could feel pain in his throat, his lungs screamed. He gathered what strength he had left and pushed her away, toward the spear she'd just fired. She spotted it and dove to retrieve it.

With her attention off him for that moment, John replaced his breathing tube. Then, reaching around behind his back, he pulled the phosphorus flare from his weight belt. The flare had a pulltab ignition. While Burger picked up the spear and started to turn around, John kicked with his legs, propelling himself toward her, snapped off the pull tab, and inserted the flare between her weight belt and the small of her back. Before she could complete her turn, the flare sputtered to life and then burst into pyrotechnic brilliance.

John knew that phosphorus will burn wherever there is any oxygen. And there is a ton of oxygen in water. There is another aspect about burning phosphorous: like a constant stream of sulfuric acid, it will burn a hole right through the human body.

The white-hot flare lit the room with incredible brightness. Burger seemed disoriented for a moment, and then began thrashing in the water like a speared fish. The flare ate through her wetsuit and began to burn her flesh. She dropped the spear and reached back to extract the flare from her belt.

She held it in front of her, seemingly confused by the flaming, star-bright object. She twisted and turned, trying to find the source of her continued pain. John saw that the flare had left fiery remnants of phosphorous embedded in her lower back. She dropped the flare to the floor, continuing to watch it burn, her face etched with agony. She opened her mouth in a silent scream--her breathing tube popped out—and John knew he stared at death. Then her body went limp—the phosphorous eating into her spinal cord had turned her into a paraplegic just seconds before she died.

CHAPTER SEVENTY-ONE

May 12

John swam to the doorway. The cargo net was stretched to the point of tearing. The strongboxes had bunched around the hinge. He grabbed the bottom of the net and let his weight pull it down, creating just enough slack to pry it loose from the hinges. The net and its contents snapped upward and moved like an articulated caterpillar through the passageway to the staircase. With the safe added to the three strongboxes, getting them through the staircase became even more difficult for John than it had been with the earlier load. He had to move quickly, continuously jockeying from the bottom step to the top step to keep the cargo line moving. His worsening vision made the job even more difficult. He knew what was happening to him and he knew he had to get out of the water as quickly as possible. But he had to keep the cable moving. As long as that line moved upward toward the *Aphrodite,* Leidner would assume everything was okay. He needed Leidner's attention focused on the winch and cable.

John calculated it would take about fifteen minutes for the winch to raise the load up to the boat. He'd been underwater for over thirty-five minutes, right after a deep-water dive of similar duration. In addition to blurred vision, he began to feel pain in his joints, and weakness and numbness in his fingers and toes. He knew if he didn't get out of the water, he could slip into a nitrogen narcosis that would impair his judgement and perception. That's how divers die. He knew he should allow for a decompression stop on his way to the surface, but he didn't have the luxury of stopping for more than about five minutes. He couldn't spend more time underwater, and he had to get to the boat before the net reached the surface. He was still lucid enough to realize he had to deal with Leidner while the man was occupied with the winch.

He surfaced on the far side of the *Aphrodite*. Holding onto a line hanging from the fishing boat, he stripped off his scuba gear. Then he dumped his tank and buoyancy control device and shed his mask and fins. His equipment disappeared below the water's surface.

The groaning of the winch covered any noise he made while he climbed part way up the ladder and peeked over the rail. Decompression sickness was wreaking havoc with his eyesight. Two Leidners—their backs to him—operated two sets of winch controls. Two of everything. He closed his eyes and shook his head to try to clear his vision. When he opened them again, there were still two men across the deck. He realized that waiting for his vision to clear would be futile. Time was running short.

Two Nicks still sat on the deck, tied up a few feet from where two Christos lay unconscious. When he peered over the rail, John saw Nick's eyes widen. The hopeful looks on both his faces were unforgettable.

John climbed dizzily up the rest of the ladder, pulled himself over the rail, and stood on the deck. The two Leidners who leaned over the rail on the far side of the boat seemed to be miles away.

With each step he took, John expected Leidner to hear him and to turn around. If the man had a gun… But thanks to the noise of the winch and Leidner's total focus on the rising cable, John was able to walk right up behind him without being detected. Then he reached out and tapped Leidner on the shoulder.

The man jumped and screamedHe looked around as though he was waiting for his Amazon to come to his aid. Then Leidner recovered his arrogance and put on a superior scowl.

"I think we can come to a satisfactory monetary arrangement, Mr. Hammond," he said.

John slugged him in the mouth, knocking him back against the rail while the safe and strongboxes rose dripping from the sea.

Leidner slid off the rail and down onto the deck, blood seeping from his nose and mouth.

John staggered over to the winch's control panel and shut down the lifting mechanism. He untied Nick and looked around for something to sit on. And then he collapsed.

When John came to, the same two Nicks hovered over him. They looked pale, but otherwise all right. "Christo?" he said.

"Not good," Nick responded. "We've got to get him

to the hospital."

John groaned and closed his eyes. He felt dizzy and nauseous. He seemed to feel slightly better when he closed his eyes.

The next things he heard were footsteps, then the sound of the boat's engine, and Nick's voice shouting for an ambulance to meet them at the dock.

John opened his eyes to test his vision. Still blurred. He saw Leidner tied to the metal boxes—a wonderful irony. Those boxes had become his ball-and-chain. Then everything went black.

CHAPTER SEVENTY-TWO

May 12

Zoë, Nick, Christo, and John had become a unit that had bonded and—for the most part—worked effectively together. So it seemed fitting for all four of them to be hospitalized. All for one and one for all. The Four Wounded Musketeers.

John knew he was damn lucky to be alive. If it hadn't been for the fact the Greek Navy had a commando base on *Samos* equipped with a hyperbaric recompression chamber, he might have died.

Up and about again, he prowled the Greek Army Hospital. He visited Nick's room, directly across the hall from his own. Nick had suffered a serious concussion, but was too hard-headed to realize it and too tough to give it much credence. He looked as good as new to John. Although recovering nicely—in the hospital for observation only—Nick had found that the staff treated him like a hero. He was getting more attention than he needed, but enjoying every bit of it, nonetheless.

"Hey, Nick," John said when he entered his room. "How about coming with me to look in on Christo and Zoë?"

"I just got back from their rooms," Nick said. "Besides, I'm feeling a little dizzy." He groaned and the two nurses in the room immediately began cooing at him.

John did a quick about-face to hide his smile. God forbid that Nick's wife, Ariana, shows up now and catches her husband enjoying himself, John thought.

Christo was in critical condition. He'd lost a lot of blood and his gunshot wound had become infected. The beating Theo Burger had given him had ruptured his spleen and damaged one of his kidneys. He was so sedated that conversation was out of the question. John looked at his face, partially covered with an oxygen mask, and didn't like the death-like color of his skin.

John said a prayer for Christo before he left the room.

Zoë's room, in a wing of the hospital separate from the rest of them, was his last stop. Her doctor had assured him there was nothing physically wrong with her. In the U.S. she would probably have been tagged with Post-Traumatic Stress Syndrome, but John didn't believe this to be the problem with Zoë. Of course, she'd been through a terrible ordeal, one that would affect even the strongest person. But he believed her emotional condition was grounded more in a historical context.

In Greek legend, women commited suicide rather than submit to rape. John knew that a national holiday was even based on an incident when all the women of a village threw themselves off a cliff rather than submit to a marauding enemy army. In Greek culture, blame lies with a violated woman. No wonder Zoë was in a near-catatonic state.

But John hoped another aspect of Greek culture might offer salvation to Zoë—its belief in revenge. Her eyes were clearly communicating a sickness in her soul. Each time he saw her, that sickness had become more and more evident. He was losing her; of that he was certain. He knew he had to do something drastic. He had to break her out of her emotional prison.

CHAPTER SEVENTY-THREE

May 13

I t took John a couple hours to drive to the Pythagorio docks in a borrowed car, locate the *Aphrodite,* find his knapsack, and return to the hospital. Zoë's doctor seemed pleased with his suggestion that "Zoë might benefit from a drive around the island." A nurse helped dress her and move her out to the car.

During the drive to Vathi, Zoë remained in her own world. She wouldn't talk or even look at John. But she communicated despair through her posture and her seeming inability to connect with her surroundings. A pathetic figure, she slumped in her seat, her head leaning against the window. Dark circles accentuated the dullness in her eyes, and her lack of interest in her appearance was obvious. Her hair was a tangle of out-of-control curls and she wore no makeup. She looked like a forlorn waif in her clothes. For the first time, John realized she had lost a great deal of weight.

The ride back to Pythagorio lasted fifteen minutes.

He drove past the block of buildings that had been destroyed by explosions and wondered again what motivated Leidner. After parking the car near the police station, John reached over the back seat and grabbed his knapsack. Rummaging in the bag, he felt the grip of the 9mm and wrapped his hand around it. He slipped the pistol behind his back, under his jacket, in the waistband of his trousers. Zoë never once looked at him, but continued to stare out the passenger-side window. He walked around and helped her to get out. She moved listlessly, shuffling her feet, never taking her gaze off the pavement directly in front of her. She showed no interest in where they were or what they were doing.

Taking Zoë's hand, he guided her into the station. Their entrance caused an immediate silence to fall over the office. Their reputation had preceded them—the man who'd captured the murderer Leidner, and the woman who'd been silent under torture. They'd become folk heroes on Samos. The station was packed with policemen. Since the destruction of the police building in Vathi, the Pythagorio station appeared to have become the headquarters.

John moved Zoë to a chair, then crossed the room and talked with a man in a suit. "As you can see, Miss Vangelos is not well," John said. "I thought if she could see her torturer locked up in a prison cell…." He hunched his shoulders in a "who knows" gesture.

Those men in the room who spoke English translated for the others. Many men were nodding their heads, murmuring among themselves.

"Of course, Mr. Hammond," the man in the suit

said. "If you think it would help Miss Vangelos recover." He snapped an order to one of the uniformed cops.

John assisted Zoë to stand and hooked his arm in hers. The uniformed policeman escorted them through a steel door to the jail cells at the back of the building. There were six cells—three on each side of a central aisle. A jailer sat at the head of the aisle.

Seeing the cells seemed to penetrate Zoë's mental fog. She clung to John as a small child might cling for safety to a parent. He intentionally obstructed her view of the only occupied cell—Leidner's. He asked their escort if they could be alone with the prisoner for just a few minutes. The man hesitated, then signaled the jailer to leave the cell area. After they closed and locked the door behind them, John slowly stepped aside, allowing Zoë to catch sight of Leidner.

At first, she showed no sign of recognizing the man who'd orchestrated her father's death, her own kidnapping, beating, and rape. But then her face became animated for the first time in days—fire returned to her eyes and her face became flushed. She stepped to the cell and wrapped both her hands around its bars. She didn't speak. She just glared at him, while he slowly rose from his cot and, seemingly pushed back by the hatred in her eyes, moved to the far end of the cell.

John drew the pistol from his waistband and pried her right hand from the bar she was trying to crush. He put the gun in her hand and raised her arm until the barrel pointed directly at Leidner's chest.

He planned for Zoë to shoot Leidner. Then he would take the pistol from her and claim he'd done it out of rage and revenge. He would have to spend some time in prison, but it would probably not be forever—and Zoë would have her mind back. In retrospect, he realized she hadn't been the only one driven to madness by Leidner.

Zoë continued to stare at the prisoner, seemingly unaware of the weapon in her hand. "Shoot him, Zoë!" John whispered. "Shoot him! Make him pay for what he's done. It's time you got payback for what he did to you and your family. *Ektheekeesee! Revenge*, Zoë!"

⧓

Her gun hand started to shake. The motion caused her to look at the weapon for the first time. She brought the shaking under control and slipped her index finger into the trigger guard.

Leidner glared at Zoë. "You don't have the guts to pull that trigger," he growled. "Your father's dead. We nearly killed your mother." His features became demonic when he added, "And my men played with you like some whore. Go ahead, shoot me," he screamed. He laughed and spat at her. "You're weak like the rest of your family."

Zoë's finger tightened on the trigger. She felt the curved piece of metal move against her finger. And then the realization of what the Swiss psychopath really wanted her to do struck her. She smiled at the man while lowering the pistol. "That's much too easy," she said.

All of his power, all of his arrogance seemed to dissipate. Leidner devolved into nothing. He appeared about to crumble. He trembled, his hands shaking like leaves in a storm. Saliva drooled down his chin. He pissed in his pants and began to sob.

That was all the revenge Zoë needed. She understood what Leidner had become. She dropped her chin onto her chest and began to weep.

John heard the key inserted into the cellblock door. Stepping between Zoë and the entry, he took the gun from her hand and put it back into his waistband. The jailer and their original escort came through the door. Both expressed their apologies for disturbing them and then they seemed extremely embarrassed when they noticed Zoë's tears. John thanked them for their kindness and started to lead her out. He noticed for the first time that the safe and the six strongboxes were stored in the cell directly opposite Leidner's windowless cell. The bastard's only view was of the containers he would never be able to claim.

They walked out into the glorious Aegean sunlight. Zoë looked exhausted. She stopped on the sidewalk and looked across at the bay. The water glittered as though diamonds had been sprinkled on its surface.

She looked up at John with a sparkle in her eyes, but she was still so haggard, so pale and weak. While they drove back to the hospital, they didn't talk. John kept stroking her hair while she leaned against him. It was communication enough. The simple act of touching affirmed their love for each other.

⧫

In the days that followed, Zoë seemed to find John's attitude toward her incredible. She was amazed he didn't consider her "spoiled" as a result of her being raped. His reaction helped her to talk about what had happened. Talking about it facilitated her healing. Hearing about it sent a chill through John that he thought would freeze his heart and numb his brain. It took all the willpower he had to keep from going back to the jail and murdering Leidner.

In the end, Zoë's recovery was all he needed. But he had to admit that Leidner's mental demise and the deaths of his cohorts gave him added pleasure. It gave him even more gratification to learn that, with the assistance of reinforcements sent from Athens, the police had swept the island and taken five other men into custody. All had Swiss passports and criminal records. Two of the men had explosives in their possession. All were armed when arrested.

"*Ektheekeesee!* Revenge!" John said to himself. Perhaps I'm becoming more Greek, he thought.

CHAPTER SEVENTY-FOUR

May 30

It took Athens seventeen days to decide which part of the governmental bureaucracy would be responsible for taking a cut out of whatever they found inside the safe and the strongboxes.

On the day the hospital released Christo, still pale and weak, twenty pounds lighter, the Vangeloses got word the Greek government had made its decision regarding the safe and strongboxes. The government scheduled a public ceremony for ten the next morning at the Pythagorio Police Station.

Nick and Christo each was at his own home. Zoë and her mother—since being released from the hospital—were staying at the Vangelos house in Kokkari. John had moved back into his hotel room in Vathi.

John slept fitfully that night, more from being alone for the first time in weeks than because of excitement over the "loot" in the Pythagorio jail. And then, of course, his dream returned. But this time it went further than usual. He experienced the explosion, the death of his men, and watched the black pajama-clad man approach him in slow motion. He once again felt the muzzle of the man's rifle press against his forehead, and saw him pull the trigger. Misfire. And, as always, he pulled his pistol from its shoulder holster and pointed it at the head of the Viet Cong soldier. But, unlike every other episode of this personal horror show, it didn't stop there. This installment carried him through to the end, as it had really occurred three decades earlier.

He woke bathed in sweat, and crying inconsolably. When he had pulled his pistol, his enemy had dropped to the ground in front of him and tried to surrender. *"Chieu hoy! Chieu hoy!"* the little man had screamed, begging for his life. John could have taken him prisoner. Instead, out of the corner of his eye, he saw the mutilated bodies of his two men hanging over the sides of the Jeep. John put a neat hole in the front of the Viet Cong soldier's head and blew his brains out the back. How often would he have to kill him, he wondered.

CHAPTER SEVENTY-FIVE

May 31

The police sent a large van to pick up the Vangelos family. They'd all congregated at Nick's house, including Nick's brother, Pavlos, who had flown in from his military base. For all of them, the upcoming event wasn't about money. It would be vindication for Petros, proof his death in the defense of the map had meant something. At least that was their hope.

Layla Vangelos' all-black widow's dress seemed to express the mood of all the van's passengers. Each of them seemed to have retreated into their own thoughts. When the van pulled up in front of Police Headquarters, John was waiting on the sidewalk.

Nick helped his mother out of the vehicle. Zoë took her mother's other arm. They walked abreast to the building entrance. Layla suddenly stopped in front of John. She shook her arms loose from her children's hands, leaned over, and put her right hand on his chest, over his heart.

She told him in Greek that he was a good man and she thanked him for all he had done. Saying "you're welcome" didn't seem sufficient to John. But, from the look on her face, she didn't need a response.

The police had set up a double row of chairs to accommodate fourteen guests in the building's small reception area. They all took seats.

A minute later, Christo hobbled in on crutches to a spontaneous outburst of applause and cheers from the police. This was the first time he'd been in the station house since his injuries. Christo had lost a great deal of weight and had still not recovered his former coloring. He looked pale. The shouting and applause had barely died down when three men in custom-tailored suits and slicked-back hair walked briskly into the room. One of the men strode over to Christo, who instantly struggled to rise from his chair. They looked at each other for a moment, then embraced.

Christo introduced him to the others as Panayiotis Argyres, his first cousin and the Greek Minister of Taxation and Revenue. It crossed John's mind that half the bureaucrats in Greece must be related to Christo. Argyres chatted briefly with Layla, Zoë and John. Then he shook Nick and Pavlos' hands.

Argyres started to make the government's announcement while a standing-room-only crowd continued to file into the reception area. All the cops on Samos seemed to be in the room. Argyres spoke slowly, as though his words were too important to rush. John found the pace of the man's Greek easy to follow. Argyres spent a couple minutes on amenities and then began reading from an official looking document:

"The duly elected and democratic government of the Republic of Greece has on the date inscribed below determined that its rights to any and all salvageable items taken, or to be taken, from the ship known as the Sabiya, registered to a Mister Mehmet Arkoun, and sunk in the Aegean Sea on or about January 17, 1945, in a location detailed on Addendum #1 to this statement, are as follows: In accordance with Greek Maritime Law and International Maritime Salvage Law, one-half of the appraised value of all items salvaged will be paid to the Greek government. Additionally, any income from the sale of any salvage items will be taxed according to current laws of Greece. The remaining one-half of the salvage rightfully belongs to the Vangelos family and will be turned over to them."

Argyres then recognized the courage of the Vangelos family. He expressed condolences over Petros' death and praised the bravery of the local police and Coast Guard, especially noting the names of the officers and sailors who'd been killed. He then looked at John and thanked him for his courage and sacrifice. Finally, Argyres ordered that the strongboxes and the safe be brought into the reception area.

The seven containers were hauled into the room by cops who were obviously struggling under their weight. The safe had been placed on a dolly. When the containers were all lined up in front of the audience, Argyres ordered them opened. One of his aides, armed with a bolt-cutter, put his entire weight into the task of snapping the padlock off the first strongbox. When the lock fell away from its hasp and clattered to the floor, he moved down the line, breaking all of the locks, but opening none of the strongboxes.

Then starting at opposite ends of the line of strongboxes, two officers began prying around the edges of the boxes with hammers and crowbars, loosening the rusty seal of five decades of corrosion. Argyres gave the signal to open them.

Beginning at the left, one of the aides put both of his hands on the lid of a strongbox and lifted. The hinges were stiff with rust, so it took some effort for the man to raise the creaking lid.

When they saw what that first box contained, several of the police officers forgot themselves and cursed out loud from shock. Diamonds—thousands of them—filled the first box.

The next strongbox contained an incredible assortment of precious gems, including rubies, emeralds, and sapphires. The next three boxes were filled with gold bars and coins. The sixth strongbox, similar to the first one, was piled to the lid with more diamonds. Even the polished and poised Argyres could only sit there with his mouth hanging open while staring at the astonishing treasure.

Two officers carried an acetylene torch into the room. The crowd was ordered to turn away from the torch's brilliant, blue-white glare while a technician wearing protective goggles worked on the safe's hinges. John and the Vangeloses followed Christo to his office, where they sat, or stood, or paced for over a half-hour until the sound of shouts reached them.

When they returned to the reception area, the safe's door lay on the floor. Stacks of what looked like banknotes were piled high inside the vault. A book of some sort rested on the banknotes. On top of the book, a single sealed envelope. Argyres reached inside the safe and picked up the envelope. The paper appeared yellowed and fragile. He carefully opened it, stared inside momentarily, then set it aside. He picked up the book and scanned through its pages. "Does anyone read German?" he asked.

One of Christo's men stepped forward.

"What are these things?" Argyres asked.

After a brief examination, the policeman declared, "The book is the captain's log. Its last entry is from the sixteenth of January, nineteen forty-five."

"What's in the letter?" Argyres said impatiently.

The young cop seemed to labor while he read the handwritten letter. When sure he had it right, he turned to Argyres. "The letter was written by a General Franz von Leibecht and is addressed to Mr. Friederich Leidner."

"Well, what are you waiting for?" Argyres demanded. "Read it to us."

The policeman translated the letter into Greek:

"My Dear Friederich:

I regret to inform you this will be the last shipment I expect to make. The war is over for all intents and purposes and I must concentrate on avoiding the madness that will surely accompany the defeat of the Third Reich

Although this last shipment is smaller than the previous two consigned into your capable hands, it will still be worth your time and effort. As with the other shipments, my instructions are the same. Kindly liquidate the jewels and gold and invest the cash proceeds in securities you deem appropriate. On this occasion, I wish you to open accounts in the names of my three children, Katerina, Siegfried, and Lisle. My share of the proceeds should be put into those accounts.

As always, your part of the shipment is thirty-five percent. I am sure you will enjoy this wealth appropriated from the vile Jews and other mongrels who had a stranglehold on Germany's economy. They will never be able to enjoy it anyway, now that we have exterminated them.

Best regards for the future."

The German general had signed it and had written the initials "SS" after his name. The postscript below the signature read: *"Heil Hitler!"*

A pall replaced the exuberant mood that had just a moment ago filled the room.

John now knew what Fritz Leidner had been so anxious to keep hidden—what he'd been so willing to murder over. The man's father had been a Nazi collaborator. He had built his financial empire on a foundation of millions stolen from murdered innocents.

PRESENT YEAR

CHAPTER ONE

August 10

The release of the German general's letter caused an international furor. There was immediate reaction against Switzerland. The denials the country and its bankers had been making for decades about having had nothing to do with laundering or hiding assets taken from Holocaust victims were now revealed as evasions.

The Greeks did not fare much better. When the news media reported that the Greek government would grab a hefty cut of the blood money—plus taxes on the remainder—it was vilified in the international press. Things got even worse when the Vangelos clan held a news conference in Vathi that CNN carried to every corner of the planet. Layla announced that the family had donated its share of the loot to two funds: one for the families of the policemen and sailors murdered by Leidner, and a second to aid the resettlement of refugees, including Jews wanting to immigrate to Israel. "I could never take money that belonged to persons who suffered at the hands of the Nazis," she said. "This is a decision we have all made together."

The picture of this simple peasant woman donating tens of millions of dollars to assist people she would never meet inspired others who poured millions of dollars into relief organizations. Letters, cards, and gifts addressed to Layla Vangelos and Family deluged the post office in Vathi. Thousands of travelers cancelled vacation plans that included Greece or Switzerland. It didn't take long for the Greek government to come around and change its position. Whatever it would have gained from its one-half share of the salvaged wealth was being eaten up in lost tourism revenue.

It took six weeks to appraise the contents of the six strongboxes. The banknotes, as it turned out, according to a note found between the pages of the ship's log, had been payment to the *Sabiya's* captain for transporting the booty from Turkey to the Italian coast along the Tyrhennian Sea. How the cargo was to be transshipped from there to Switzerland was anybody's guess. The government turned the captain's money over to the Greek Orthodox Church, with the stipulation that the funds had to be used to help the poor.

The appraised value of the jewels and gold in the salvaged boxes was announced in the middle of August— more than ninety-eight million dollars.

When Nick heard that figure, he looked sick for a moment—but only until Layla scowled at him. Then he sheepishly declared, "Oh, what the hell. I can still salvage the rest of that boat. It ought to be worth a million or two."

Based on General von Leibecht's letter to Fritz Leidner's father, it was determined that the total current value of all the assets confiscated by the SS officer was at least three hundred million dollars, because, as von Leibecht's letter had said, 'this shipment was the last and least valuable of three shipments.'

The German government immediately froze all of the von Leibecht family's assets. The general had died in a freak automobile accident just before the end of the war, while fleeing the advancing Russian Army. But his wealth had been transferred to his heirs, whose place in Germany's financial and social circles now changed suddenly and considerably.

The scandal precipitated by the discovery of the *Sabiya* destroyed the Leidner family almost overnight. The Swiss authorities applied a new law that allowed the government to appropriate the assets of any Swiss citizen or company proven to have collaborated with the Nazis. The capital base of the Leidner family's bank, *Banque Securité de Swisse,* determined to be the equivalent of ten point eight billion dollars, was, after the liquidation of debts, added to a fund the government and the country's banks had already established for the families of Holocaust victims. Depositors received their funds, then *Banque Securite de Swisse* disappeared at the stroke of a pen wielded by the Commissioner of Finance and by the Justices of the Supreme Court of Switzerland. the Greek government shipped Fritz Leidner to a prison on Crete where the facilities were the worst in Greece. It was generally believed by police authorities, due to Leidner's physical and mental collapse, that the man would be lucky to survive a trial, let alone incarceration in a Greek prison.

John, of course, had discovered his own treasure— non-taxable and a whole lot more fun to wrap his arms around

CHAPTER TWO

August 17

John sat in the back of the taxi and dropped the newspaper and his briefcase on the seat next to him. He looked out the window at the wall-to-wall traffic clogging Athens' streets. He couldn't get over the changes that had occurred in the city in the thirty years since he'd lived here before. Then he smiled. *There's been a lot of changes in my life, too,* he thought. He'd come to Greece to find himself. *My God! I did that, and a whole lot more.*

He looked at his watch. *It takes about thirty minutes by cab to get to the Olympic Airlines terminal,* he thought, then another hour to fly to Samos. All things considered, it's not much of a weekly commute, especially for someone who daily drove an hour-and-a-half from Palos Verdes to Newport Beach and back for fifteen years.

He smiled while he pictured Layla Vangelos still living in her house on Samos, spending most days with the other black-clad widows of the village. The old women would go to church every morning, and then sit around talking about whatever it is that old women talk about. John guessed if the conversation ever got boring, Layla could regale her friends with the story about her brave son and daughter and her fabulous new son-in-law. And, of course, she would relate Petros' part in the whole adventure.

John's mind turned to the business he and Nick had started. He had invested $800,000 and pooled it with a like amount of Nick's proceeds from the salvage of the *Sabiya,* and they now ran a fleet of four small tour boats. Their office was in Piraeus and their boats left from there for cruises through the Greek Islands, as well as to other tourist sites in Italy and Turkey. The administrative duties had fallen to him, while Nick supervised the boats' schedules and maintenance. John would rather have been out on one of the boats, but Nick claimed total ignorance about finances and accounting. John didn't believe him in the slightest. But the business was thriving and they were talking about buying two more boats. They called the company Vangelos Tours.

He picked up the newspaper and wasn't surprised to see Zoë's picture on the front page—again. Her position as head of the Antiquities Department at the University of Athens put her in direct conflict with the contractors working on the new Athens subway system. The project going on in the Greek capital had created more opportunities for her department than anyone could have imagined. It had turned into an archaeologist's dream— and a contractor's nightmare. Ancient graveyards, streets, houses, temples, statuary, pottery, jewelry—all continually being unearthed. Zoë was proud to have her name keep showing up in the local newspapers as the person responsible for another construction delay.

It was Friday evening and John was on his way to meet Zoë at the airport. They would fly to their home on Samos, spend time with Layla, Christo and his wife, Demetria, Nick and Ariana, and Pericles and Marika. They would be altering this schedule a couple months before the baby was born. They planned to spend Zoë's seventh month on Samos, and then the two of them would fly to the United States and stay with John's folks. They wanted Zoë to have the benefits of American health care and they wanted their son, Peter, born in the States.

John placed the newspaper back down on the seat, closed his eyes, and reflected on the last year. Truly remarkable, he thought. Zoë always greets me with a smile that not only lights up her face, but warms my heart almost more than I can bear. It makes me dizzy with happiness to see her. I haven't once had the nightmare from Vietnam since we married.

Before Petros Vangelos' death, John hadn't thought much about destiny. A true son of his culture, he'd always believed hard work led to success—relying on luck meant losing. But the old Greek fisherman altered everything. John knew no one could have planned for the odyssey Petros set in motion.

He felt sad that Petros and he never had the chance to know one another. But the more he learned about him, the more he realized how remarkable the man was. Petros had changed his life and telling his story barely did justice to the man's memory.

John's eyes snapped open when the taxi lurched to

a stop. Zoë stood just outside the door to the terminal building, showing him her radiant smile. For the thousandth time, John thought that his initial translation of Petros Vangelos' words was right all along—*Ee Zoë mou* does mean "my life."

THE END